MEDICINE CREEK CLAIM

On the Dakota Frontier

**By
CK Van Dam**

Medicine Creek Claim

This is a work of fiction. Names, characters, places and events are products of the author's imagination. Any resemblance to actual persons or events is coincidental.

Copyright © 2024 by CK Van Dam

All rights reserved. No part of this book may be used or reproduced without written permission, except in the case of literary reviews.

Published in the United States in 2024 by Pasque Publishing

www.ckvandam.com

Cover design by Douglas Moss

Dedication

While writing a book is a solitary endeavor, publishing a book takes a team of historians, editors, proofreaders, designers and beta readers. This novel was inspired by the women homesteaders who understood that the Homestead Act was their opportunity to control their lives and their destinies.

Thank you to the friends and readers who let me know that you enjoyed my earlier novels – you inspired me to write another story about the strong women who went before us.

Table of Contents

Author's Note 1

Chapter 1: October 27, 1861 – Springfield, MO 2

Chapter 2: July 1861 – Ward Farm 9

Chapter 3: September 1861 – Ward Farm.............. 17

Chapter 4: November 1861 – Springfield, MO 23

Chapter 5: Spring 1862 – New Madrid, MO 38

Chapter 6: May 1862 – Ward Farm 52

Chapter 7: May 1862 – Callaway County, MO 64

Chapter 8: June 1862 – Jameson Ranch................. 73

Chapter 9: June 1862 – Jameson Ranch................. 88

Chapter 10: August 1862 – Independence, MO..... 97

Chapter 11: Oct - Dec 1862 – Ward Farm 110

Chapter 12: April - May 1863 – Missouri River .. 119

Chapter 13: April 1863 – Cape Girardeau, MO ... 129

Chapter 14: July 1863 – St. Louis, MO 141

Chapter 15: Summer 1863 – Yankton.................. 148

Chapter 16: September 1863 – St. Louis, MO 160

Chapter 17: October 1863 – Dakota Territory 171

Chapter 18: November 1863 – Shady Bluffs 185

Chapter 19: November 1863 – Medicine Creek... 195

Chapter 20: December 1863 – Medicine Creek ... 209

Chapter 21: January 1864 – Medicine Creek 226

Chapter 22: Spring 1864 – Medicine Creek 236

Chapter 23: Spring 1864 – Shady Bluffs 249

Chapter 24: Summer 1864 – Shady Bluffs 263

Chapter 25: September 1864 – Medicine Creek .. 272

Chapter 26: Autumn 1864 – Shady Bluffs 281

Chapter 27: Winter 1865 – Dakota Frontier 298

Chapter 28: April 1865 – Shady Bluffs 312

Chapter 29: April 1865 – Shady Bluffs 327

About the Author 345

Author's Note

During the Civil War, Missouri saw more than 1,200 battles and skirmishes. Only Virginia and Tennessee exceeded this level of combat.

Missouri played a unique role during the War Between the States. It began with the Missouri Compromise of 1820, which drew an imaginary line along the 36th parallel, allowing states south of the line to be slave-holding. The Compromise admitted Missouri into the Union as a slave state, while Maine was admitted as a free state. Fast-forward to 1850, when the Kansas-Nebraska Act repealed the Missouri Compromise, allowing for popular sovereignty and the possibility that slavery could be extended into lands where it had once been banned.

Because of this history, Missouri was deeply divided into pro-slavery and anti-slavery camps. Claimed by both the Union and the Confederacy, Missouri held a unique position and was the site of both conventional battles and guerrilla warfare. In addition to conflicts between Union and Confederate forces, "private armies" of Bushwhackers and Jayhawkers fought in the state. These citizen militia groups did not abide by the "rules of war," often attacking non-combatants.

Chapter 1: October 27, 1861
Springfield, MO

"We've got 'em on the run, men. Keep after 'em," the sergeant yelled to the battle-weary Union soldiers under his command.

On a warm October day, Major General John Fremont's regiment encountered Confederate forces retreating south. The Union soldiers, marching toward Springfield in the early days of the War, were surprised by the enemy. The Rebs dug in, taking a stand on the hilly terrain.

Private Charlie Ward was among the Union soldiers, but Charlie focused on another soldier in the unit. Charlie's brother, Max Ward, was at the front of the advancing troops.

"Stay low, Max," Charlie whispered. But Max didn't hear his sibling's warning. He concentrated on the Confederates, who were returning fire from a nearby hill.

Max, the youngest of the three Ward children, grew up hunting grouse, turkeys, and the occasional deer on the family farm near St. Joseph, Missouri. Even though he was only seventeen when he enlisted, the Army of the West welcomed the tall, lanky farm boy without question.

Charlie – Charlotte, actually – had followed Max into the Army with the intent of watching over her "little brother." Of course, her fellow comrades did not realize that Charlie was, in fact, a woman. Charlotte found it wasn't difficult to pass as a man. Like her brother, Charlotte was tall and slim. She had chopped off her chestnut-colored hair without a second thought. Vanity was not part of Charlotte's character. She didn't possess a curvy figure like her younger sister, Elizabeth. What she did possess was a single-minded determination to protect those whom she loved.

Now, that single-mindedness was focused on her brother. Max was in the vanguard of the Union Army. He and his unit led the charge and took most of the enemy fire.

The Rebs were retreating but giving the Yanks a run for their money. As Charlie watched the firefight, it reminded her of a dance. The two sides would move forward, then scramble back. The back-and-forth movement was punctuated with Rebel yells. The Union soldiers were not as vocal, but they did call out encouragement to their comrades.

"Good work, Elijah!" called the company's sergeant, "Keep it up, Joe. Shake it off, Max!"

That got Charlie's attention. Max? Her brother Max! Charlie spotted her brother lying on the ground after the troops continued to advance. He wasn't moving. That got Charlie moving.

Crawling on her belly, Charlie Ward made her way through the rank and file of the soldiers behind the lines. Her goal was the front line, where she could see her brother lying motionless. Despite the deafening sounds of battle, both rifles and cannon fire, Charlie kept her eye on her brother. Now, the Union soldiers were moving forward, chasing the Confederates over a distant hill. Max remained where he was, but Charlie was relieved to see her brother only grasping his thigh.

That's a good sign, Charlie told herself. He's not dead. That's good. I can help him.

Finally, she was able to reach the battleground where her brother lay on the blood-stained ground.

"Max, Max – it's me, Charlotte," she said softly into her brother's ear.

"Char, you can't be here." His sister's face loomed over his.

"Don't tell me what I can and cannot do, brother. And since we're talking about who can and can't be here, you were still seventeen years old the last time I checked. I came here to bring you home. It took a while for me to find you. Let's not fight right now. There's been enough fighting here today. I can see that you're bleeding. Looks like it's your right leg."

"It hurts, Char. It hurts."

"Let's get you back to the hospital tent. Can you use your other leg?"

"I think so." Charlotte helped Max stand, and he swung his right arm over Charlotte's shoulder. With the battle still raging, they made their way through the dead and dying soldiers that littered the battlefield.

Arriving at the field hospital, Charlotte called for a doctor to attend her brother.

While they waited, Charlotte ripped open the leg of Max's uniform pants. She probed the wound and could tell that the minié ball was still in Max's leg.

Patiently, Charlotte waited for an Army doctor to examine her brother, but the doctors were pulled in too many directions. Initial assessment determined that Max's wounds were not life-threatening, so he would have to wait. Charlotte watched as the surgeons amputated arms and legs. She was determined that would not be her brother's fate.

As night fell and the flow of wounded men did not subside, Charlotte took matters into her own hands – literally.

Spotting a tray of medical instruments, she laid Max flat on a cot and went to work.

"This is going to hurt, but I can't find any laudanum. I'm sorry for that. You can bite on this stick. That might help some."

He nodded and put the stick between his teeth.

Charlotte rinsed the wound in whiskey, and Max groaned. "Yell if you have to. Nobody will notice," she told her brother.

Surveying the surgical tools, Charlotte selected a thin, pointed instrument to probe for the minié ball. After some digging, she found it lodged in her brother's upper thigh. The wound had since stopped bleeding, so she didn't think it had struck a blood vessel.

"We're making progress, Max," she assured her patient. "Now I just need to remove the ball without doing more damage." For that procedure, Charlotte reached for the forceps on the tray.

"This would work better." An Army surgeon handed Charlotte an extractor made specifically for removing the minié balls.

Even though she was shaken that she had an audience, Charlotte didn't take her eyes off the open wound. She took the proffered instrument and caught the minié ball. Carefully, Charlotte removed the ball from Max's thigh. The metal ball made a clang as she dropped it onto the surgical tray.

"Nicely done, Doctor…." The Army surgeon waited for a name.

"I'm not a doctor, but it seemed like everyone else here was busy and my brother needed help." She saluted the surgeon. "Private Ward, sir. Charlie Ward."

"We don't stand on formalities here, Ward. I'm Dr. Bernard, a colonel by rank, but you can call me Thomas." He nodded to Max's leg. "Go ahead and close it. Then we'll talk."

Charlotte nodded and proceeded to suture the wound with a needle and thread she found on the tray. While she focused on stitching the wound, Charlotte gathered her thoughts. She wondered if she'd been discovered. Now what?

Thomas brought over a bottle of laudanum and a spoon. "Here, give him a spoonful of this. It will help him rest. That's all we can do now – that and watch for infection. We're losing more boys to infection and dysentery than we are to Rebel bullets." The surgeon shook his head in disgust.

Dr. Bernard examined Max's leg. "That was a nice piece of doctoring you did there, Charlie. You've had experience."

"I took care of my ma when she was sick after my baby sister died in childbirth. When my pa got kicked in the head by a mule, I tended to him. My 'doctoring,' as you call it, didn't do much to save either of them, but I learned some of the basics. Growing up on the farm, I fixed a few broken bones and stitched up bad cuts."

"You have a talent for it, Charlie. Would you like to work in the hospital tent? We could use another set of hands."

"I could watch over my brother?"

"That would be part of your duties, Charlie."

"You can count on me."

"I'll warn you, it's long hours and hard work," Thomas said.

"So is soldiering. But there aren't so many bullets flying around in here. I'll need reassignment orders to show my sergeant."

Dr. Bernard scribbled something on a scrap of paper. "If he has a problem with it, send him to me."

"Thank you again."

With that, Dr. Bernard left to attend to other wounded soldiers. Charlotte sat by Max's cot, relieved that she'd found her brother and that they were both away from the front lines of battle – for now.

Charlotte was exhausted. While she watched over her brother, she recalled the day she had discovered that Max had joined the Army. That was the day that changed the course of her life.

After-Action Report – Battle of Carthage

July 5, 1861

The Battle of Carthage gave Missouri its first taste of War. Union Colonel Franz Sigel's force of 1,100 men attacked a larger contingent but poorly armed Missouri militia led by the state's governor, Claiborne Jackson. The battle culminated with a firefight in the Carthage town square. Although Jackson's men did not dislodge Sigel's force, the Union troops retreated that evening. The battle buoyed Confederate hopes in Missouri.

Chapter 2: July 1861
Ward Farm, St. Joseph, MO

"Papa would have wanted me to join up, sis," argued Max. "He always said slavery was an abomination." Maxwell Ward was tall for his age, with shaggy, light brown hair bleached from the Missouri sun. Working on the Ward farm since he could walk, he had built muscle and appeared older than his seventeen years.

"You're too young, Max," Charlotte countered. "Enlistment age is eighteen. Wait until next summer."

"What if the War's over by then? Jimmy Potter and his brother joined up and they got to fight at Boonville with General Lyon. The Blue Coats routed the Rebs. I don't want to miss out, Char."

"I thought Papa's anti-slavery beliefs were inspiring you to go to War. Now you say you don't want to 'miss out.' Neither Papa nor Mama would cotton to you joining the Army," his older sister said. "I'm head of the family now, and I'm saying no. Besides, Lizzy and I need you on the farm. It'll be harvest time soon."

Max stomped off, but Charlotte knew this wasn't the end of the argument. Too many of their neighbors had joined, and not just on the Union side. Missouri was one of the most divided states in the country. Missouri Governor Claiborne Jackson was pushing for the state to secede, even though in February the state convention had voted 98-1 to stay in the Union. And then the Rebs fired on Ft. Sumter in April, signaling the start of the War.

Elizabeth Ward watched her siblings take up the familiar clash, but, as the middle child, she tried to stay neutral. Elizabeth, "Lizzy" to her family, was three years older than Max and two years younger than Charlotte. For as long as she could remember, Lizzy had worked beside her father while Char helped in the house and nursed their ailing mother after yet another pregnancy that ended in a stillbirth.

"You're both stubborn as mules. He's going to run off, you know," Lizzy said to her older sister.

"I know. But I don't have to give him my blessing."

Lizzy clicked her tongue and re-positioned her wide-brimmed hat. Her thick, dark blonde hair was tied in long braids to keep it out of the way while she worked. Unlike her sister, Lizzy's figure was curvy, and she was at least a head shorter than either of her siblings. People said Lizzy was "the pretty Ward girl," thanks in part to her unusual hazel-colored eyes and long lashes. But it was Lizzy's dimples that people remembered about the young woman. Her dimples were deep set and appeared on her rosy cheeks whenever she broke into a smile.

Since the death of their father three years ago, Lizzy had been managing the farm. Her pa said she was the "real farmer" in the family. Lizzy could calm a mare about to foal, and she seemed to sense when rain was coming. But more than that, she loved working the fertile soil in northwestern Missouri.

"I'm moving the cows into the west pasture this morning. Can you collect the eggs?" she asked Charlotte.

"I will. We have enough to sell, so I'll make a trip into town."

In a gesture of conciliation, Charlotte invited Max to ride into St. Joseph on that hot July day. She had hoped the ride would give her time to talk some sense into her brother. It was a decision that Charlotte later regretted. The town was abuzz with war news, which only fed Max's hunger to enlist.

Charlotte conducted her business at the general store, pleased that the price of eggs was adding to the family's savings account. Since the Wards grew most of what they needed, Charlotte only purchased a few supplies.

"Char," Max called as he rushed up to her on the street. "Boonville was just the beginning! Governor Jackson and the Rebs pursued the Yanks to Carthage last week. And this time the Rebs won."

Seeing that his sister was unmoved by the urgency of the situation, Max continued. "They're calling it the Battle of Carthage, Char. The Union needs me, Charlotte. I've got to join up."

"It's just the three of us on the farm. You're needed on the farm, Max. No more talk of War."

The ride back to the farm was silent. Charlotte was making mental lists about the chores that awaited her. Max was planning his escape.

August 1861

The War continued to favor the Confederate troops that summer. Pro-Southern sympathizers called the Battle of Carthage their first victory in the state. Soon after, the two forces met again, this time in Springfield, Missouri.

On August 9th, Union General Nathaniel Lyon's forces faced off against superior numbers of Confederate troops under the command of General Sterling Price at Wilson's Creek. Following Confederate counterattacks and General Lyon's death, the new Union commander, Major Samuel Sturgis, ordered a retreat. Even though the Rebel army did not pursue, the Battle of Wilson's Creek was called a Confederate victory and buoyed Southern sympathizers in Missouri.

The Battle of Wilson's Creek was a call to arms for Max Ward. After reading an account of the battle in the Kansas City newspaper, Max was more determined than ever to enlist.

Just days later, his chance came. In the distance, Max could hear the roar of cannons. Riding to the top of a hill, he saw the smoke. After dark, Max saddled his horse and rode away, heeding the siren call of battle.

When Charlotte and Lizzy discovered that Max had run away to the Army, they debated what to do.

"There's no question that I have to go after him, Lizzy," Charlotte said. "He's only seventeen and, like all boys, he thinks he's invincible. Pa's last words to me were, 'protect them, Char.' I hate to leave you, but can you handle the farm without me for a few days?"

"You've kept the house running, Charlotte. But you're not a farmer," Lizzy replied. "Go after Max. Don't worry about the farm. Go fetch Max – if he'll come home."

"Are you sure?"

"Of course. But how will you do it? You can't just ride into an Army camp and demand they hand over a soldier."

Charlotte thought about it for a moment. "I'll join the Army if I have to."

"I've heard of women following the armies, but…" Lizzy said, referring to the laundresses and camp followers who tagged behind the troops.

"I'm not about to wash somebody else's underwear, Lizzy. Besides, that won't get me close enough to Max. I'll cut my hair, lower my voice, and enlist as a man.

"Say hello to Max's brother, Charlie Ward." Charlotte straightened to her full height and held out her hand to shake in greeting.

"It will never work. How will you tend to your…personal needs?"

"I'll figure it out when I have to," Charlotte declared. Then, with a wry smile, she said, "I believe Charlie Ward is a very private person. My greatest challenge will be finding Max among all the Union troops."

"What's your plan?"

She bit her lip, then said, "Hmm. Still working on that."

"When will you leave?" Lizzy asked.

"Let's get as much done around the farm as we can. I'll need to enlist somewhere that's not close by. I don't want anyone recognizing me."

In preparation for her deception, Charlotte found some of Max's cast-off clothes, which were just about the right size. She began wearing them around the farm and practiced more "manly" mannerisms when she walked or stood. She trained herself not to use her hands when she talked and to look directly into the eyes of people she spoke with. Lizzy, however, was the only person she could practice on to this point.

Charlotte's height and features helped with her disguise, too. Her eyes were a deep, dark brown rimmed with short lashes. Her light brown hair, usually worn in a bun, was striking but not as memorable as her sister's golden mane. And being slender meant she would not have to bind her breasts to complete the transformation. To her dismay, though, the freckles that sprinkled across her thin nose gave her face a softer, playful look that contrasted the soldier's appearance she was trying to project.

"I refuse to spit, though," she told Lizzy one day.

"A disgusting habit," her sister agreed. "Even so, you make a fine man, Charlie Ward."

The two sisters smiled.

"We have to do something about your hair," Lizzy said.

Charlotte handed her sister a pair of scissors. "Start cutting."

When she was done, Lizzy stood back to take in the new Charlie Ward. "I couldn't bear to cut it all off, but your hair is short enough to pass for a man," she said. Lizzy handed a mirror to Charlotte.

"I'm as ready as I'll ever be," Charlotte said. "I'll ride out tomorrow. If I head east, I should run into a Union outfit sooner or later. I just need to steer clear of the Confederates and the State Militia."

"Send me word when you find him," Lizzy asked.

Charlotte rode toward south and east, looking for blue-coated Northern troops. Instead, she encountered Confederate troops marching toward the Kansas border. Major General Sterling Price, the victor at Wilson's Creek, was gathering recruits to march on Lexington, Missouri.

The last thing Charlotte wanted was to be forced to join the Army of the Confederacy. Hastily, Charlotte found the skirt in her saddle bag and pulled it on over her trousers. She tied a long scarf into a bow at her neck and put a pretty smile on her face. Luckily, the wide-brimmed hat covered her short hair.

The Rebel soldiers marched by Charlotte and her horse on the side of the road. Recognizing several of the Missouri soldiers in the regiment, Charlotte waved and wished them good fortune. What she was really thinking was how fortunate she'd been to pack the skirt for just such an incident.

Back in her Charlie Ward disguise, she came upon a company of Blue Coats. The 13th Missouri Infantry, commanded by Colonel Peabody, was stationed in

Lexington. Finding a likely officer, Charlie introduced himself and asked where he could enlist. The Union forces struggled to gain a foothold in Missouri, so every enlistee was heartily welcomed.

As a new recruit, Charlie Ward spent his days drilling, cooking meals, and cleaning equipment. Some soldiers, like Charlie, wrote letters home in their free time.

Charlie kept an eye out for her brother and asked fellow soldiers if they had seen Max. Sooner or later, she realized, she would be faced with battle. She steeled herself for that eventuality.

After-Action Report: Battle of Wilson's Creek
Aug 10, 1861

The Battle of Wilson's Creek, called Oak Hills by Southerners, was fought ten miles southwest of Springfield, Missouri, on August 10, 1861. The battle pitted a smaller but aggressive Union Army of approximately 5,400 soldiers against the 11,000 combined forces of Confederate soldiers and the pro-secessionist Missouri State Guard.

The Southern Army's victory at Wilson's Creek secured southwestern Missouri for Confederate forces. Politically, the Wilson's Creek victory energized pro-secessionists to pass an unofficial ordinance of secession.

For the next three and a half years, Missouri was the scene of fierce fighting, mostly guerrilla warfare, such as Quantrill's Raiders, that destroyed anything of military or civilian value that could aid the Federals.

Chapter 3: September 1861
Ward Farm

The Siege of Lexington, as it became known, gave both Union and Confederate soldiers a real taste of War – and many found it distasteful. Deserters were common, and since many were good ol' Missouri boys, they knew the lay of the land and struck out for home.

Lizzy Ward became accustomed to seeing lone riders in the distance. Once in a while, the deserters would be bold enough to ride – or walk – into the farmyard looking for a handout or a job. That was how Lizzy met Frank James.

Lizzy was milking cows when she saw the "walking scarecrow" enter the farmyard. He looked somewhat familiar. She finished with the last cow and left the barn to intercept the drifter.

"Howdy, ma'am," he said. "I'm lookin' for Max. This is the Ward place, isn't it?"

Relieved that the stranger might simply be a neighbor, she answered, "This is the Ward farm, but Max isn't here. How do you know my brother?" She hoped that the stranger could provide some information about Max's whereabouts.

"I'm Frank James. My family's from over in Clay County. Max was a year behind me in country school. But that was a few years back."

"Yes, it was," she said, warming up to the stranger. "Max joined up a few weeks ago. Are you... were you in the Army, too?"

"Yes'm," Frank answered. "In the Missouri Guard, fighting under General Sterling. I was at the Battle of Lexington. Got left behind in the infirmary when my outfit pulled out. Now I'm bound for home to heal up."

Realizing that Frank James and the Wards were on opposite sides of the conflict, Lizzy didn't ask about Max's whereabouts.

"I'm just looking for a place to rest tonight, if it's all the same to you, Miss Ward," Frank continued.

"Of course. I'm Lizzy – Elizabeth Ward – Max's older sister. You're welcome to stay in the barn, Mr. James."

"Thank you, kindly. I'd be pleased to help with chores in return."

"I was just about to gather the eggs, but if you want to help, I'll start dinner," Lizzy said, motioning to the hen house.

Over dinner, Lizzy and Frank James talked about their families. Lizzy didn't clarify that Max had joined the Union Army or any details about Charlotte at all.

"You're working the farm all alone, Miss Lizzy?" he asked.

"The crops are mostly in, so I'm just taking care of the animals now. And next spring, well, a lot can happen between now and next spring."

As good as his word, Frank James left the next morning. As Lizzy watched him walk down the path, she hoped he would be one of the lucky ones who survived the War.

November 1861

Frank James wasn't the only soldier who made his way to the Ward farm that autumn. Young men who thought that War would be exciting or had imagined they would make a name for themselves came away with entirely different perspectives about army life and combat. Sometimes these deserters came alone; sometimes, they arrived in small groups. Sometimes, like Frank James, they had been injured and needed to recuperate. They were all hungry, tired, and disillusioned.

In early November, two Union soldiers, deserters actually, wandered into the farmyard as Lizzy was feeding the cows. She had put up hay for winter feeding, but the grass in the pastures wasn't providing enough grazing for her small herd.

Lizzy was considering selling or butchering one or two head of cattle when she saw the stragglers. Because deserters were becoming commonplace, Lizzy carried a shotgun with her when she was out of the house, just in case.

The visitors were dirty. The taller of the pair had a bandage around his head. The other deserter was walking with a limp.

She wiped her hands on her apron, sighed, and greeted the men.

"Gentlemen. This is the Ward farm. Would you like a dipper of water? Please help yourselves." She nodded to the well.

Both men eagerly availed themselves of the fresh well water. For too many days, they had been drinking from streams and creeks – some of which had a suspicious tinge of pink in the water.

"Mighty neighborly of you, ma'am," said the shorter man. He still wore the dark blue trousers but had changed the more recognizable blue sack coat for a brown jacket. His partner wore the blue coat but had removed the military insignia. Both men had dark brown beards and long, shaggy hair. Lizzy thought they might be brothers. She was correct.

"Neighbors, you say. Are you from around here?" she asked.

"We're headed home. Iowa," said the shorter man.

"Joe, we're forgetting our manners." Both men removed their hats, and the taller man said, "I'm Rob Taylor. This is my brother Joe. Thank you kindly for the water. Could we trouble you for a night's rest in the barn?"

Lizzy thought about her own brother. What if Max were on the road, making his way home, too? What if he needed shelter for a night? While it might not have been the wisest of choices, Lizzy's charitable nature won out.

"You may."

"We'd be willing to clean the barn or muck out the stable for a hot meal," Rob continued.

"I won't turn down willing labor," Lizzy said. "Tonight's meal is chicken and dumplings. Clean up at the well when you're done working."

Lizzy had an ulterior motive for inviting the men to her table. She wanted news of the War. And, they might have served with Max.

As it turned out, the Taylor brothers had served with Max.

"Wasn't there a 'Ward' at Linn Creek last month, Joe?" Rob queried his brother.

"I think you're right. He was with the Missouri Volunteers, if I recall," said Joe.

Lizzy was thrilled to get news of her brother, even if it was second-hand. "Max? He was there?"

"Can't say for certain, Miss, but I seem to recollect a tall, lanky kid from Missouri, and I heard someone refer to him as 'Ward.'"

"That's wonderful news, gentlemen. Any word about my brother is much appreciated."

"If that was the right soldier, he was still upright," agreed Rob Taylor.

"Glad we had good news for you, Miss," said Joe.

The Taylor brothers stayed in the barn that night. In the morning, they thanked Lizzy again for her hospitality and continued their trek north toward Iowa.

News that Max was still alive and well buoyed Lizzy's mood. Even with the occasional deserter showing up at the farm, she was lonely. Lizzy had always worked side-by-side with her father and, when he was old enough, her brother Max. Now, she talked to the farm animals. But mostly, Lizzy talked to her cat, Butter.

Butter had been part of a litter a few years ago. As time went on, the other farm cats disappeared — either they ran away or, well, Lizzy didn't want to consider the other options.

The yellow tabby had started as a barn cat, but she soon became a house cat. Butter craved affection. On winter nights, Lizzy would read a book with Butter curled on her lap. Lizzy had found that knitting or needlework with a cat on her lap didn't work well.

Still, Butter earned her keep. She was a good mouser and kept the house and barn free of rodents.

After-Action Report: Siege of Lexington
September, 1861

Following their victory at Wilson's Creek on August 10th, the pro-Confederate Missouri State Guard continued to march on Union forces. The Siege of Lexington began when the Missouri State Guard advanced on the Union fortifications in Lexington, Missouri. On the afternoon of September 20th, the Southerners rushed the lines, forcing Union officers to surrender.

The victory won by the Missouri Guard bolstered the Southern support in the area and consolidated Missouri State Guard control of the Missouri River Valley in the western part of the state.

Chapter 4: November 1861
Springfield, MO

The War touched the lives of the Ward siblings, all in different ways.

Max was injured in the Springfield skirmish.

Charlotte, also known as Charlie, was now working in the Union field hospital.

And Lizzy, back on the farm, was constantly on the lookout for deserters.

Still, she was comforted by the news from the Taylor brothers that Max had been seen a few weeks back in Linn, Missouri. Then she received the letter that Max had been shot.

Dear Lizzy,

I found Max! We were both at the Springfield skirmish. Max was wounded in action. I was at the back of the company, but I heard someone call his name. After he was shot in the leg, I was able to get him to the field hospital. The injury wasn't too severe. I removed the rifle ball, and he's recovering now. We are so close to the farm – about a half-day's ride. I'll try to convince Max to leave with me.

Everything you've heard about War is true, Lizzy. It's loud and dirty. There aren't enough doctors to tend to the sick and wounded. This brings me to my next news: I've been reassigned to the field hospital. Apparently my "medical experience" in removing the bullet impressed one of the surgeons. The good news is that I'll be able to keep an eye on Max while he heals. The bad news is that he's eager to return to the fight. If you have any words of wisdom for me, please write back. I will be in General Fremont's battalion.

I will try to write more regularly. Oh, how I miss the quiet days on the farm.

Char

Lizzy took the news with mixed emotions. Her brother was injured, but he was alive. And her sister was no longer on the front battle lines, even though the field hospitals weren't always safe havens.

As for "quiet days on the farm," not all the visitors were as congenial as Frank James or the Taylor brothers. Lizzy kept the cows in the nearby pasture; the pigs were in a pen next to the barn. More than once, she had discovered deserters attempting to make off with a pig or a couple of chickens. Lizzy knew it was only a matter of time before one of her cows was killed by scavengers.

In the field hospital, Charlie Ward kept busy assisting Dr. Bernard with amputations. Oh, how she hated amputations. Piles of arms and legs were stacked up like cordwood as doctors tried frantically to save patients at the expense of their limbs. Battlefield medicine did not allow physicians the luxury of repairing injuries.

But, Charlotte learned, it wasn't battlefield injuries that killed most of her patients. Disease and dysentery were the biggest killers. Infections ran rampant in the military hospitals, both in the rough field hospitals and in the general hospitals that were far from the front lines.

Charlie was spoon-feeding a new amputee when Dr. Bernard called her.

"Ward, I need some assistance here," the surgeon said.

Immediately, Charlie put down the bowl and spoon and hurried to the table where Thomas Bernard was cauterizing a deep wound. The smell of burning flesh was overwhelming, but Charlie had become accustomed to this and other medical procedures.

The one smell that Charlie would never get used to was gangrenous flesh. Of all the conditions that Civil War doctors encountered, gangrene was one of the most fearsome. Charlie tried to keep wounds clean and was constantly washing equipment. "Almost done," Thomas said when Charlie arrived at the table. "Hand me that cauterizing iron and I'll finish the work. Hopefully, this will prevent gangrene from setting in."

Charlie nodded and handed Thomas the heated instrument. The patient was sedated, so he couldn't hear the warning about gangrene and hopefully couldn't feel his skin and muscles burning. Even so, Charlie had to immobilize the patient during the procedure to prevent involuntary movements.

"That should do it, Charlie," said Thomas. "Now we wait. That's the hardest part of being a doctor, in my opinion. Watching and waiting to see if our efforts are successful. And if they're not successful, what should we do next."

He continued, "You know, you seem to have an instinct for healing, Charlie. Have you ever considered going to medical school?"

"Me in medical school?" Charlie replied. "No, I've never thought about it. Most of what I know I learned on the farm. I could set a broken bone or stitch a deep cut. But when my father was hurt in a farm accident, I couldn't save him. I'm not sure I have the skills to be a doctor."

Thomas heard the uncertainty in Charlie's voice. "Nothing beats on-the-job training. If you're interested in medicine, this is the place to be. The flow of incoming wounded has slowed down. I think I'll walk through the tent and check on patients. Care to join me? Consider it part of your medical training."

"Thank you. There are a couple of patients that need your attention."

"Lead the way, Dr. Ward," Thomas said.

Charlie smiled inwardly. She liked the sound of that.

They stopped at Max's cot. "Private Ward, how's that leg doing?" Thomas asked. "Is it giving you any pain?"

"I'll be up and out of here in no time, doc," Max answered.

"Your brother here did a fine job of field surgery," Thomas nodded to Charlie.

Charlotte knew that Max still had a hard time seeing his older sister as a man. "Yes, I guess sh…I guess so," Max amended his response.

"If I may, Dr. Bernard," Charlie interrupted. "I'd like Max to stay around until there's no chance of infection."

"Caution is good, Charlie, but we'll need this bed when more casualties start coming in from the next skirmish." Thomas turned to Max, "You mind your brother, Private Ward. He's in charge of you."

"Always has been, Colonel Bernard," Max said with a smile.

Thomas and Charlie moved down the row of hospital cots. "Who's next on your list, Charlie?"

"This is an unusual patient, Doctor." Then, in a whisper, Charlie said, "I think he's a Reb."

That got Thomas Bernard's attention. "What makes you think so? His uniform?"

"It's more that he's *not* in uniform. Most of our boys are in blue. The Confederates – at least the ones I've seen on the front – were wearing gray or butternut. And to make it more confusing, some of them wear Union blue they've found on the battlefield." Charlie paused, then said, "It's more a feeling I have about this one."

"What's he here for," Thomas asked.

"Head wound," Charlie replied.

"Is he conscious?"

"He drifts in and out. It's some of the things he's said that makes me think he's a Confederate."

"Our duty is to treat all patients, regardless of the uniform. Let's take a look. Do you have a name?" Thomas headed toward the cot of the patient in question.

"I found his name – I think it's his name – scratched on his belt buckle," Charlie offered. "It says 'Luke Jameson.'"

Thomas unwrapped the bandage to reveal a deep gash on the side of the patient's head. "That's a nasty injury, soldier," Thomas said to the man on the cot.

Luke Jameson had a strong, thin face with a long, bushy mustache the same color as his chestnut hair. Charlie couldn't guess his height, but judging from Jameson's arms and chest, Luke Jameson had a muscular build.

"Yes, sir," the patient answered.

"Do you know where you are, soldier?" Dr. Bernard began the familiar litany of questions used to determine the severity of head wounds.

Luke Jameson looked around and said, "A field hospital, sir?"

"What's the last thing you remember," Dr. Bernard continued.

"I was on the front lines by Springfield. Heavy incoming attack, then I went down. That's about it, sir."

"What's your rank?" What company are you in?"

Cautiously, Jameson answered, "Sergeant, sir. The rest is a little fuzzy. I was reassigned to a new unit a couple of days ago. Can I think on that?"

Not satisfied but ready to move on to the next patient, Dr. Bernard said, "Let's give it another day or so. Head wounds can play with our memories, soldier. Charlie, see to his wound with clean bandages when we're done here."

Charlie nodded and continued on with Dr. Bernard. When they completed their rounds, Dr. Bernard left the medical tent in search of a meal. Charlie returned to Max's bed.

"I've written to Lizzy, Max. She knows you've been wounded. We could slip out tonight and head to the farm. It's less than a half-day ride. There's no disgrace in going back home."

"You can't boss me around here, Char, even though the doc says you can," Max replied. "The War will be over soon. We've got the Rebs on the run. I enlisted and gave my word to fight for the Union. I'm bound to stick it out."

"You're only seventeen, Max. You can't make decisions for yourself. That's my job. Pa said so."

"Pa's been gone for three years. I'll be eighteen in the spring. Besides, there are a lot of soldiers younger than me in this Army."

"He's right," Luke Jameson called from the nearby cot. "There are two boys that are sixteen serving in my unit."

Charlie glared at Luke. "I thought you couldn't remember which unit you were in. Stay out of this fight, soldier."

Luke shrugged his shoulder and just smiled as the siblings continued to argue.

"After my leg heals enough to walk, I'm headed back to the lines, Char," Max said. "You won't be able to keep an eye on me out there. If you haul me back to the farm before that, I'll just run away again."

"Incorrigible, that's what Mama called you," Charlie said. "Incorrigible and stubborn." She grabbed clean bandages from a nearby basket and went to Luke Jameson's bed.

"I think your memory is better than you're letting on," she said to Jameson as she unwound the bloody bandages on his head.

"It comes and goes," he answered. "Where abouts are you and your brother from," he asked Charlie.

Charlie concentrated on tending to Jameson's head wound. "We farm by St. Joe," Charlie answered, using the nickname for her hometown.

"My family's from St. Louis County," he said. Charlotte knew better than to believe him. A common pastime for soldiers was to look for mutual friends.

"Mmm. Don't know anyone over that way," Charlie said. She was just about done applying the clean bandages.

"There, that ought to do it. Dr. Bernard said to rest." Charlie gave Jameson a critical look, "And maybe work on that story of yours."

Luke knew he should be more wary of Charlie Ward. The medic asked a lot of questions — questions that Luke didn't want to answer. If anyone in the field hospital figured out that Luke was a Confederate officer, he would be recuperating in a prisoner of war camp. Still, something about Charlie's disturbing deep-brown eyes haunted Luke.

Military engagements were light in the days after Springfield. Charlie, Thomas Bernard, and the rest of the field hospital staff were thankful that the lull in fighting gave patients time to recover before they were sent back to their respective military units. It also gave Lizzy's letter time to find her siblings. In her greeting, Lizzy continued the ruse, addressing the letter to Charlie Ward.

Dear Charlie,

I was so happy to learn that you found Max and that, aside from the bullet wound, he is well. I trust you will keep him safe until he returns home soon. Please assure him that since he is not of enlistment age, he will not be deserting.

I have, however, "entertained" quite a few deserters in the past few months. Some were local men and boys who had their fill of War. Others were returning to their farms to help with harvest, intending to rejoin their units when the farm work was done. All of them – Union and Confederate – were tired, dirty, and hungry. I've made it a habit always to have a pot of soup cooking. Lately, (I hesitate to write this lest you worry about me) I've noticed chickens and pigs missing, so I keep my shotgun handy at all times. I haven't had to shoot anyone yet, but I believe those days may be coming. It would be good to have Max at home. Perhaps that might convince him that he's needed here.

One of my earlier guests was a local man, Frank James, from Clay County, who was returning home to recover. He said he knew Max from their school days. There have been other deserters passing through, too. Because of that, I've decided to move the livestock to a nearby cave this winter to keep them more secure.

Please give my best to our brother. I look forward to the day that both of you are safe at home.

Your loving sister, Lizzy

Charlie read the letter to her brother, emphasizing how much Lizzy needed him to come home. Max only responded, "Sounds like she's doing just fine without me. I'm staying put, Charlie."

Charlie thought she heard a chuckle from Jameson in a nearby cot. She ignored it.

Missouri was admitted to the Confederacy in late November, even though the state never officially seceded from the Union. That act riled up the Union forces in Missouri and surrounding states.

Several days later, Max declared he was fit to rejoin his outfit. And even though he was walking with a limp, he pulled on his blue wool trousers with the repaired *minié* ball hole, buttoned up his dark blue wool coat, and donned his forage cap. Despite Charlie's insistence that he wasn't ready for combat, Max Ward reported for duty.

Spotting the empty cot on morning rounds, Charlie didn't cry. Of course, Charlotte Ward rarely cried either.

"It was only a matter of time, I guess," Charlie said to no one in particular.

"He was craving to rejoin fight, Charlie," said Luke Jameson.

"I suppose you'll be leaving soon, too."

"The headaches are fewer and the hole in my head is nearly gone," Luke responded. "It's time for me to leave, too."

Charlie's dark eyes squinted. "So, where is your outfit again? All this time in the infirmary and you've not completed any paperwork."

"Hmmm, it is a quandary, isn't it? If only I could remember…"

Charlie nodded. She glanced around to make sure no one was in earshot. "When you arrived at the medical tent you were delirious. You said some things that made me wonder what side you're fighting on."

"Did you tell anyone what I said?"

"I may have said something to Dr. Bernard in the beginning, but he believes we should treat all patients, whatever color their uniform. Nothing more was said. Now, I need to follow the doctor's orders. It's time to change that bandage."

Charlie expertly unwound the strips of cloth, tossed them into a laundry bag, and began re-bandaging

Luke's head wound. "Your injury *is* healing nicely," Charlie said.

Luke watched intently as Charlie completed the procedure. He was mesmerized by Charlie's ebony eyes. Most disturbingly, when Charlie touched Luke, he felt a thrill of electricity. Luke had lain awake at night, trying to decipher the feelings he was experiencing. He had never been attracted to a man before. It was uncanny and unnerving. Why did he feel these things about Charlie Ward? Was it the head wound?

Putting his hand to his injured head, "The headaches are getting better," Luke repeated.

Dang it, Luke thought. *I sound like a tongue-tied schoolboy.*

"Mmm, you said that. How is your vision?" She moved a candle flame in front of Luke's face and stared directly into his slate-gray eyes.

"Stop that. My vision has always been fine," Luke growled. He pulled away from Charlie to put some distance between them.

"Ah, you're getting testy. That's a sure sign that you're feeling better," Charlie observed. "I'll talk to Dr. Bernard about a discharge tomorrow. We'll get that paperwork started."

Luke considered this. He would have to slip out during the night before the paperwork proved that he wasn't actually in the Union Army.

"About that paperwork…" he began.

"Armies run on paperwork – both armies, Luke."

Luke Jameson arched an eyebrow. "So, you think you know my secret."

Charlie had accepted that Luke was an enemy combatant. It was simply a fact of life in the divided state of Missouri. Many of the Ward's neighbors had chosen to fight for the Rebels.

"Why?" Charlie asked.

"Why return?"

"No, why are you fighting for slavery? Does your family have slaves?"

Luke gave a wry smile. "My family has a small horse farm. No slaves. But a lot of our neighbors own slaves. I didn't really have a choice when the unit in our county was formed. I was expected to join up." He sighed. "And now you know my dark secret. Will you turn me in?"

"That's not my job. My job is to change bandages and bed pans, dispense medicine and assist the surgeons when needed."

Luke looked directly at Charlie and said, "Will you look the other way tonight? Just for a few minutes?"

Charlie did not respond at first, then said, "If you are uncomfortable at any point, please call out. Otherwise, I will be attending to other duties."

"Thank you, Charlie Ward. I won't forget this."

When Charlie made her rounds the next morning, she found Luke's cot empty.

Luke discovered it was easy to walk away from the army hospital. Now that the shelling and bombardments had ceased, it wasn't unusual to see medical staff or patients out for an evening stroll. The doctors encouraged patients to take short walks and "stretch their legs." It was easy to simply disappear into the darkness on the edge of camp. It was as simple as that.

What wasn't so simple were Luke's feelings for Charlie Ward. Luke was confused and, to be honest, a bit worried. He'd never been attracted to another man. Hell, he'd been an eligible bachelor back in Boone County, and he'd enjoyed the company of more than one young lady. He knew that War changed men, but he didn't think he had changed *that much*.

For weeks after his secret departure, Luke had romantic thoughts about Charlie Ward. Those deep, dark brown eyes. The sprinkling of freckles across Charlie's nose and cheekbones. The easy conversations they had. He had admitted to himself that maybe he was attracted to Charlie Ward.

After-Action Report – Skirmish at Springfield
October 25, 1861

After the Battle of Wilson's Creek, Missouri's pro-Confederate State Guard met and defeated Union forces in Lexington, Missouri. Following that battle, General John C. Fremont initiated a campaign to push into southern Missouri. On October 24, 1861, Union troops were sent on a scouting mission toward Springfield, Missouri, where they encountered Missouri State Guard soldiers under the command of Confederate Colonel Julian Frazier. Two days later, the State Guard retreated, and Federal troops occupied Springfield, Missouri.

Chapter 5: Spring 1862
New Madrid, MO

The pause in casualties did not last long. In the spring, skirmishes around Kansas City created a steady stream of injured soldiers at the field hospital. Charlie continued working at Dr. Bernard's side, assuming a greater role in treating patients. In doing so, she grew more confident in her role as a medic.

The tide turned in the Union's favor by December 1861. On December 18th, Union forces surprised Confederate regulars and militia near Milford at Shawnee Mound, south of Kansas City. The Federals captured just over 1,300 Confederate troops and shipped the prisoners by train to St. Louis.

Charlie thought fleetingly about Luke Jameson, wondering if he was among the captives.

More often, she worried about her brother. Max had never been one for writing letters, so she didn't expect any communication from him. But she knew that his unit had been dispatched to the Milford skirmish. Each day, when casualty reports arrived, Charlie scanned the documents, hoping to not see her brother's name on the lists.

Sometimes, Charlie wondered why she didn't just give up and return to the farm. It wasn't easy to keep her secret among the male soldiers she served with. Still, working in the hospital allowed her a semblance of privacy that was not possible in fighting units. She had private quarters near the field hospital and enjoyed more freedom to move around the camp. Besides, she loved being in the hospital, working side-by-side with Dr. Bernard and the other Union doctors.

Her curiosity and interest in medicine began when Charlotte was young. She was only five when she watched the midwife bring Max into the world. It wasn't unusual for older children to assist midwives during deliveries in rural parts of the country.

Each pregnancy became increasingly difficult for Blanche Ward. As the oldest daughter, Charlotte assumed more and more household duties when her mother was too tired or sick to care for her family.

When a family member was sick or there was a farm injury, it was Charlotte who nursed them back to health. Until she didn't. Charlotte still carried the awful burden of not being able to "save" her mother after a particularly difficult delivery that resulted in a stillborn birth. After the midwife left, Blanche began to hemorrhage. Try as she might, Charlotte could not staunch the blood loss. Her mother lingered for two days before slipping away. Charlotte had been only fourteen at the time.

With his wife gone, Jacob Ward relied on Charlotte to manage the household while he, along with Elizabeth and Max's help, did the farm work. In 1858, just five years later, a mule kicked Jacob in the head. He lay in a coma for nearly a week before he died. Again, Charlotte felt her caregiving was inadequate. She had failed a family member.

In his passing, their father left Charlotte, age nineteen, Elizabeth, age seventeen, and Max, age fourteen. The three siblings became a tightly-knit group. Each sibling brought their own skills and strengths to the family farm – until Max decided to break those bonds by enlisting.

Charlotte had promised herself that someday she would learn all she could about medicine so that she could better protect her loved ones. That time came when Thomas Bernard asked Charlotte to work in the field hospital.

Thomas gave Charlie a great deal of responsibility. As Thomas said earlier, this was on-the-job training for someone like Charlie, who had an interest in medicine. In addition to assisting with surgical procedures, Charlie learned about medications, anesthesia, and treatment for a variety of maladies. She learned how to diagnose and treat dysentery, cholera, and typhoid. She became familiar with the surgeons' tools: forceps, tourniquets, and, of course, scalpels.

After Christmas, Union and Confederate soldiers met again at the Battle of Mount Zion Church in Boone County, Missouri. The Union Army claimed another victory at Mount Zion, forcing the Rebels to curtail recruitment and Bushwhacker activities in the Confederate-friendly region.

March 1862 – New Madrid, Missouri

Then, in March 1862, the armies of the North and South clashed at New Madrid, Missouri, a small town on the Mississippi River bordering Tennessee. The focus was Island Number Ten, a river fortification used to prevent Union troops from invading the South by river. For three weeks, Southern forces defended Island Number Ten from a steady bombardment.

As the Union Army marched across the state of Missouri, the field hospital followed, now situated in an abandoned barn near the New Madrid battle site. Both sides knew the strategic importance of Island Number Ten, and the fighting was fierce. Injured soldiers began pouring in soon after the first engagement.

Charlie was assigned to receive patients outside the barn. As she examined soldiers to assess the severity of their injuries, she found her brother on a stretcher. He had taken a bullet in his lungs. This injury was much more serious than the shot in his leg.

"Max!" Charlie exclaimed. "Max, can you hear me?"

"Charlotte, is that you?" Max drifted in and out of consciousness.

"Don't you worry, Max. I'm here now. You're in good hands." She completed her evaluation of her brother's injuries and then asked an orderly to prep him for surgery.

Despite being distracted by her brother's injuries, Charlie completed her duties. She immediately went to the surgery to check on her brother.

Thomas Bernard was finishing an amputation when Charlie found him.

"Dr. Bernard, I've assessed the wounded. There are several who will require surgery, including my brother Max."

That got Thomas Bernard's attention. "How bad is he?"

"He has a minie ball in his right lung. I've had him prepped for surgery. Can you take a look? I'm hoping that you'll be able to do the surgery. This is beyond my skills, but I'd like to assist."

"Bring him in." Dr. Bernard motioned to two orderlies to bring Max's stretcher into the surgical theater.

Charlie watched as Thomas probed her brother's chest for the minie ball. "Forceps," he ordered. Charlie selected the instrument requested and handed it to Thomas. She mopped the surgeon's forehead as he extracted the bullet from Max's chest.

"Got it," Thomas said, holding up the bullet. "There is a lot of damage to his lung. Good thing it was the right lung, away from the heart."

Charlie sent a private prayer to the angels and to her parents in heaven to look after Max.

"Can you close the incision so I can go on to the next one?" the surgeon asked.

"Of course," Charlie replied. She reached for a needle and thread from the tray and began the procedure.

Out of Dr. Bernard's hearing, Charlie said, "Damn you, Max Ward. Why did you have to go and get yourself shot – again? This time I'm bringing you home whether you like it or not."

For Charlie, the days and nights ran together. She grabbed an hour or two of sleep when she could. After she completed her duties, Charlie sat vigil at Max's cot. She understood the complications that could arise from chest wounds, primarily infections and pneumonia.

Two days after Max's surgery, he developed a high fever and a cough. Charlie spent a sleepless night applying cool cloths to bring down the fever. She also changed Max's position, helping him rest in a reclining position rather than lying flat on the cot. That seemed to help for a while. Still, the fever and cough persisted, and then Max's breathing became shallow. He complained of stabbing pains when he coughed.

"I'm worried, Thomas," Charlie told Dr. Bernard. "He doesn't seem to be improving." Charlie listed the symptoms she observed.

"What's your diagnosis?" he asked.

Charlie took in a deep breath. "Pneumonia?"

Thomas nodded. "I think you're correct. We'll keep him comfortable. Make sure he has plenty to drink: tea, soup, and water. Boil the water and let it cool before he drinks it. We don't have a lot of reliable water sources here."

The surgeon put a hand on Charlie's shoulder. "We'll do everything we can to help your brother through."

Charlie nodded mutely.

During the next few days, Charlie was diligent in caring for Max. She followed Dr. Bernard's recommendations, and, for a time, her efforts seemed to be working. Then, a week after Max was wounded, his fever spiked. He passed away after a fit of coughing. Charlie was by Max's bed the entire time.

After Max was gone, Charlie sat in stunned silence. Inwardly, she berated herself for allowing yet another family member to die on her watch.

"You did everything in your power to save him," Thomas said when he learned of Max's death. "Doctors are not miracle workers, Charlie. We're not gods – although some may think they are. You cannot blame yourself for your brother's passing. Pneumonia can be a death sentence, despite everything we do to fight it."

He paused, then said, "Take some time for yourself. Go for a walk. We can manage the hospital without you for a while."

Charlie nodded. She had done everything possible to save her brother. In the end, it wasn't enough. But could she accept that?

The walk helped Charlotte clear her head. She had decided on a course of action. That night, she wrote to Lizzy about Max's death.

Dear Lizzy,

I am writing this letter with news of Max. The field hospital followed the Army to New Madrid, a long distance from our previous posting. But, amid the chaos and commotion of battle, the field hospital and Max's unit were stationed together, and that's how I found Max.

He was wounded in the chest during the Battle of New Madrid. The surgery was successful, but there were complications. While he was recovering, he developed pneumonia. I did my best to treat him, Lizzy, but my best wasn't good enough. Max died early this morning. I wanted to bring him home to the family plot, but the travel made it impossible. However, I am done with this War and will return home soon.

In case I do not make it through the Confederate-held lands on the way there, I hope this letter will find its way to you, dear sister.

Charlotte

After patient rounds the next morning, Charlie found a chance to tell Thomas about her decision. Charlie brought two cups of coffee to the table where Thomas was updating patient charts.

"Dr. Bernard, may I have a minute of your time?" Charlie began.

The doctor smiled and said, "After all this time, we're back to 'Dr. Bermard,' Charlie?"

"Well, this is official Army business."

"Alright, then it's Colonel Bernard, to be precise," Thomas said with a bit of self-derision.

Charlie sat down. "Max's death is, well, it's hard. Max was the reason I joined up, you know. To watch over him if I could."

"That's pretty difficult during a war, Charlie."

Charlie nodded and said, "When I first found my brother at Springfield, I thought maybe I could bring him home before he…"

"You are not your brother's keeper," Thomas intoned.

"Well, I am, sort of. At least those were my Papa's last words to me. And, after seeing to Max's funeral and such, I aim to go home, sir."

"What about your work at the hospital? Someday you'll be a fine doctor if you stick with the training. You already know more about doctoring than some of the Army quacks I've encountered. Besides, your enlistment isn't up yet."

"Yes, sir. I've learned a lot, working by your side. But the Army isn't for me."

Thomas tilted his head and assessed his assistant. "Charlie – is that your given name?"

"Sir?" Charlie nearly spit out the mouthful of coffee.

"Did you really think that you fooled me? Granted, you did have me thinking you were a man for a while. But some of your mannerisms…"

"You knew? You knew all this time? Why didn't you kick me out?"

Thomas chuckled. "It's hard to find good help, especially in an Army hospital. It didn't bother me that you were serving under false pretenses. Yes, let's call it 'false pretenses' for now."

He continued, "Didn't you wonder why you were assigned private quarters? Or why you had more time to…" Thomas motioned to the latrine in the distance.

"Oh. I didn't think… I didn't realize…"

"But now it's time for Charlie Ward to go home," Thomas said.

"It's Charlotte, actually. Charlotte Ward," she said.

"You realize that you'll be riding through Bushwhacker territory. The road from New Madrid to St. Joe is straight through the successionist stronghold in Missouri."

"I've thought about that. Charlie Ward, the Union soldier would likely be waylaid by the Bushwhackers. But Charlotte Ward, who has been visiting a sick aunt, might – would – be able to cross enemy lines."

The physician gave it some thought and said, "I believe you may be on to something, Charlotte. I'll submit the paperwork. The Army runs on paper."

Charlotte smiled to herself. She'd said those same words to Luke Jameson a few weeks back.

April, 1862 – New Madrid, Missouri

Charlie Ward waited until hostilities ceased and Island Number Ten officially fell to General Pope. During those last days at the field hospital, she continued to follow Dr. Bernard on rounds, completing her duties competently and even helping some of the soldiers write letters home to their loved ones.

At the end of her shift, Thomas presented Charlie with the paperwork she needed to cross through Union-held lands. "Not sure if you should keep the papers when you get to secesh territory," Thomas said. "But I'm sure you have a plan for riding through that area. What is it?"

"My 'secret weapon.'" With that, Charlotte shook out the skirt and bonnet that were packed in her saddle bag.

"Good thinking. I have something else for you, too. Something to thank you for your service and to help you reach your goal of becoming a doctor." He handed Charlie a burlap sack with something heavy in it. "Open it."

Charlie gasped as she pulled a worn, black leather satchel out of the burlap sack. Her fingers caressed the brass plate on the bag engraved with "C W" just below the handles.

"Who…how…why?" Charlie said, having trouble forming the right question. Instead, she just looked up at Thomas.

The surgeon shrugged. "This was ol' Doc Fontaine's bag. I had the brass plate added to encourage you to continue in medicine. Doc Fontaine passed away from a heart attack before you arrived. I don't think it's bad luck to inherit another doctor's medical bag. In fact, I think it's probably good luck. You're getting instruments that have proven their worth. Just as you've proven your worth, Charlie. Can I still call you 'Charlie'?"

"I will treasure this forever. Thank you. I won't let you down. You've shown me a path to follow. And yes, you can always call me 'Charlie.'"

The following morning, Charlie Ward set out for home. St. Joseph, Missouri, was the nearly farthest destination in Missouri that one could travel from New Madrid. Charlie planned to cross the state diagonally from the southeast corner to the northwest corner, a trip that could take several weeks by horseback, especially during wartime.

If only, she thought, *I'd been able to convince Max to leave when we were at Springfield. He would be alive now, and we would be much closer to home.*

The first few days, Charlie encountered Union troops patrolling the flanks, ensuring that raiders didn't pick off soldiers standing guard or delivering much-needed supplies. When these patrols stopped Charlie, the official paperwork from Colonel Bernard ensured safe passage through the lines.

The further Charlie traveled from New Madrid, the more likely she was to encounter hostile patrols — Bushwhackers or actual Confederate soldiers. It was time for Charlie to become Charlotte Ward again. She had decided to avoid Missouri's big cities, which would only slow down her journey, but smaller towns would provide a refuge for the weary traveler. And, while it was unusual for a woman to be traveling alone, Charlotte's story about visiting a sick relative would elicit sympathy from anyone questioning her journey.

A week after leaving New Madrid, Charlotte reached Fredericktown and decided to stay for the night. Fredericktown was still recovering from a battle the previous fall when the Missouri State Guard, fighting for the Confederacy, had engaged the Missouri Infantry, part of the Union Army, just outside of town. Although the Union forces triumphed, some of the Blue Coats believed that locals had assisted the Rebels. This resentment led to retaliation against the town by Union soldiers. At least seven homes were burned, and other buildings were damaged in the aftermath.

Charlotte learned all this as she checked into a boarding house, using some of her Army pay to cover expenses.

After-Action Report – Battle of New Madrid

February-April 1862

The Army of the West clashed with Confederates for over a month. And, while casualties were comparatively light, in the end, more than seven thousand Rebel soldiers and officers surrendered to the overwhelming strength of the Union. Even so, the under-staffed field hospital was busy treating injuries, exhaustion, and other maladies of War.

Union forces included infantry, cavalry, artillery units, and engineering regiments from Illinois, Indiana, Iowa, Michigan, Ohio, Missouri, and Wisconsin under the command of Brigadier General John Pope. The Confederates, commanded by Brigadier General John McCown, fielded a combined force from Alabama, Arkansas, Louisiana, and Tennessee.

In the end, the North's overwhelming numbers forced the Confederates to surrender. The Battle of New

Madrid marked the first time the South lost a position on the Mississippi River in battle.

Chapter 6: May 1862
Ward Farm

Springtime was Lizzy's favorite season. It was a time of new life and regrowth. She had just finished plowing and planting corn on the one hundred or so acres of tillable land on the Ward farm.

Lizzy loved working Missouri's rich, loamy soil. She loved the earthy smell and the feel of the moist soil after plowing. Papa had said it smelled like hope. With timely rains, the corn would grow straight and tall across the gentle hills and rolling valleys.

But Lizzy's work was far from done. The huge family garden was next. As she did every year, Lizzy had saved seeds last fall for planting this year. Packets of seeds lined the shelf in the cool root cellar behind the barn. Several varieties of bean seeds, along with carrot, cabbage, beet, and pea seeds, were waiting for Lizzy to plant and nurture this spring.

West of the garden was the orchard. Lizzy saw that the apple and plum trees were fully covered in leaves. Soon, the fruit trees would bloom, promising sweet fruit this fall. At least, Lizzy thought, the fruit trees would need scant attention in the spring.

This morning, Lizzy had already turned the cows and calves out into the nearby pasture to graze. Sizing up the cows' milk bags, Lizzy knew the calves had already had their fill. There were pigs and chickens to feed, eggs to gather, and horses to tend. The sun's first purple and pink rays showed on the eastern horizon.

"Oh, it's going to be a glorious day, Butter," she said to the yellow-striped cat that had already staked out a sleeping spot near the barn. Butter appeared to be napping, but Lizzy knew the feline was on the hunt. The cat kept the barn and house free of the pesky rodents that might devour the family's precious grain.

With the eggs collected and the animals fed, Lizzy returned to the house to cook her own breakfast. Jacob Ward had built a fine home for his family many years ago. He and his wife Blanche had hoped to fill the house with six or eight children and had planned the house accordingly. The two-story wooden structure featured a generous front porch with two rockers on it. Lizzy wished she had someone to share the rockers with.

Inside, the center of the sitting room had a braided rag rug on the wooden plank floor. The floor, which used to be "polished within an inch of its life," as Jacob would say, now had a dull sheen but was clean, nonetheless. Several chairs, small tables, and a settee circled the rug. A large clock on the fireplace mantle marked the hours of the day with melodic chimes. The bedrooms were located upstairs, five in all. The largest bedroom, Jacob and Blanche's room, had a cushioned chair and a small table by the window. Blanche would sit there when she was recuperating. The other four rooms were intended for the children that Jacob and Blanche hoped for. Max had his own room, while Lizzy and Charlotte chose to share a bedroom.

The heart of the Ward home, though, was the kitchen. Blanche had loved to cook and bake when she was in good health. Lizzy still recalled the smell of breads and muffins that wafted through the house from this warm place. Now, there was a single pot of coffee on the wood-burning stove. Lizzy set about making breakfast for herself.

Over a plate of eggs, side pork, and fresh strawberries, Lizzy considered which chores to tackle first. There was butter to churn, and the garden could stand some weeding. There was always work to keep her occupied. Even though she missed Charlotte and Max's company, she was content on the family farm.

Later that morning, Lizzy was in the garden weeding a row of peas when she heard the pounding of horse hooves and, more disturbingly, Rebel yells in the distance. The sounds grew closer as the riders raced up the road to the Ward homestead.

Ten, maybe twelve, riders galloped up the road and reined in at the garden's edge.

"'Morning, gentlemen," Lizzy greeted the riders.

"Gentlemen, she calls us," said one of the men. He sported a large handlebar mustache and wore a long, gray coat, tall leather riding boots, and a wide-brimmed hat. He swept the hat off and executed a mocking bow from the saddle of his horse. "'Morning, ma'am," he said in reply. "Who do I have the pleasure of conversing with?"

"I am Elizabeth Ward. This is my farm. And you are…"

"Captain William C. Quantrill, ma'am. My comrades and I are in need of shelter and sustenance."

Elizabeth recognized the speaker's name. William Quantrill led a band of Confederate guerilla fighters who had been terrorizing Union sympathizers across Kansas and Missouri. In March, his raiders attacked and looted Aubry, Kansas, just across the Missouri border. Elizabeth had read accounts of the raid in the Kansas City newspaper just a few weeks ago. Three people had been murdered in the raid.

Striving to keep her voice steady, Elizabeth said, "Of course, Captain Quantrill. You're welcome to water your horses." She motioned to the well. "I'll bring out coffee and biscuits."

One of the raiders followed Lizzy into the house. "My apologies, Lizzy," the raider said. Lizzy whirled around and gasped. It was Frank James, although now he had a full beard and wore a slouch hat pinned up on one side with a Confederate flag pin.

"Mr. James! I did not recognize you. So, you're riding with Quantrill now?"

"I wanted you to know that I did not direct the boys to your farm. But I assure you that you will come to no harm."

Before she knew what she was saying, Lizzy replied, "Is that what you told the good citizens of Aubry?"

Frank James stepped back as if he'd been physically struck. "I wasn't part of that, Lizzy. I swear I....you have my word of honor that I wasn't at Aubry."

Lizzy's face softened. "I believe you, Frank. But you're part of the gang now."

"Soldiering wasn't for me. Too many rules and too much marching," Frank explained. "Riding with Quantrill is different. We're still fighting for the South, but in our own way."

He paused and then said, "Is your brother still with the Blue Coats?"

Lizzy pursed her lips. "I don't believe I said he was with the Union, Frank."

"Everyone knew your family was pro-Union," Frank said.

"Does Captain Quantrill know?"

"Nope, and I'm not going to enlighten him. Let's just keep it friendly. We'll stay the night in your barn and head out at sunrise."

Lizzy nodded in agreement. "I'll bring out the coffee if you get the biscuits." Together, Lizzy Ward and Frank James fed the notorious Quantrill Raiders.

"Thank you, kindly, Mrs. Ward," said William Quantrill. "Is your man off fighting?"

"I'm not married. My father passed a few years back. My sister is with relatives." Lizzy didn't think she needed to explain that both her brother and her sister were soldiers in the Union Army.

"Hmmm. That's a lot of work for a lady to do."

"It's wartime, Captain Quantrill. We all do what is required to survive."

"That we do, ma'am," Quantrill replied. "Speaking of surviving, the boys and I thank you for your hospitality."

"Of course, Captain. May I say that you sound like an educated man."

"That I am, Miss. I was a schoolteacher in Ohio before I came to Kansas back in '57."

Lizzy poured the rest of the coffee. "Now, if you'll excuse me, I'd better begin dinner."

In the kitchen, Lizzy collapsed at the kitchen table and thought, *William Quantrill and his Raiders! In my front yard! What would Charlotte do?*

Elizabeth knew the answer. Her sister would put on a pleasant face, feed the hungry horde, and wave goodbye to them in the morning. *Thank goodness,* she thought, *that Frank James is with the Raiders. Or is that a good thing? He knows where the root cellar is and where the cows graze.*

She shook off the thoughts of foreboding and started planning a very large meal.

Even though cooking wasn't her favorite activity, Elizabeth served the raiders a wonderful dinner: pork roast, potatoes, and fresh greens. For dessert, she made bread pudding sweetened with raisins and dried apples. Her guests heartily thanked her and retreated to the barn for a good night's rest.

Before William Quantrill left to join his men, he sought out Lizzy in the kitchen.

"Sorry to intrude, ma'am. I wanted to thank you one more time for the dinner you prepared. We're fixing to head out before sunrise tomorrow, so we won't be imposing on you any further. Good night, Miss Ward."

"Good night, Captain Quantrill."

Elizabeth was pleased to see that the Raiders were, indeed, gone before sunrise.

"Didn't get much gardening done yesterday, but I think we can finish the work today," she told her faithful cat.

Midmorning, Lizzy's chores were interrupted by sounds of gunfire in the distance. She scooped up the cat and ran for the root cellar. Although tornados were less frequent in Missouri than in neighboring states, the Wards sometimes used the root cellar during threatening weather. Because of that, the retreat was stocked with blankets, a lamp, a chair, and even several books.

Lizzy felt safe in the underground shelter. Indeed, she was safe for several hours – until Frank James opened the cellar door. "Lizzy, we have a situation," he said. "One of the boys got shot by Jayhawkers."

"Where is he now?" Lizzy asked.

"He's in the barn, but he's bleeding something fierce."

"Bring him into the parlor. I'll get the medical kit."

The injured raider was a boy – young enough that he could barely grow facial hair, Lizzy observed. "Why, he's younger than my brother Max," she whispered to Frank.

"He just joined up," Frank nodded.

Although Lizzy didn't ask for details, Frank explained, "We met up with a bunch of Jayhawkers down by the river. We wanted to cross into Kansas, and they didn't much like that."

"We gave 'em a good fight," said one of the men who had carried the injured boy into the parlor.

"I'm going to boil some water to clean the wound," Lizzy said as she left the room.

That's when the gunfire started up again.

"Those damn Jayhawkers must've followed us here," one of the men shouted.

"It's too late to get to the root cellar," Frank called to Lizzy. "Get on the floor, away from windows."

Quantrill's men took up stations inside the house, along the outer walls. If the window glass hadn't already been shot out by the pro-Union riders outside, Quantrill's men intentionally knocked it out for better accuracy.

The gun battle lasted only a few minutes – but it seemed like an eternity to Lizzy. As Frank James had commanded, Lizzy hid in the hall closet among winter coats and piles of quilts.

Eventually, the gunfire ceased. Lizzy emerged from the closet to find several wounded, possibly dead, raiders lying on her floors. All the windows on the first floor had been shot out or broken. The mantle clock had a bullet mark on the wooden base, but the faithful timekeeper was still ticking.

"Are you the fainting type, Miss?" Quantrill asked her.

"Haven't been for a long time, Captain Quantrill," Lizzy replied.

The leader of the Bushwhackers nodded. "That's good. Apologies for the mess. You'd better start boiling that water."

She retreated to the kitchen, which had also been shot up. Glass chimneys on lamps were broken. Two of her mother's favorite bowls lay in pieces on the floor. That's when Lizzy started to cry. "Mama's bowls," she said, kneeling to try to fit the pieces back together.

Frank James entered the kitchen and saw Lizzy weeping on the floor. "I am so sorry that we drew those bastards here – begging your pardon, Elizabeth."

Lizzy sniffed and said, "I don't know why I'm crying about broken pottery when there are dead men in my parlor." She wiped a tear from her cheek.

"It's always the little things that get us, Lizzy. It's not the big things that start wars. It's the shoving in a bar room, or a slight to a family member. Those grievances build up, and, well, it's Jayhawkers against us Bushwhackers.

Lizzy gave a weak smile.

"I'm riding light, so I don't have a handkerchief for you," Frank said. "But I'll help clean up the kitchen if you want to rest a spell."

Lizzy held out her hand, and Frank helped her get to her feet. "We'll do it together if you're willing."

As the day wore on, Quantrill sent men out to scout for the Jayhawkers. The two men who had died were buried in the orchard. Even Quantrill's Raiders understood that they did not belong in the family cemetery.

Instead of cooking another large meal, Lizzy warmed up what remained from yesterday's dinner. That was sufficient for the gang, as none of them were particularly hungry. Before nightfall the scouts returned, reporting that the Jayhawkers had ridden south.

"Then we'll take another route," William Quantrill decided. Looking at Lizzy, he said, "Ma'am, it's not that I don't trust you with our plans. But, if you don't know which way we're headed, you can truthfully attest to that."

"I hope no one stops here and asks about it," Lizzy said.

Quantrill did not respond, and Lizzy understood that he was fairly certain that someone — friend or foe — would visit the farm soon for details about the shoot-out.

"I hope so, too, ma'am. We'll be on our way tomorrow morning."

And the next day, Quantrill's Raiders rode away from the Ward farm. Lizzy could see they were headed west but assumed they would soon alter their course.

Lizzy was not ashamed to admit to herself that the encounters with the Bushwhackers had shaken her. Until now, the War had been somewhat abstract to her, even though her brother and sister were soldiers in the War of the Rebellion.

Even though Lizzy had not received a letter from Charlotte in more than a month, she decided that she should write to Charlotte about Quantrill's Raiders and the gun battle.

Dear Char,

I pray that this letter finds you and Max safe and well. Spring planting is nearly completed, and we have two new calves.

But I wanted to write you about the visit from Bushwhackers. Two days ago, Quantrill's Raiders arrived, requesting shelter for the night. I didn't think it would be wise to refuse their "request." Frank James, whom I have written about before, was among the group. They stayed in the barn and then left in the morning, bound for Kansas, I believe. Before long, though, they returned – with Jayhawkers on their heels. Our farm became a war zone, with several men on both sides killed. The house has been shot up. There is not a window that has escaped damage. But I am safe, and that is all we can ask for.

I hope to hear from you soon. Even better, I hope that you and Max are on your way home.

Your loving sister, Elizabeth

Lizzy sealed the letter. The following day, she took the buckboard into St. Joe. After a stop at the lumber yard for lumber to cover the broken windows, she mailed the letter to Charlotte.

While in town, Lizzy learned that President Lincoln had signed a new law called the Homestead Act. The newspaper reported that the government was giving away 160 acres of land to anyone over the age of twenty-one who hadn't fought against the Union. The promise of new land was enticing, but the fact that, for the first time, women could hold land in their own name excited Lizzy.

It's about time, Lizzy said to herself.

News from the Front – Guerilla Forces and the Confederacy

Pro-Confederate guerrilla fighters, also known as Bushwhackers, played a significant role during the Civil War. The most well-known of these groups was Quantrill's Raiders, led by William Quantrill. Members of Quantrill's Raiders included Frank and Jesse James.

Relying primarily on ambushes, Quantrill's guerrillas attacked Jayhawkers, Missouri State Militia, and Union troops. The Raiders attacked Union patrols and supply convoys, seized the mail, and terrorized towns in both Kansas and Missouri.

The Confederate government granted William Quantrill a field commission as a Captain under the Partisan Ranger Act. By 1864, Quantrill had lost control of the group, which split into small bands. Some, including Quantrill, were killed in various engagements.

Chapter 7: May 1862
Callaway County, MO

In her time on the battlefields, Charlotte thought she had become used to the horrors of war. But as she traveled the backroads of her home state, she realized that the war was not just soldiers fighting soldiers. The War of the Rebellion brought destruction to non-combatants as well. Women and children became homeless when their towns and even their houses were casualties of the battles. She passed homes in ruins. Farm fields stood barren because there were no farmers to plant or work the land. Pens that used to hold farm animals were empty because armies had stolen the cows, pigs, and chickens for food.

The road home would take Charlotte through Jefferson City, the state capital, in the heart of secessionist Missouri. During the early days of the war, the citizens of Jefferson City took to the streets demanding that Missouri secede from the Union. General Nathaniel Lyon and his Federal troops crushed that demand. Lyon's forces entered the capital, declared martial law, and occupied the city until the end of the war.

Because the state capital was still a hotbed of dissidents and turmoil, Charlotte decided it was best to avoid Jeff City, as the locals called it. Instead, she rode north, which led her directly into secessionist territory. This was the heart of Missouri's pro-slavery faction. Many of the citizens had joined the Missouri State Guard. The

Guard, considered part of the Confederate States Army, often fought alongside Confederate troops.

Still, Charlotte didn't see how she could reach St. Joseph without passing through "enemy territory," as she thought of it now. In preparation for this leg of the journey, she became Charlotte Ward again, a young woman returning home after visiting a sick relative.

Charlotte missed the freedom that the man's clothing offered. The trousers and jacket were much more sensible than the voluminous skirts when riding horseback. She found the bonnet, tied with ribbons, to be fussy. But she needed the bonnet since her hair was still a boyish length, not the fashionable style with chignons and curls.

She had just crossed the Missouri River east of Jefferson City when she heard gunfire. Dismounting, Charlotte led her horse into a grove of trees. The tall oaks provided welcome shade from the scorching noon sun. She also hoped the trees might hide her presence or at least give some cover from the shooting.

While most of the battles had moved into Tennessee and further east, there were still skirmishes in Missouri, particularly between the guerilla forces. Bushwhackers and pro-Confederate forces were intent on retribution for the Union's occupation of the state capital. And as the guerrilla fighting wore on, the hostilities between the two sides became increasingly inflamed.

Over a slight rise, Charlotte could see a group of riders retreating even as they fired upon another group in pursuit. She was alarmed to see that both forces were directly coming her way! The thundering sounds of the gunfire and the racing horses reminded Charlotte of the battles she had hoped to leave behind.

The soldiers passed within yards of Charlotte's hiding spot. So close, in fact, that stray bullets filled the air. Even though she was crouching in the grove of trees, Charlotte realized she was not safe. She had been hit.

Charlotte watched as blood blossomed red over her left shoulder. Her first instinct was to call out for help. Instead, leaning into her medical training, she began to staunch the bleeding. She ripped a piece of fabric from her petticoat into a bandage – at least the undergarment was good for something. The location of the bullet wound on the back of her shoulder made it difficult to hold a bandage over the injury. Knowing that she had to stop or slow the bleeding, she tried leaning against the tree to apply pressure to the wound. The pain was horrible.

Eventually, Charlotte passed out. When she woke, she could hear voices.

"Captain, I think she's coming to," one of the soldiers said.

"You've lost a lot of blood, miss," said the officer.

Charlotte's vision was fuzzy, but she could make out the gray uniforms. The soldiers were Confederates.

She heard another soldier say, "Sir, I've sent Thompson back to let General Bragg know that we've chased the Blue Coats away from the river."

"Good. Let's make camp here for the night," said a familiar voice. Charlotte couldn't quite place the voice; then it struck her. It was Luke Jameson speaking.

Oh, dear Lord, she said to herself, *I've gotten myself captured by Confederates! And Luke Jameson can identify me!*

She hoped that she had kept a poker face when the realization of her situation dawned on her. More than that, Charlotte hoped that Luke hadn't recognized her.

"Miss, we're going to need to get you to a doctor. You've been shot," Luke now addressed Charlotte. "Do you live nearby?"

She was grateful that the sun was setting. The twilight might give her some anonymity. Turning slightly away from Luke, Charlotte said in a soft voice, "I'm afraid I live quite a distance from here. I was visiting a sick relative. How badly am I wounded?"

"As I said, you've lost some blood. But I'm more worried about the bullet. We need to get it out."

Charlotte's eyes flew wide open. "Yes, I'll need a doctor."

Luke recognized those dark brown eyes that could only belong to Charlie Ward.

"Charlie? Charlie Ward?"

Charlotte turned to face Luke. "Am I your prisoner?"

"We don't generally take prisoners out here."

"Does that mean you're going to kill me?"

"No, we won't kill you. But I'm still trying to figure out why you're dressed like a woman. You are Charlie Ward, are you not? Are you on a spy mission?"

Charlotte grimaced. "I'm not 'dressed' like a woman. I *am* a woman. I was dressed like a man to get into the Army."

"Wait. Let me get this straight. You're not Charlie Ward? So that means…" Luke's mind was racing with possibilities.

"My given name is Charlotte. Charlotte Blanche Ward. When my brother Max joined up, I followed to watch over him. The only way I could do that was by enlisting and pretending to be a man."

"Well, don't that beat all! And all this time, I thought…." he shook his head and changed topics. "So, did someone figure out that you weren't a Charlie? Is that why you're not in uniform?" He gestured to the skirt covered in delicate peach flowers.

"I exchanged my Union blues for a dress so that Confederates and the State Guard wouldn't shoot at me, Mr. Jameson. I guess that didn't work out so well. I still got shot."

"It's Captain Jameson," he corrected her. "And you still haven't explained why you're riding through secesh country. Why did you leave the army hospital?"

"Max died at New Madrid, Luke. He was my reason for being in the Army. I'm going home."

"I'm mighty sorry that your brother's dead. A lot of good men are dying in this rotten war."

Charlotte shifted and groaned with pain. "Is there a doctor in your unit? Someone who can remove a bullet and patch me up?"

Luke calculated the options. "I wouldn't trust the boys in this unit to do any doctoring." He nodded to himself, then said, "The closest help is a half day's ride from here. Are you up to it?"

Charlotte sucked in her breath and said, "Bind my arm in a sling and I can ride for a couple of hours. Where are we going?"

"My family's ranch is in the next county. Ma has plenty of practice taking out bullets. You're going to meet the Jameson family, Charlie…er, Charlotte."

"Yes, I should be Charlotte Ward for this encounter. When do we leave?"

"In the morning. Try to get some rest tonight. Tell me how to bind up your arm."

"There's a medical bag on my saddle," she said. "I want you to clean the wound first, then put a fresh bandage on it.

Charlotte ripped off more pieces of her petticoat and instructed Luke on how to clean and stabilize the wounded shoulder.

"It's gonna be tricky riding with one hand," he said as he finished tying up the sling.

"At least it's my left shoulder," Charlotte said. "You did a passable job with the bandage and the sling." She leaned against the oak tree and closed her eyes.

Even in the moonlight, Luke could see how drained Charlotte looked.

"You look exhausted," he said. "You should sleep." He put a folded saddle blanket behind Charlotte's head.

"I doubt I'll sleep, but the rest is welcome." Her body proved her wrong; soon, Charlotte was softly snoring.

Back in his role as Captain, Luke assessed the unit's location and ordered his men to take sentry duty. Then he settled his bedroll near Charlotte.

A woman! Luke's thoughts were a jumble. *All this time, I thought I was attracted to a man – which was something new for me.* He knew it wasn't unusual for soldiers to form relationships, but he'd never thought he'd be among them.

As Luke recalled Charlie's presence in the field hospital, he wondered what had attracted him to the medic. Was it how he – she – moved through the rows of cots with a grace that men just don't have? Was it how she looked at him, her dark eyes seeming to reach deep inside Luke? Maybe…then he remembered the moment she had first touched him. It was like an electric shock. *That's it,* he thought. *It was – it is – her touch that awakened those feelings of desire.*

He'd felt that same electric shock when he had cleaned her bare shoulder today. Comforted that his romantic feelings were for someone of the female persuasion, Luke breathed a sigh of relief.

Then, his thoughts turned to the coming day's journey. His mother wouldn't be a problem. She had been the county's midwife and healer for as long as Luke could remember. Mary Jameson would take care of Charlotte's gunshot wound.

It was his pa, Will Jameson, who might take issue with Luke bringing a stranger to their farm. Will had settled in Missouri a few years after the territory became a state, declaring he wanted the "open spaces" that Missouri offered. Originally from the slave-holding state of Kentucky, Will was accustomed to the "peculiar institution," as John Calhoun called slavery, even though he did not own any slaves himself.

Will Jameson and his new bride, Mary Jameson, settled in the Ozark Highlands of Missouri in 1838. Declaring that he had no intention of "dirt farming," Will thought the rolling hills of his newly adopted home were perfect for raising horses. Over the years, he and Mary built a comfortable home for themselves and their seven children. But Will often declared that he'd choose horses over people any day. And strangers were not to his liking.

Sun was dawning when Luke gave final orders to his second in command. He promised he would return in three days or less. Then he helped Charlotte on her horse, and they set out for the Jameson horse ranch.

News from the Front – Missouri State Guard

At the beginning of the hostilities in 1861, Missouri Governor Claiborne Fox Jackson disbanded the Missouri

Volunteer Militia and reformed it as the Missouri State Guard. The State Guard was formed to resist invasion by the Union Army.

Shortly after the First Battle of Springfield, pro-Southern elements of the Missouri legislature voted to secede, and the Confederate Congress welcomed Missouri as the twelfth Confederate state. In his winter encampment, Confederate General Sterling Price began converting members of the State Guard into the Confederate Army.

Chapter 8: June 1862
Jameson Ranch, Boone County

The day promised to be warm, but Luke hoped to have a good portion of the ride behind them by then. He thought they could be at the Jameson ranch by early afternoon if they could keep up a steady pace. He looked over at Charlotte. She seemed to be sitting her saddle all right for now. Luke knew that Charlotte's injury might require frequent stops, and he was prepared for that.

Riding in silence seemed awkward, and both riders started speaking at once after they'd left the last sentry behind them.

"Tell me about your ..." Charlotte began.

"How'd you get that...?" Luke asked at the same time.

They both laughed. "You first," Luke said.

Charlotte completed her question, "Tell me about your family. You said they raise horses?"

"We raise and train horses," Luke said. "Pa and Ma were from Kentucky – that's horse country. He brought a couple of horses with them when they moved to Boone County back in the '30s. Before the war, he also did a brisk business in mule teams. Mules and oxen are better suited for pulling those Conestoga wagons that homesteaders are using."

She nodded at that information. "Do you have brothers or sisters?"

"Yep," Luke said with a laugh. "Three brothers and three sisters. Ma named the boys after the apostles: there's Matthew, Mark, Luke, and John."

Charlotte laughed, too. "You're all saints, I assume."

That made Luke grin. "Not exactly, but that was the intent. The girls – my sisters – are Mary Jane, Martha, and Nellie. Mary Jane is named for Ma."

"Wait – Nellie?" Charlotte asked.

"Pa said Nellie was the last of the brood. He wanted to name her 'Whoa, Nellie,' but Ma would have none of that."

"Your mother sounds like a woman with sound judgment."

"That's a fair assessment," Luke agreed with a laugh. "I think you'll like Ma. And I think she'll like you."

Charlotte shifted in her saddle, turned, and looked at Luke. He was wearing his gray Confederate coat, which she noticed was the same color as his eyes. Tufts of chestnut-colored hair poked out from his uniform cap, and a long mustache framed the corners of his mouth.

"How will your family feel about you bringing a stranger home," she asked.

"Pa doesn't cotton much to outsiders, but Ma will mother-hen you to death if you let her. And Ma runs the house, so you'll be welcomed with open arms."

Changing the subject, Charlotte asked, "Are your brothers in the war, too?"

"Yep. Matt is fighting in Tennessee. Mark and John are with Governor Jackson and the Missouri State Guard."

"You're all fighting for the right to own slaves, but your family doesn't own slaves. I don't understand it," Charlotte said.

"Nothing to understand. Even though we don't have slaves – and never would – most of our neighbors do. It wouldn't be smart to join up with the blue coats. Ma, Pa, and the girls wouldn't be safe."

This admission gave Charlotte a glimpse into the internal struggles that some of the Confederate soldiers must have.

"At least you haven't lost a brother in the war," she said, thinking of Max.

"Oh, the war has touched our family," Luke said. "Mary Jane's husband, Silas, died at Wilson's Creek. That was a bad one, even though General Price and the Confederates won. Martha's husband, Ben, was wounded in action there. He was fighting with General Lyon and the Union."

"You have family fighting on both sides?"

"That's not unusual, especially here in Missouri."

Charlotte had heard others talk about how the war had split up families.

"I've talked enough," Luke said. "It's your turn to answer questions."

"Fair enough," Charlotte said.

Luke pointed at the medical bag tied to Charlotte's saddle. "How did you come to have that doctor's bag? The last time we talked at the field hospital, you made it clear that you were not a doctor. I imagine there's a story connected to that bag."

She nodded. "Thomas...er Dr. Bernard gave me the bag before I left."

"Thomas, huh? That sounds cozy."

Charlotte glared at Luke. "It's not what you think."

"Did he know you weren't a man?"

"Apparently he did, but he never let on that he knew. Anyway, the bag's previous owner was a doctor who died in the early days of the war. Dr. Bernard gave me the medical bag along with the suggestion that I should go to medical school."

Luke burst out laughing. "A woman doctor?"

Charlotte glared at Luke again. "I'm glad I could amuse you, Captain Jameson. Dr. Bernard didn't think it was funny. Even if I don't go to medical school, I can still help people." She patted the medical bag. "I learned a lot watching the Army doctors. Dr. Bernard thought I could put the bag to good use."

"Look, I didn't mean to offend," Luke apologized. "Don't tell my ma that I laughed about you being a doctor. She'd thump me."

Charlotte swayed in the saddle.

Luke reached over and grabbed the reins of Charlotte's horse. He caught Charlotte just as she was about to fall out of the saddle. After steadying her, Luke jumped off his horse and pulled Charlotte from her mare.

"Let's get you into the shade." He carried Charlotte to a large oak and carefully set her down. Then he fetched the canteen from his saddle and handed it to Charlotte.

"Here, drink this. Careful, not too much at first."

Charlotte took a few sips, and then Luke poured water into his cupped hands. He bathed Charlotte's forehead with the cool water.

"Oh, that feels good," Charlotte murmured.

"We'll rest here a while," Luke said softly.

"I need to get the bullet out," Charlotte protested, remembering the festering wounds of soldiers who did not get medical attention in time.

"And you will. We're not far from the ranch."

She nodded and mustered her strength. "Help me on to my horse."

Luke did as she commanded. "If you feel like you're going to faint…"

"I don't faint," Charlotte said with gritted teeth. "How much further?"

"Just a few miles more. We can be there in an hour or so."

"Fine." With steely determination, Charlotte told herself she could do this as she mounted her horse.

Charlotte had beads of sweat on her forehead, and she was fading fast by the time Luke said, "The ranch is just over that ridge."

She breathed a sigh of relief when she saw the tidy ranch house next to a large corral.

"Usually there are a lot more horses in the corral," Luke said. "The Confederate Army bought a lot of our stock for pennies on the dollar when the war broke out."

A rider raced toward them. "Brace yourself. You're about to meet Nellie. She's a force of nature."

"Luke! Luke! You're home!" With dark red braids flying, a girl of about fourteen came into focus for Charlotte.

Nellie reined up when she reached Luke and Charlotte. Breathlessly, she said, "Is the war over? Do Ma or Pa know you're coming home? How long will you be home? Who is your lady friend?"

Luke turned to Charlotte and said, "And now you know why we *still* call her, 'Whoa, Nellie.'

"Nellie, this is Miss Charlotte Ward. She will be our guest for a few days while she recuperates."

Nellie eyed the sling on Charlotte's arm. "What happened?" Nellie asked.

Before Luke could respond, Charlotte said, "I got in the way of a bullet during a skirmish. Your brother found me on the side of the road and brought me here."

Charlotte and Luke had already agreed to keep secret the fact that they had first met at a Union field hospital – on opposite sides of the conflict. Charlotte's affiliation with the Union Army, as well as her pretense as a soldier, would be difficult for Luke's family to accept. Instead, they would use Charlotte's story that she had been visiting a sick relative and was on her way home. Luke fervently hoped the story could remain that simple.

"Nellie, run back to the house and let Ma know that she has some doctoring to do," Luke instructed his youngest sister.

"She does look a might flushed," Nellie said. "I'll warn Ma." Nellie wheeled her horse around and sped back to the ranch house.

Charlotte watched as the girl galloped home. "I don't remember ever having that much energy."

"Being the youngest of the brood is part of it," Luke replied. "She gets all of Ma's and Pa's attention these days. And both of 'em dote on her something fierce, even though they won't admit it."

When they reached the ranch house, Mary Jameson stood on the front porch, ready to welcome her son and the visitor.

"Let me look at you, Luke," Mary addressed her son. "Are you getting enough to eat? You look thin. Well, we'll take care of that soon enough. Now, introduce me to your friend."

"Ma," Luke said as he helped Charlotte off her mount, "this is Charlotte Ward. Charlotte, this is my mother, Mary Jameson. Charlotte needs your doctoring, Ma. She caught a stray bullet yesterday. We can fill you in on the particulars later, but now she needs that bullet removed."

And, just as Luke had predicted, Mary Jameson began "mother henning" Charlotte immediately.

"Bring her in the house, Luke," Mary said, "and put her in Mary Jane's and Martha's old room. There's good light in there so I can see what I'm doing – and she'll have some privacy."

Luke did as he was told, then left to tend to the horses.

"You just sit on the bed, Miss Ward," Mary said.

Charlotte complied and untied her hat. Rather than draw attention to her short hair, Charlotte decided that no explanation would be better than a lie. There could be any number of reasons for the unconventional length, often the result of illness. Charlotte counted on Mary to be a genteel, Southern woman.

Mary didn't seem to notice Charlotte's hair. She was focused on Charlotte's injury. "I'll unwrap the sling and see what we're dealing with. And don't you worry, this isn't the first bullet I've had to remove."

Charlotte thought about her "new" medical bag. "Mrs. Jameson, there's a bullet retractor in that medical bag if you need one."

"And how did a young lady such as yourself come to be in possession of a doctor's bag?" Mary asked as she opened the large black satchel.

"It was a gift from the doctor who was tending my family member," Charlotte explained. "The bag belonged to a doctor who died a while ago. Dr. Bernard – he was tending my relative – thought I showed a talent for medicine. He gave me the bag and told me to put it to good use."

Charlotte winced as Mary began probing the wound for the bullet. "I didn't think I would be its first patient."

"Found it." A few minutes later, Mary pulled the bullet from Charlotte's shoulder. "Seems to have missed the shoulder blade," Mary observed. "I'll just stitch up the wound, put a fresh dressing on it and leave you to rest. Lord knows how you were able to ride with that shoulder."

"I was lucky that Luke – Captain Jameson – found me when he did."

"You didn't say, but I'm guessing it was his unit that was doing the shooting in that skirmish Nellie mentioned."

"I thought I was safe behind a big, old oak tree," Charlotte confessed. "I don't know if it was a Confederate or Union bullet that got me. It doesn't matter. I was in the wrong place at the wrong time.

"Thank you for your kindness today," Charlotte concluded. "You're right. I do need to rest now."

Mary pulled a colorful quilt over Charlotte and said, "I'll bring in some soup later. You should sleep now."

When Charlotte woke up, she could hear talking and laughter in the outer room. Rather than joining the Jamesons, Charlotte let the sounds of a happy family roll over her. She missed those sounds.

Eventually, the bedroom door opened, and Mary quietly entered to check on her patient.

"I feel much better, Mrs. Jameson," Charlotte said. "I didn't realize how much I needed a good sleep."

"It's the best medicine for you now," Mary whispered. "I'll bring in some soup and biscuits if you're up to it. First, I reckon you might like to use the privy."

"You read my mind," Charlotte confirmed.

As Mary ladled soup into a pottery bowl, Charlotte re-entered the house.

"That looks and smells delicious," Charlotte said. She indicated a place at the table, "May I sit here?"

"Of course," Mary answered. She brought the soup, biscuits, and a jar of jam. "These early strawberries were in the garden last week," she said.

When she finished her second bowl of soup, Charlotte said, "That was the best chicken soup I've ever had."

"Don't let your ma hear you say that," Mary said. "There's nothing better than a mother's soup."

"You're right about that," Charlotte agreed. "My mother passed a few years back, and I'm afraid I'm not half the cook that she was – or that you are."

"I'm sorry to hear that, Miss Ward," Mary began.

Charlotte cut in, "Please call me Charlotte, Mrs. Jameson."

"Then it's Mary that you'll be calling me," Mary Jameson said. "Now, tell me about yourself."

Carefully, Charlotte picked out facts that would not be too revealing.

"Well, my parents died a few years back. My sister, brother, and I have been running the farm since then. Now it's just Lizzy and me. My brother died after the Battle of New Madrid."

Mary patted Charlotte's hand. "This has been a terrible war. I pray that it will be over soon. Where do your folks farm?" Mary continued her questions.

Luke chose that moment to enter the house. "It's good to see you're feeling better. I told you Ma would fix you right up."

"Her color is much better, too," Mary added. "All it took was a little chicken soup. We were just getting acquainted."

"Were you now?" Luke said. "And here I was hoping that our guest might enjoy a short walk."

Charlotte was glad to escape Mary's probing questions. "A little exercise might be good for me. I'll get my bonnet."

Away from the house, Luke held out his arm for Charlotte to hold. "I thought you might need rescuing," he laughed.

"She is curious about my whereabouts and family. You were just in time." She lifted her face to the sun, closed her eyes, and deeply breathed. "I've missed fresh country air. For too long, all I've smelled is gunpowder, disinfectants, and the odor of men dying."

For a moment, Luke was mesmerized by Charlotte's simple presence as she glowed in the summer sun.

Then he gathered himself and said, "War is no place for a woman."

"War is no place for anyone," Charlotte amended.

"You're right, but I'll be headed back to my unit tomorrow. I hate to leave you here, but I can't accompany you back to St. Joe."

"I'll be fine in a couple of days." Charlotte paused, then continued, "I've been thinking about that ride back home. Instead of wrangling these skirts, I might change back into trousers. Besides, being an unaccompanied female isn't particularly safe these days."

"Pretending to be a man could get you conscripted. I've heard the Confederacy is low on recruits," Luke warned.

"You've never ridden in a skirt, have you?" Charlotte countered. "And with a bad shoulder…well, trousers would be easier to ride in."

Luke thought about that for a moment, then said, "I might have an idea."

Back at the house, Will and Mary were in matching rockers on the front porch, enjoying the last rays of the June sun. Luke took the opportunity to formally introduce Charlotte to his father.

"Pa," Luke said, "this is Charlotte Ward. Charlotte, this is my father, Will Jameson."

"Thank you for your kind hospitality, Mr. Jameson," Charlotte said. "You have a beautiful ranch and horses."

"Yep. Just wish the Army hadn't taken most of my livestock – even the mules," Will grumbled. "But our boys in gray need good mounts." He changed the subject slightly, "Your mare seems to be from fine stock."

"I've had Belle since I was Nellie's age. She's a good horse," Charlotte agreed.

Luke took this opportunity to make his request. "I have to return to my unit tomorrow, and Charlotte is determined to continue home on her own."

Charlotte wondered where Luke was leading with this conversation.

"I watched her ride here with her arm in a sling. It didn't look easy what with that fancy dress and all." He shook his head.

Mary understood where her son was headed. "Western saddles weren't meant for hoop skirts and such. I think we have one of Martha's old riding skirts in a trunk. That might be just what she needs."

Will said, "You mean those trouser skirts that Martha was partial to?"

Mary nodded. "A riding skirt would make your journey much easier, Charlotte." Mary said.

"That's what I was thinking, Ma," Luke said enthusiastically.

His mother hurried inside to search through Martha's trunks.

"You two set a spell," Will said to Luke and Charlotte. "I'm going to check the stable before turning in."

Alone now on the front porch, Charlotte said to Luke, "Nicely done. And thank you. Your family is very kind. I *am* looking forward to getting home, though."

"You know you're welcome to stay."

"I know, but I'm hoping to leave by the end of the week."

Luke nodded. "Stay safe, Charlie…Charlotte."

"Call me Charlie. It sounds right coming from you."

Luke wanted to take Charlotte's hand, but he wasn't certain that she shared his romantic feelings for her.

Instead, they sat in companionable silence, enjoying the pinks and lavenders of the setting sun.

News from the Front – Conscription

When the War of the Rebellion began in April 1861, neither the Union nor the Confederacy had conscription laws in place to recruit soldiers. Neither side needed a draft to fill the ranks because men on both sides initially volunteered enthusiastically for what they believed would be a brief conflict. However, as the war dragged on, men were less willing to enlist in the increasingly bloody, violent war. As a result, the Confederate States of America and the Union enacted conscription laws in 1862.

The Confederacy was the first to pass laws regarding compulsory military service. Twelve months after the South fired on Fort Sumter in April 1861, the enlistments of "Men of '61" were expiring. The Confederacy needed more soldiers. President Jefferson Davis authorized the first Conscription Act in April 1862, requiring all white men between eighteen and thirty-five to serve for three years if called.

Chapter 9: June 1862
Jameson Ranch

Despite Mary Jameson urging Charlotte to stay longer, Charlotte declared she was fit to travel.

"Thank you for your hospitality. You and your family have been so kind," Charlotte said when she announced she would be leaving the next day. "I have a long journey ahead of me, and I'm eager to get home."

"The girl is right," Will agreed. "I've drawn out a map for her. She'll be using backroads to reach her farm, with stops in small towns along the way. I reckon Miss Charlotte will be hugging her sister in about two weeks – if she doesn't dilly-dally."

"Oh, I do worry about you, Charlotte," Mary said. "A woman alone on the road. It's just not safe…"

The following morning, Charlotte proved to Will and Mary that she could, indeed, saddle her horse. She promised to write to them when she reached home. With hugs from Mary and Nellie and a pat on the back from Will, Charlotte set out for home.

Charlotte had enjoyed her time with Luke's loving family. While Mary and Will obviously doted on Nellie, they also had a close relationship with Luke. This was a side of Luke Jameson that Charlotte had not seen before.

At the field hospital in Springfield, he'd been guarded and sometimes a bit prickly. The Captain Jameson she'd encountered when she was shot was all business as he commanded the soldiers in his unit. At home with his family, Luke was more relaxed. Friendlier. She liked this Luke Jameson.

Ward Farm – St. Joseph, Missouri

Back on the farm, with planting season done, Lizzy kept busy milking the cows, feeding the chickens and pigs, and tending the garden. It was shaping up to be a warm, dry summer – not the best for growing. But, like every farmer, Lizzy was optimistic for a good harvest.

She had replaced some of the broken windows after the shootout between the Bushwhackers and the Jayhawkers. Other windows had been patched with boards. Standing back to assess her work, Lizzy thought she had done a passable job of repairing the worst damage.

"At least it will keep the bugs and the rain out," Lizzy commented to Butter, the cat.

On one of her trips to St. Joe for supplies, Lizzy found a letter from Charlotte waiting for her. It had been more than a month since Lizzy had last heard from her sister.

Eager for news, she sat on the bench outside the post office and tore open the letter.

She read, "*.... there were complications. While he was recovering, he developed pneumonia. I did my best to treat him, Lizzy. But my best wasn't good enough. Max died early this morning.*"

Lizzy was devastated. Max was gone. Then she put herself in Charlotte's place. *"But my best wasn't good enough."*

Oh, poor Charlotte. Her sole reason for enlisting had been to find and protect their younger brother. Lizzy knew that Charlotte would blame herself for Max's death.

But the good news was that Charlotte was coming home! *"I am, however, done with this War and will be returning home soon."*

There were no details about how or when Charlotte would return. Lizzy tried calculating when Charlotte might arrive home, but there were too many variables. She would just have to be prepared for the homecoming – whenever it happened.

On her wagon ride back to the farm, Lizzy thought about Char. Her sister had always been the protector and had carried the weight of the family on her shoulders. *Well, no more,* Lizzy promised herself. *We will be equal partners in this family.* And she had a plan to propose to her sister.

About a week after getting Char's letter, Lizzy was in the kitchen when she spotted a lone rider in the distance.

She couldn't make out the rider's identity, but just in case it was raiders again, Lizzy sprang into action. She didn't want to lose more livestock to hungry deserters. And she certainly did not want to face raiders again.

The cows and their calves were already in the far pasture. Lizzy had relocated the pig pen behind the orchard several weeks ago. That left the poultry. Quickly, Lizzy gathered the hens and their chicks and put them in a cage on the wagon. She considered chasing the rooster, but he was an ornery creature, so she left him behind. Then, she drove the wagon into a cave behind the orchard.

The cave opening faced northwest, making it invisible to anyone approaching from the east or south. Lizzy figured that's where most of the trouble came from. After Quantrill's raiders had departed, Lizzy knew she might not be so lucky the next time – and chances were good there would be a "next time."

Lizzy furnished the cave with a cot and a small table. She'd moved the food stocks from the root cellar to the cave. Now, inside the cave, Lizzy lit a lantern and unhitched the horses from the wagon.

"There, that should keep you content for a while," she said to the two horses who were now stabled in a makeshift stall complete with a feed bunk.

The only thing that needed to be added to the cave was a water source. Lizzy had solved that dilemma by keeping a large crockery container filled with water from a nearby creek.

Generally, deserters would pass by once they discovered the house was abandoned and there was no food to be had. Sometimes, they'd search her house for money or valuables, but she knew there was nothing left to steal.

The cave was her refuge. Her safe place. Lizzy settled in to wait.

The rider who had put Lizzy on high alert was Charlotte. After weeks of travel, including the stop at Jameson's house, Char was eager to be home and to see her sister. Coming up the path to the house, Charlotte could see the damage done by the raiders. Windows were boarded up. Bullet holes riddled every wall. The cows and pigs were nowhere to be seen.

The farm was deserted.

Charlotte was devastated. What had happened to Lizzy? The house had obviously been the scene of a firefight. Did Lizzy get shot or killed?

She dismounted and raced into the house.

"Lizzy! Lizzy! Elizabeth, are you in here?" Her voice boomed throughout the empty house. Even so, Charlotte went from room to room, looking for signs that Lizzy had been there. Then she saw the sliced bread on a plate next to a new jar of preserves. She checked the coffee pot. Still warm.

Someone's been here, and they left in a hurry, Charlotte thought. *If it's Lizzy, where would she go?*

Charlotte checked the root cellar. It had been cleaned out.

Back in the kitchen, Charlotte poured herself a cup of coffee and sat at the table. She needed to think. She thought about hiding places they'd used as children. *Where would Lizzy go?*

She needed a plan. Re-mounting her horse, Charlotte began searching for likely places to hide. Then she remembered the cave. She guided her horse through the thicket toward the creek. The mouth of the cave faced away from Charlotte, so she wasn't sure if it was still usable.

The cave's opening came into view. Still on her horse, Charlotte called out, "Lizzy, Elizabeth Ward…are you in there? I sure hope you're in there!"

"Charlotte! Oh, Charlotte, I'm so happy to see you!" Lizzy exclaimed as she rushed from the cave.

Charlotte dismounted and wrapped her sister in a one-armed hug.

The two sisters finally pulled apart.

"What happened to your arm?" Lizzy asked.

Charlotte laughed ruefully. "I was in the Army eight months, fought a handful of battles and even more skirmishes, and never got a scratch. On my way back here, I was caught in the crossfire between Union soldiers and Rebs. A stray bullet hit me in the shoulder. I'm on the mend now, though. I'll tell you all about it back at the house. We can go back to the house, can't we?"

"Yes, of course! After Quantrill's Raiders and some Jayhawkers had the shootout at our farm, I've been retreating to this cave when I see strangers coming."

"Quantrill's Raiders!" Charlotte exclaimed. "We *do* have a lot of catching up to do!"

Leading their horses, the two sisters walked back to the farm.

Over the following days, Lizzy and Charlotte fell into their old routines. Charlotte was glad she could take some of the burden from Lizzy. And Lizzy became the nurse, cleaning and re-bandaging Charlotte's shoulder. Soon, Charlotte declared she no longer needed the sling.

And, although her shoulder ached when she overexerted it, she knew that was part of the healing process.

The healing process also extended to Charlotte and Lizzy's grieving for their brother. Even though Max was buried in a grave on the other side of the state, the sisters decided that a memorial headstone should be added to the family plot. The headstone was placed next to Blanche and Jacob Ward's grave.

"We'll have a brass plaque engraved when we can afford it," Charlotte promised her sister.

"I think he'll be at rest," Lizzy agreed.

Charlotte had again taken up her former household duties, although she knew she would never match Mary Jameson's talents in the kitchen.

One night, over a dinner of fried chicken, biscuits, and collard greens, Lizzy brought up a subject she'd considered for several months. She pulled out the newspaper with the story about President Lincoln signing the Homestead Act.

"Charlotte, I've been thinking that we should start fresh," she began. She handed Charlotte the newspaper.

"But this is our family farm…our land," Charlotte countered.

"For now, it is, but what about after the war? If the South wins, we could lose the farm," Lizzy said. "Besides, I want to leave the war behind. I want to leave the battlefields and the hatred that has torn our state apart. I'm tired of neighbors fighting neighbors." A tear trickled down Lizzy's cheek.

She took a breath and brushed away the tear.

"This Homestead Act," Lizzy tapped the story in the newspaper, "says that women can legally own their land. Maybe you want to stay in this house, but for me it's full of memories – and they're not all good memories. Mama and Papa died in the corner room upstairs. There's been joy, but there's been a lot of sorrow here, too. I want to start fresh, on new land."

Charlotte considered what her sister said and uttered one word: "Ghosts."

Lizzy looked at her sister. She knew that Charlotte was in agreement.

"You've given this a lot of thought, Lizzy," Charlotte said. "What's your plan?"

Lizzy chewed her lower lip, a habit she'd had since childhood. "The law doesn't go into effect until next January. Then claim offices will be 'open for business,' according to the newspaper. We can use the next few months to prepare, pack up and get ready to move."

"Move where?" Charlotte asked.

"I've thought about that, too. We follow the Missouri River up to Dakota Territory. There's plenty of good farmland up there and the war didn't touch those lands. We can each stake a claim for 160 acres of land. Imagine, Charlotte, 160 acres of land – that's more land than we have here."

"Lizzy, we have a lot of work to do between now and next year," Charlotte said.

"Yes, we do! Charlotte, but it will be a new beginning for both of us," Lizzy said.

"No more ghosts," Charlotte said.

News of the Day – The Homestead Act of 1862
May 1862

In a speech on July 4, 1861, President Abraham Lincoln said the purpose of America's government was "to elevate the condition of men, to lift artificial burdens from all shoulders and to give everyone an unfettered start and a fair chance in the race of life."

That was the idea behind the Homestead Act. Lincoln signed the Homestead Act into law on May 20, 1862. Homesteaders – both men and women – who were head of a household, twenty-one years of age, and had not borne arms against the United States met the qualifications of the Homestead Act.

To successfully "prove" a claim, homesteaders were required to live on the land for five years, build a home on it, and work the land through farming or ranching.

Chapter 10: August 1862
Independence, MO

The summer of 1862 was long and hot. It was so hot, in fact, that the sisters often sought refuge in the cool cave at night.

"I could live in this cave year-round," Charlotte said on an especially sweltering night. "Maybe we could add a couple of windows for sunlight."

"Then you'll feel right at home in Dakota Territory," Lizzy replied. "I've read that a lot of homesteaders up there live in dugouts and something called a 'soddy.'"

"What's a 'soddy?'" Charlotte asked.

"Settlers cut up the prairie sod and stack it like bricks to make walls," Lizzy explained. "Apparently, there's not much wood for building so they make do."

"A 'soddy,'" Charlotte repeated. "We're in for an adventure, aren't we, Lizzy?"

Lizzy could keep only a fraction of her corn fields watered, but she was more successful with the smaller garden plot.

One hot summer day in August, Lizzy heard what she thought was gunfire in the distance. Afraid that Bushwhackers and Jayhawkers might be bringing the fight to her farm again, she ran into the house to alert Charlotte.

Breathlessly, she said, "Charlotte, I hear gunfire."

Charlotte hurried from the house, wiping her hands on her apron. She tilted her head toward the blasts, then said, "No, that's more than gunfire. I recognize that sound. It's cannons. There's a battle going on somewhere over there." She pointed toward Kansas City and Independence, where smoke bloomed on the horizon.

"Should we go to the cave?" Lizzy asked.

"Cannons are so loud that they can be heard for miles. If it gets closer, we'll take to the cave," Charlotte counseled.

"All right, but let's keep a watch for strangers," Lizzy said. "There are always deserters."

Charlotte nodded in agreement.

The next day, Lizzy's prediction came true when a rider galloped down the road to Ward's house. Lizzy emerged from the barn where she'd been gathering eggs. She didn't recognize the rider at first. *I knew we should have retreated to the cave*, she thought with regret.

"Lizzy!" He yelled.

Then she saw it was Frank James riding as if the devil was on his tail.

By now, Charlotte was on the front porch with the shotgun. She watched the rider tie his mount to the fence railing.

Frank looked up to see the slim, dark-haired woman on the porch. He didn't recognize the woman.

"Frank, what's going on?" Lizzy called out.

Frank looked over his shoulder to see Lizzy approaching from the barn. "There you are!" he said. "We've got some wounded men."

"Where?" Charlotte asked.

"There was skirmish. Colonel Hughes and Will Quantrill went up against a troop of Yankees. We won the battle, but a lot of men were wounded. I was sent out to find a doctor, or a nurse."

"Charlotte's a doctor. And I can help as a nurse."

"But it's a battlefield, and a woman shouldn't…" he began.

"I've seen my share of wounded men on battlefields," Charlotte countered. "I'll get my bag. Lizzy, you stay here at the house. We'll be gone several days at least, and the animals…"

"You're right, of course. I'll saddle your horse while you get ready to travel."

A few minutes later, Charlotte emerged from the farmhouse wearing the practical split skirt and carrying her black satchel. She tied on a wide-brimmed straw hat for shade before mounting her horse.

They rode quickly in the direction Charlotte had seen the smoke yesterday.

"Tell me about the battle," she asked.

"We were short on ammunition. When scouts found the Blue Coats camped in Independence, Captain Quantrill and Colonel Hughes ordered us to take the city." Frank shook his head, "Even though we outnumbered 'em two-to-one, we took a lot of casualties, including several officers. It was a bloody battle."

"They all are, Mr. James."

"Yes, ma'am. But we lost Colonel Hughes and it's not looking good for Colonels Hays and Thompson. You say you have some experience in doctoring, Miss Charlotte?" Frank asked.

"Yes, I was at Springfield, and later, I worked in the field hospital at New Madrid."

"We lost a lot of good men in those battles," he said.

Frank James was impressed by Charlotte's experience even though he assumed she had been assigned nursing duties. They could see Independence in the distance now.

"Is there a field hospital set up?" Charlotte asked.

"The wounded are laid out in the Baptist church. That's where we're headed," Frank replied.

Church pews had been converted into hospital beds. Charlotte was used to the Union Army's orderly field hospitals with assessments set up separately from the patient ward and surgical theater.

All Charlotte could see were rows upon rows of bloody bodies; some of the men were moaning. Others were deathly still.

"Where are the surgeons?" she asked as she scanned the hospital ward for doctors.

"We're a little light in that department, ma'am," Frank said. "Quantrill – er Colonel Quantrill – sent a couple of us local boys out to bring back help. I was hoping that Lizzy could do some nursing…then I found you," he shrugged.

"Fine." Charlotte became all business. She tied on an apron, picked up her medical bag, and started going from church pew to church pew to begin triaging the wounded. And just as Dr. Bernard had done in the Army field hospitals, Charlotte began calling out orders. Some soldiers were prepped for surgery – usually amputations. Other soldiers were given laudanum to ease the pain in their final hours. And yet others – the lucky ones – had their wounds dressed and were sent back to their units.

There were very few doctors or nurses in the Confederate field hospital. Charlotte saw one surgeon and took the initiative to introduce herself. The blood-spattered man was amputating a soldier's leg when Charlotte approached the surgical table.

"May I be of assistance, doctor?" Charlotte inquired.

"Hand me that bone saw," he ordered, not looking up from the surgery.

Sensing this was a test of her medical knowledge, Charlotte selected the pistol-grip saw from the tray and handed it to the surgeon. The surgeon grunted in acknowledgment, and she knew she had passed the test.

It was dusk when Charlotte finally sat down. Someone put a plate of cornbread and gravy in front of her.

Mechanically, she ate the meal as she considered how to get through the night.

"You know your way around bone saws, missy." The surgeon Charlotte had assisted a few hours ago sat beside her. He began mopping the gravy with a hunk of cornbread.

"I'm Forrest Lee, Doctor Forrest Lee. No relation to General Lee," he introduced himself. "And you are…"

"I'm Charlotte Ward."

"You've been in a field hospital before. I watched you examine soldiers and call out orders. Where did you train?"

Charlotte recalled Thomas Bernard's "on-the-job training" statement. "I've learned as I go but worked under Dr. Thomas Bernard. My last assignment was at New Madrid. After that, I returned home. That's where Frank James found me and brought me here." Charlotte hoped Dr. Lee wouldn't pry for details or wouldn't ask questions about Thomas.

"You did well today. It's good to have you on our side."

Charlotte realized that the "side" he referred to was the Confederacy. "Dr. Bernard – my teacher – believed the war stopped at the hospital door. Every patient – no matter if they wore blue or gray – received his best efforts."

"Ah, the Hippocratic Oath. You learned from a good one. It's important to remember our oath at times like these." He patted Charlotte on the back. "Now get some rest. I believe we have seen the worst of the injuries. But *our battle* is just beginning." Dr. Lee referred to the enormous number of soldiers who died from infections and disease after they had been wounded.

Charlotte and Dr. Lee worked tirelessly for the next several days. She administered laudanum for pain and quinine for fevers. Dr. Lee spent his days cauterizing wounds to prevent gangrene from setting in or spreading.

She was applying cool compresses to the forehead of a soldier who suffered a chest wound similar to Max's when she heard a familiar voice behind her.

"Miss, excuse me, miss. That's my sergeant. How's he doing?"

"He had a rough night, Captain Jameson." She turned to face the questioner.

"Charlie? What in the blue blazes are you doing here?" exclaimed Luke Jameson.

"Shh. Keep your voice down, Captain. We're trying to heal these soldiers, not scare them to death," Charlotte scolded. "But you're right. My presence here is a bit," she fumbled for the correct term, "unexpected, isn't it? Yet here I am."

"You do turn up in the most unexpected places, Charlie," he said.

She responded with a crooked smile, pleased that he still called her Charlie. "But to answer your question, Sergeant Driscoll has developed a fever, probably due to his chest wound. I'm hoping we've turned the corner."

"I feel better knowing that Dr. Ward is on duty. Speaking of which, when are you 'off duty?'"

"I'm just starting rounds. It will be a while."

"I'll come by for you at the end of the day," Luke promised.

The day flew by. Charlotte continued on her rounds until twilight.

Dr. Lee watched as Charlotte finished cleaning and re-bandaging the amputated arm of a young private. "We've done all we can for one day," Dr. Lee said to Charlotte.

"Yes, doctor." She removed her apron and hung it on a peg by the door. When she left the former Baptist church, she saw Luke on a bench waiting for her.

"There is actually a decent diner left in Independence, and I've reserved a table for us," he said.

"Luke, I'm exhausted," Charlotte protested.

"Too tired for some real southern fried chicken, grits, and garden-fresh peas?"

"Garden fresh, you say. It's been a while since I've eaten anything that wasn't covered in gravy. Lead on."

"How did you find this place?" Charlotte asked as she finished the last morsel of crispy chicken.

"Being an officer does have its advantages," he admitted. "Now, tell me how *this place* found you!" He gestured to the whole of Independence, Missouri. "The last time we saw each other, you were bound for your family farm near St. Joe."

"I made it home. It was so good to be home. But the war came to our farm while I was gone. Quantrill's Raiders and a troop of Jayhawkers had a skirmish there. The house was shot up pretty badly.

"Actually, one of Quantrill's men – a school mate of Max's – brought me here. Seems Frank James and Lizzy struck up a friendship a while ago. That's why Quantrill's Raiders were at our house before the skirmish. The Jayhawkers tracked them there. I'm here because the Confederate hospital was short on staff. Frank came to the farm to fetch Lizzy. I convinced her to stay home. So here I am." She shrugged.

"Hmm. You do seem to find trouble."

Before Charlotte could protest, Luke continued, "My ma will have my hide if I don't ask after your shoulder."

She rubbed her left shoulder and said, "It still aches now and then, but I seem to be able to move it just fine. Tell your mother again how much I appreciated her doctoring me."

Luke nodded. "With seven young 'uns and pa – she had plenty of practice in doctoring."

Luke thanked the proprietress and paid for their meals.

"Will you join me for a stroll before I return you to the hospital?" Luke asked, holding out his arm in invitation.

"Thank you for dinner," Charlotte said as she tucked her hand in the crook of Luke's arm. "A stroll sounds like something in a world apart from this war. I like the sound of it."

Together, they walked to the edge of town, where they could see the flat plains spread before them.

"The plains do seem to go on forever and ever," Charlotte said. "I guess I'll get to see more of them in a few months."

Luke tilted his head. "What do you mean?"

"Lizzy and I are leaving Missouri. We're bound for Dakota Territory next spring."

"What's in Dakota that you can't find here?"

"Peace, I hope."

"The war will be over soon, Charlie. Where will you go? Are you joining a wagon train?"

"No wagon train," Charlotte answered. "We'll follow the Missouri River north into Dakota Territory. It will keep us on course and leads directly to Yankton, the capital of the new territory. We've looked into the Homestead Act, and as single women, we can each stake a claim for 160 acres."

"I haven't heard much about this Act," Luke admitted. "And I know less about Dakota Territory." He shrugged. "That's not something that we Rebs talk about."

Charlotte continued. "Lizzy and I talked with some folks in St. Joseph. Our banker told us to start with the Claims Office in Yankton. As the Territorial Capital, there's sure to be a Claims Office. We'll file claims next to each other and then set out to prove our claims."

"Next to each other?" Luke said. He wanted to keep her talking so the night wouldn't end.

"We can share tools, supplies, and the workload, just like we do now on our family farm. Besides, we both want our sister to be 'next door.' Lizzy wants land in her own name. Land that no one can take away from her. And I want to leave the ghosts behind us."

Luke would have argued with Charlotte about the wisdom of leaving a working farm in Missouri for a new place on the frontier. But her comment about ghosts stopped him.

"How will you get there?" he asked.

"We'll follow the river north to find our new home. A place where neighbors aren't fighting neighbors. A fresh start."

"We can all do with a fresh start, I reckon. I'd best get you back to the hospital," he said with regret.

At the converted church, Luke took his leave. "Thank you for a lovely evening, Miss Ward." He swept off his slouch hat and executed a formal bow.

He hoped that Charlotte might honor him with a kiss – at least a kiss on the cheek. Instead, she patted his hand and said, "Yes, it was very nice. Thank you."

The next morning, during hospital rounds, Dr. Lee asked, "Did you have an enjoyable evening with your beau?"

"Beau? Luke isn't my beau. I think you're mistaken, Dr. Lee."

Forrest Lee shook his head, "No, Miss Ward. I believe you're mistaken."

Charlotte considered the conversation but was certain that Luke only thought of Charlotte as a friend. For her entire life, boys and now men had always been drawn to Lizzy, the pretty sister, not to Charlotte.

Later that week, Dr. Lee approached Charlotte with news. "The troops are pulling out, Miss Ward. And we are leaving without you. You were the answer to my prayers, but I cannot impose on you any longer. The Confederate Army may be conscripting fighting men, but I will not allow our Southern women to be treated in that fashion."

"I'm glad I could be of help, Dr. Lee. But to be honest, I'm also glad to return home. Our farm is less than a day's ride from here."

"Then I believe you will be home in time for dinner," the surgeon said.

Charlotte smiled. "Thank you, Dr. Lee."

Nothing felt as good as coming home, Charlotte thought, as her mare began trotting up to the Ward homestead. *Even Belle was excited to be home,* she thought, gently patting the horse's withers.

Ever vigilant for riders, Lizzy heard the horse coming up the path. She was overjoyed to see that it was her sister returning again from the war.

After-Action Report – The First Battle of Independence, Missouri

August 11, 1862

The First Battle of Independence, Missouri, was fought on August 11, 1862. After a string of Confederate defeats in Missouri, the Confederate strategy shifted from fighting for control of Missouri to using the region as a source for supplies and recruits. Union forces had been tasked with finding and destroying these moving bands of Confederate troops and Bushwhackers under the control of William Quantrill. The combined force of 800 Southern troops staged a two-pronged attack on approximately 350 Union soldiers who were now trapped in the town of Independence. Eventually, Union Lt. Colonel James Buel surrendered to Confederate Colonel Gideon Thompson.

The Confederate victory at Independence and a subsequent victory at Lone Jack, Missouri, just a few days later bolstered Confederate morale for the military, the Southern sympathizers, and the newly commissioned Captain William Quantrill.

Chapter 11: October - December 1862
Ward Farm

"That's the last of the corn harvest." Lizzy stood back and gazed at the field of shocked corn. Turning to her sister, she said, "It wasn't our best year, but it will take us through the winter, and we'll have seed corn for Dakota."

Planning for the journey north had absorbed both sisters. While there was some money in the bank from years when the harvests were bountiful, and the sisters intended to sell some of the livestock for other expenses to supplement their savings. They had started making lists and had consulted with folks in St. Joe about what they should pack for the trip.

"The frontier won't have stores like here in St. Joe, Miss Lizzy," said Ezra Bloom, the owner of Bloom's Mercantile, the largest general store in St. Joseph. "You'd better stock up whilst you can."

The sign above the store's entrance boasted, "Dry Goods – Produce – Fripperies." A second sign read, "If you can't find it here, you don't need it."

"Mr. Bloom, I know we'll miss the convenience of shopping at Bloom's. But I'm afraid there's only so much room in our wagon."

Charlotte couldn't help adding her "two cents" to the conversation. "We're not leaving until spring, Mr. Bloom. It's early and we're still making our lists in pencil – easier to erase."

"If you need more pencils, they're over there," he pointed to a shelf behind him and laughed.

"Oh, I will miss shopping here, Mr. Bloom," said Lizzy. "If only for the entertainment."

"Before the war, we had a lot of folks jumping off from here, bound for Oregon and California," Bloom said. "Some of the wagon train bosses handed out packing lists. I might still have some of those lists in the backroom." He disappeared through a door behind the counter.

"Wouldn't hurt to see what the wagon masters said to pack," Charlotte said.

Lizzy took Charlotte's arm and said excitedly, "Oh, Charlotte, this is going to be a grand adventure! I'm so glad you've agreed."

"A fresh start is just what the doctor ordered," Charlotte replied.

A few minutes later, Bloom, a balding, middle-aged man with a slight limp, emerged from the back room. "Here it is." He handed Lizzy a wrinkled sheet of brown paper.

Lizzy scanned the list. "Let's see," she said. "Flour, rice, coffee, sugar, beans, dried fruit, bacon…" She nodded, "We'll get the dried goods here, Mr. Bloom, but some of the supplies will come straight from the farm, like corn meal, dried fruit, bacon…"

"Of course, Miss Ward," Bloom said. "Should I set aside some of these for you now?"

"Might as well," Charlotte said. "With the war, we never know what will be available. In fact, we'll take some of the supplies with us today."

"When do you ladies plan to leave for the wild and wooly frontier?" Bloom asked.

"President Lincoln signed the Homestead Act in May," Lizzy said. "It becomes a law on January 1, 1863. We'll leave before planting time in the spring."

Charlotte picked up the narrative. "We won't be the first to stake a claim in Dakota Territory, but we'll be one of the first."

Lizzy continued, "That gives us time to break ground and plant our first crops."

Charlotte patted her sister's arm, "She's the planner – and the farmer."

On the way back to the farm, Lizzy drove the wagon while Charlotte read the *St. Joseph Herald* newspaper. "Seems like the war has moved East," she observed. "Most of the battles are in Maryland, Virginia and Kentucky."

"That's a good turn of events," Lizzy said. "Missouri has seen too many battles."

"Well, here's something interesting. This story mentions a Sioux uprising in Minnesota." Charlotte put the paper down. "Lizzy, did you ever think that we might be jumping from the frying pan into the fire? When I was in the Army, I heard talk about soldiers being called up to fight Indians on the frontier."

"Oh, that's way out west," said Lizzy. She didn't want to dampen their enthusiasm for the journey ahead. "California and such."

"Last time I checked a map, Lizzy, Minnesota was east of Dakota Territory. It's just something to be aware of. I imagine that we'll see our share of Indians on the frontier."

The Ward sisters continued planning and preparing for their Dakota Adventure, as they called the homesteading plan.

"How much furniture can we take, Lizzy?" Charlotte asked one day.

"We only have the one farm wagon," Lizzy replied. "If we pack it right, I'm thinking we can take the table, two chairs and our mattresses."

"I was hoping to bring the rockers from the porch," Charlotte said.

"And mama's China," Lizzy added wistfully.

"We're going to need a second wagon," Charlotte stated.

"We could trade some of the cows for another wagon and a team of oxen. We can't herd all the cattle north, anyway. We have two drivers. We might as well have two wagons."

"Agreed!" Charlotte said.

The sisters continued preparing for their journey north. Before they knew it, Christmas was upon them. They were going to attend Christmas services at the church in St. Joseph, but a heavy snowfall changed that plan.

"It's odd having just the two of us for Christmas," Charlotte said.

"I miss Mama, Papa, and Max, too. But I can't think of anyone else that I would rather celebrate the season with. Charlotte, you've made a delicious holiday dinner. We'll sing carols, and then we'll exchange gifts, just as we've always done."

She looked out the parlor window, still cracked from the Jayhawkers' attack. "The falling snow looks like a painting, Charlotte. Come look. It's beautiful."

The sister gazed out on the farmlands, now covered with fluffy, glistening snow.

"One thing is certain," Charlotte said. "This will be our last Missouri Christmas."

"We should toast our Dakota Adventure," Lizzy suggested. She poured two glasses of hot apple cider, and they clinked glasses.

"I know what you're thinking, Lizzy," Charlotte said. "We need to pack mama's glassware, too." They both smiled.

After dinner, the sisters exchanged gifts. "Open yours first," Charlotte said, presenting her sister with a package that was obviously a book.

Lizzy carefully untied the white bow, which she would later use as a hair ribbon.

"*Great Expectations* – Mr. Dickens' latest novel. Oh, thank you, Charlotte. I hope the price was not too dear."

"I know how much you loved his earlier books, and when I saw this in Bloom's window, I snatched it before you even saw it!" Charlotte explained.

"I can't wait to start it," Lizzy said. "I'm afraid my gift to you is not as imaginative, but you've always liked them before."

Charlotte accepted a package wrapped in brown paper with a blue ribbon. Unwrapping the package, she found a copy of Godey's Lady's Book from 1860.

"It's not the latest issue," Lizzy cautioned, "but…"

"It's wonderful!" Charlotte exclaimed. "I don't need the latest fashion. Mama always said Godey's had the best dress patterns. We'll be the most fashionable homesteaders on the prairie! Thank you so much. We'll need to pack the fabric that Mama stored in the trunk."

"Our list keeps getting longer and longer," Lizzy laughed. "How ever did you go off to war with just a saddle bag?"

"I didn't have as much time to make my list," Charlotte rejoined.

Christmas 1862 was a quiet affair at the Ward farmstead. But both sisters looked to the new year with anticipation.

January 1863 was stormy in northwestern Missouri. While the snow made it more difficult for Lizzy to care for the farm's livestock, it also deterred deserters from arriving on the Wards' doorstep.

The sisters continued their preparations throughout the early months of 1863. During a break in the weather, Lizzy and Charlotte drove most of the cattle into town. They sold the livestock at a profit and purchased a second wagon and a team of oxen. This wagon, a "prairie schooner," had high sides treated with tar to waterproof the wagon for crossing rivers and streams. The Ward sisters were assured that a "well-proofed" wagon would float in deeper waters. A canvas "bonnet" was attached to several ribs on the wagon's sides. Pleased with their new purchase, they loaded up on barrels of coffee, sugar, corn meal, and bags of salt for curing meat.

Charlotte also browsed Mr. Bloom's shelves for medical supplies. She found laudanum, witch hazel, and ginger root. Not seeing any quinine, Charlotte requested Mr. Bloom to order some, if possible.

"Of course, Miss Charlotte," Bloom said. "What about leeches? 'Course, I expect you can find them along the way."

Charlotte shuddered. "Awful creatures. Dr. Bernard believed leeches did more harm than good. No thank you, Mr. Bloom. The quinine will be sufficient."

Before leaving town, they stopped at the gunsmith's shop. They purchased an additional shotgun and rifle, along with supplies of ammunition. Tallying up the purchases, the gunsmith said, "Looks like you ladies are headed to war."

Charlotte tucked the remaining money in her small handbag and replied, "No, we're headed away from war. We're bound for Dakota Territory."

"Good luck to you," he said.

Throughout those early months, Charlotte and Lizzy could sometimes hear cannon fire or see smoke from a distant battlefield. Reminders of the war just increased their determination to put Missouri and the War of the Rebellion behind them.

Lizzy visited neighbors, selling furniture and livestock. One neighbor was particularly interested in Mama's piano. And, while the sisters were reluctant to part with it, they knew it would not make the journey. Besides, they could use the cash when they staked their claim on the Dakota frontier.

Pigs were butchered; the meat was smoked and cured. Farm implements were repaired and stacked in a wagon, along with rope and other farming equipment. Lizzy fretted about how to transport Papa's plow. Finally, they dismantled it and lashed parts of it to the side of the wagon.

The Ward sisters worked steadily through the winter and spring. By April, they were ready to begin their Dakota Adventure.

After-Action Report – Battle of Fredericksburg, Virginia Dec 13, 1862

The Battle of Fredericksburg was the largest concentration of troops in any Civil War battle, involving nearly 200,000 combatants. The 120,000 Union troops were led by Union General Ambrose Burnside, newly appointed commander of the Army of the Potomac. The battle began on December 11, 1862, when Union forces crossed the Rappahannock River to engage General Robert E. Lee's 80,000-strong Army of Northern Virginia. Lee's forces turned back the Union assault with heavy casualties (nearly 13,000) but nevertheless won the battle. The battle concluded on December 15 when Burnside ordered Union forces to retreat across the Rappahannock, ending the campaign of 1862 in the Eastern Theater.

The Union Army of the Potomac suffered more than 12,500 casualties. Lee's Confederate army counted approximately 6,000 losses. The conflict resulted in demoralized Union sentiments and provided much-needed positive momentum for the Confederate forces.

Chapter 12: April - May 1863
Missouri River

"There! That's the last of the hens and chicks," Charlotte said in triumph. "An even dozen and all in cages on my wagon."

Lizzy surveyed the empty farmstead. "We've cleaned out nearly everything we can carry," she said. "I wish we could have sold the farm, but no one wants to buy land in Missouri these days."

"We're leaving our 'old lives' behind us, Lizzy," Charlotte said. "But still, we've packed some of those memories, like Mama's dishes, Papa's rocking chairs."

She looked over the two wagons and said, "There's nothing left to pack – or at least no room to pack anything on either wagon. There's not even room for a driver."

"We agreed that we'd walk alongside the teams, at least in the beginning," Lizzy said. "According to this trail guide, it's about three hundred miles from St. Joseph to Yankton as the crow flies. We just need to follow the river.

"It's the middle of April, and if we cover ten or fifteen miles a day, we'll be in Yankton by mid-May. I've heard that's not too late to plant up there," Lizzy offered.

Charlotte tied on her broad-brimmed straw hat with her new blue ribbon and said, "Let the Dakota Adventure begin!"

"Amen," Lizzy said to herself. She scooped up her cat, Butter, and placed the yellow feline on a pile of blankets in her wagon. Under the blankets, the sisters had hidden a purse of cash and coins – their "nest egg" for supplies and contingencies.

Unlike the pioneers who spent months traveling to California, Utah, or Oregon, the Ward sisters hoped that their journey would be brief. The weather should be agreeable, although spring rains could make travel treacherous along the Missouri River.

All in all, they packed a dozen chickens, three milk cows with calves at their sides, and four young pigs. The cows were tethered to the wagons, and the calves wouldn't let their mamas out of sight. The pigs and poultry were in crates that hung from the sides of the wagons. Lizzy had sold or bartered most of the other livestock, including the bull and the remaining pigs that hadn't been butchered for ham, side pork, or bacon. She had to admit that traveling with such a menagerie was challenging. Still, she wanted ready livestock when they settled down on their claims.

They had covered just under twelve miles when the sisters decided to make camp.

"It's our first night," Charlotte said. "It will take us a while to establish a routine."

Lizzy agreed. She untied the cows and set them in a nearby pasture to graze, then began feeding the rest of the animals. As Lizzy took care of the animals, Charlotte made a campfire and cooked dinner. She also stirred up a batch of biscuits for breakfast the next day.

While they considered themselves "country girls," they were not accustomed to sleeping under the stars. To their surprise, they enjoyed the sounds and sights of the night skies. Soon, the sheer exhaustion of the day caught up with both sisters, and they drifted off to sleep with the song of crickets in the air.

The morning dawned bright, incentivizing Charlotte and Lizzy to "get on the road," as Lizzy called it. On the second day, they made better progress. Lizzy estimated they walked nearly 20 miles, according to the trail guide she'd purchased from Bloom's Mercantile.

"See, here's a landmark that tells us where we are," Lizzy pointed to a notation on the guide. "As long we keep the Missouri River in sight and keep heading north, we'll get there. But the guide does provide some assurance."

A week into the journey, Charlotte spied a town in the distance. She pointed it out to Lizzy.

"I believe that's Rock Port," Lizzy confirmed. "It's a couple of miles out of the way, and it's only midday, but we can stop there if you'd like."

Charlotte considered it, then said, "No, let's keep moving. If that's Rock Port, we're nearly out of Missouri."

Lizzy said, "I think you're right. Tomorrow we should be in Iowa…or Nebraska Territory. It gets a little…" she paused, searching for the right word. "It gets a little fuzzy on the guide map. Either way, we're headed in the right direction."

The daylight continued to get longer, allowing the sisters to cover even more miles each day. Along the way,

Charlotte had noticed a shadow following them. Maybe a wolf? A coyote? No, it was a large, black and tan dog.

She began leaving bits of food for the animal when they broke camp in the morning. The dog became bolder and entered camp one evening. He sat on his haunches and watched the women by the campfire.

"Well, look who wants to join us," Charlotte said to Lizzy.

Lizzy saw the dog and said, "It's our shadow." She gathered Butter into her lap and then called to the dog, "Come on, Shadow. Come into the light."

Charlotte tossed a bone in the space between her and the dog. Shadow took "the bait" and settled down to gnaw on the stew bone. Shadow's fur was mostly black, with patches of light brown on his chest and front legs. His ears stood at attention most of the time.

"I think we have a new member of the family. Maybe his old family had to abandon him, or he just ran off. Will Butter approve," Charlotte asked.

"She's purring right now," Lizzy said. "I'll take that as approval."

After that evening, Shadow trailed along with the wagons. Occasionally, he'd stray off to chase a rabbit, but he was always back by dinner time, the sisters observed.

The next town on the journey was Nebraska City. Charlotte and Lizzy made camp outside of town for the night.

"I don't mind staying with the wagons and the animals if you want to go into town, Charlotte," Lizzy offered.

Charlotte laughed. "I was going to say the same thing to you. I guess we're getting used to life on the road. It's enough to see the lights…to see civilization. It's been a long day, and I'm going to turn in."

The sisters awoke to Shadow's growls and barking.

Quietly, Charlotte reached for her shotgun. "Don't light a lamp. It will make me a target," she whispered to Lizzy.

Shadow's barking was becoming more ferocious.

"A dang watchdog!" Charlotte heard a voice in the darkness.

"Show yourself," Charlotte crouched behind the wagon and called out.

Two men, deserters from the looks of them, stepped into the light of the campfire.

"Throw down your guns," Charlotte said as she chambered a shell in her shotgun.

One man tossed a six-shooter; the other pitched a shotgun into the light.

"What were you doing skulking around our camp," Lizzy said as she joined Charlotte from the other side of the wagon.

Now, there were two women holding shotguns on the intruders. And Shadow was still growling menacingly behind the men.

"We didn't mean no harm, misses," said the shorter man. He wore a ragged blue Union jacket, along with dark, dirty trousers and a black bandana around his neck.

"It doesn't look that way to us," Lizzy said.

"Just tryin' to make our way west. Looking for a bite to eat," said the other man. He wore a Union forage cap, the flat-topped hats that soldiers favored. "We'll keep going, if it's all the same to you."

Charlotte motioned with her shotgun at the pistol and shotgun on the ground. "We'll drop these off in Nebraska City tomorrow morning. You can claim them from the sheriff. Good night to you."

Lizzy and Charlotte kept their shotguns leveled at the strangers as the men walked toward the lights of Nebraska City.

When they were out of sight, Charlotte called to Shadow. "Good dog! Good Shadow! You've earned an extra treat!" She scratched the watchdog between the ears, and he seemed to smile at his new mistress.

They were well past Omaha and Council Bluffs when the rains started.

"Everything is getting soaked," Lizzy complained. "We need to find a place to shelter."

"A cozy cave would be just the thing," Charlotte suggested. "But I'm guessing there aren't any marked on your trail guide."

"Better yet," Lizzy said excitedly, "how about a barn? Like that one over there?" She pointed to a large structure about a half-mile from the river. "It looks abandoned, but even if it's not, we can at least check it out."

Charlotte agreed that seemed like the best option as the downpour continued. They struggled through the muddy farm fields toward the barn. The wagon wheels sank to the axles, but the teams of oxen muscled through and pulled the wagons free. Finally, as another crack of thunder threatened to spook the cows, the sisters and their wagons reached the shelter of the barn.

"It's empty," Lizzy called back to Charlotte as she led her team inside. Behind the barn, they saw the burned remains of a farmhouse.

"It's emptier than our barn!" Charlotte exclaimed. "But the fields had been plowed. Someone was recently living – and farming – here."

"Looks like they pulled up and moved out just like we did. Probably after the house burned down," she surmised.

Lizzy unpacked the wagon goods that needed to dry out while Charlotte started a small fire.

"This barn is – or was – dry as tinder. I don't want to tempt the fates with a roaring fire," Charlotte explained.

"Anything is better than that cold, drenching rain," Lizzy said. She set up a long pole and hung their clothing and towels on it to dry out.

Charlotte made a stew for dinner as Lizzy bedded down the livestock for the night. "This will be a treat for them," she said. While the cows were nursing their calves, Lizzy fed the pigs and chickens. She collected a few eggs and gave them to Charlotte. "For breakfast?"

"I'll pull out some of our salted pork. It will be a fine meal."

They discussed their Dakota adventure over beef stew. "How much farther, Lizzy?" Charlotte asked.

Lizzy consulted her trail guide. "I'm thinking we're nearly to Sioux City. We've covered about two hundred miles, Charlotte! We arrive in Yankton in just over a week if my calculations are correct."

"That's if this rain ever stops," Charlotte said ruefully.

"Oh, it will stop, and then we'll pray for rain. That's how farming works, sister.

"Charlotte, have you noticed how empty the countryside is? This isn't the first abandoned farm we've seen. Where is everyone?"

"It's the war, Lizzy. The men went off to fight, and women stayed behind. Just like we did. I'm guessing some of the women went back home – maybe back East. Others might have gone to live with relatives in town. This war has hollowed out our country."

"I'm glad we decided to move on, too, Charlotte."

Her sister nodded. "Leave the ghosts behind."

Lizzy was right about the weather. After another day of rain, the skies cleared, and the sun came out.

"It's going to be a glorious day, Butter!" Lizzy said to her cat. Charlotte, who was entering the barn after a trip to the outhouse, overheard the conversation and said, "I think Butter will miss the plentiful supply of field mice in this barn."

"She *is* a good mouser. We'll find work for her soon enough."

"Let's hitch up the wagons and head out ... but be mindful of the mud," Charlotte cautioned.

They made good progress that day and put Sioux City behind them.

"Dakota Territory, get ready for the Ward sisters!" Charlotte exclaimed.

"Dakota will never be the same," Lizzy laughed in response.

After-Action Report – Battle of Chancellorsville
May 1-6, 1863

The Battle of Chancellorsville is considered Gen. Robert E. Lee's greatest military victory despite the heavy casualties the Confederate forces sustained.

Fought in Spotsylvania County, Virginia, Lee's Army faced a force twice its size. The Union Army of the Potomac, led by General Joseph Hooker, numbered nearly 100,000 men. From May 1 to May 6, the two armies clashed on a field just beyond the Wilderness Forest west of Chancellorsville. Despite his superior numbers, Hooker had his men fall back to defensive positions, allowing General Lee to launch a brilliant and strategic offensive plan.

More than thirty thousand soldiers died in the week-long battle. Among the casualties was Confederate Lt. Gen. Thomas J. "Stonewall" Jackson, who was mortally wounded by friendly fire.

Chapter 13: April 1863
Cape Girardeau, MO

After parting ways with Charlotte at Independence, Missouri, the previous summer, Luke Jameson's unit had joined up with Major General John Marmaduke's troops. Like Luke, Marmaduke was a Missourian from the secesh region of the state. Marmaduke's troops saw action primarily in Missouri and Arkansas, including the Battle of Cape Girardeau.

The two brigades under General Marmaduke saw Cape Girardeau as an opportunity to restock dwindling supplies. Cape Girardeau, however, had been heavily fortified by General Grant in 1861. Union troops, led by General John McNeil, occupied four forts at strategic locations around the city and stood ready to defend the river town.

Rebel forces, about 5,000 men strong, advanced on the town on April 26, 1863. The fighting lasted approximately five hours, ceasing in the afternoon when General Marmaduke ordered his forces to withdraw. While only a dozen or so Union soldiers were killed or injured, the Confederates counted more than 300 casualties and losses. Among the losses were several Confederate troops who were taken prisoner, including Luke Jameson.

Luke and several other soldiers from his unit were captured before General Marmaduke's withdrawal. They were held in a makeshift prison next to one of the city's forts until provisions could be made. When no one from

General Joseph Shelby's or General Marmaduke's regiments came forward to claim the Rebel prisoners, they were shipped to Gratiot Street Prison, one of several Union prisons in St. Louis.

May 1863 – Yankton, Dakota Territory

It was just short of a month since Charlotte and Elizabeth Ward had left their family farm in Missouri and when they entered the capital city of Dakota Territory.

Like most frontier towns, Yankton was raw and rowdy, often muddy, and always full of optimism. Main Street was lined with wooden storefronts sporting tall facades to make them seem larger than they were. There were half a dozen saloons, two banks, three churches, a general store, a post office, and a livery stable. At the end of the street stood the Territorial Capitol building, which Charlotte decided was less than impressive.

They camped outside Yankton to get a "fresh start" with their business the next day. On a warm May morning, the Ward sisters entered Yankton. Each woman walked beside a covered wagon pulled by a team of oxen.

"Morning, ladies," said a portly gentleman smoking a cigar. He was standing outside the Black Bull Saloon. "Can I direct you someplace in particular?"

"Thank you, sir," Lizzy said. "We're looking for the Claims Office."

"I thought that might be the case," the man replied. "It's over yonder, next to the Post Office." He pointed to a small building with a sign that proclaimed its purpose.

"I see it. Thank you," Lizzy called back.

"If I may be so bold, could I stand you ladies a drink at the Black Bull?" he asked. "Think of it as a 'welcome to Yankton' gesture."

"Very kind of you, but no," Charlotte said.

Charlotte and Lizzy continued to the Claims Office on the far side of the street. They lashed the wagon reins to hitching posts. Lizzy took a deep breath and said to her sister, "Here we go!" She reached for the front door.

Inside the Claims Office, sunlight streamed through the front windows. A man hunched over a rolltop desk with his back to the door. He greeted his customers without turning around.

"Howdy. I'll be with you in just a minute." He stamped an official document with a rubber stamp, then turned to see two young women.

The taller woman was slim but not thin. A wide-brimmed sun hat covered her dark hair. The other woman was shorter and held a sun bonnet, showing blonde braids coiled over each ear. Both women wore dresses spattered with mud and dirt — just like most of the settlers who entered the Claims Office.

"Ladies, what can I do for you?"

"We're here to file claims for land," the shorter, blonde woman replied.

"Where are your menfolk?" the agent asked. He craned his neck, looking for the presence of husbands or fathers.

Charlotte wanted to answer, "They're all dead." Still, she refrained, remembering Mama had always said, "You can attract more flies with honey than vinegar."

Lizzy stepped up to the counter and smiled. She noticed the nameplate on the desk. "Mr. Mathews, I believe the Homestead Act states that anyone over the age of twenty-one who is head of their household is eligible to file…"

"As long as they haven't fought for the Confederacy," Charlotte added. "We're both over twenty-one and we intend to file for 160 acres each. I am Charlotte Blanche Ward, and this is my younger sister, Elizabeth Ruby Ward. Our birthdays are recorded in the family Bible if you'd like proof of our age," she offered.

"This is a first for me, ladies. I've not had any girl homesteaders file claims." He ran his finger down the lists of births and deaths in the large, black Bible until he found Charlotte's and Elizabeth's names.

"Welcome to Dakota Territory, ladies." He pulled out large plat books and said, "Now, let's see what's been surveyed and ready to claim."

"There are a number of claims available directly west of here," he suggested.

"We want two claims with a common border," Charlotte requested.

"And water. We want a creek or stream running through the claims," Lizzy added.

"How about Claims 168 and 170?" Mr. Mathews indicated two parcels of land. "These have been surveyed and have a common property line. Looks like there's a fine stream running through both claims." He scrutinized the plat map, "Hmmm, I don't see a name on the stream."

"Neighbors?" Charlotte asked.

"Not for a few miles, although the Sioux often camp by the river. I heard there's a new town starting up a few miles west of your land. It's called…," he squinted and looked at the ceiling as if he'd find the town name in the rafters. "Shady…Shady Bluffs. That's it," Mathews said.

"Shady Bluffs," Charlotte repeated. "Sounds like a friendly town."

The sisters looked at each other, and Charlotte said, "Ready?"

"I am," Lizzy said with more than a hint of excitement.

The sisters paid their filing fees, and then Mr. Mathews began reciting the requirements for proving their land. "You understand that to own the land permanently, you'll need to 'prove' the claim."

Lizzy was about to protest that she understood the requirements, but Mr. Mathews raised a hand. "I'm confident you ladies understand the rules, but I'm required to review the regulations with new homesteaders."

He continued, "You must build houses on your land, live on the claims at least six months out of the year, and work the land. Can you do that?"

"Yes," Lizzy and Charlotte said in unison.

"Dandy," Mr. Mathews said. "Now, sign here."

With that, Charlotte Ward and Elizabeth Ward were officially Dakota homesteaders.

"I can ride out to the claims with you, if you like, to make sure you're on the right parcels."

"That's very kind of you, Mr. Mathews," Charlotte said.

"Are you available tomorrow?" Lizzy asked.

"It would be my pleasure," Mr. Mathews said. "Oh, and the name's Mike Mathews. You can call me Mike."

After they left the Claims Office, Charlotte said, "I think we deserve a night in a real feather bed." She pointed out a hotel across from the Claims Office.

"After hot baths in a real tub," Lizzy added. "First, let's tend to the animals. We haven't even unhitched them yet!"

They inquired at the livery and were able to stable the horses, oxen, and the farm animals inside the horse barn. Grabbing their carpet bags from the wagon, the Ward sisters headed to Yankton's finest hotel.

Later, as Elizabeth brushed through her shampooed hair, Charlotte luxuriated in the large copper bathtub. "This is pure pleasure," Charlotte said. "We'll probably regret spending money on this extravagance."

"Nonsense," said Lizzy. "I sold our livestock in St. Joe for a good price. We deserve this after a month of travel and rough camping."

"You've always been the practical one," Charlotte teased her. "This doesn't seem practical."

"It's more than practical. It's our reward for making the journey. And on those days when we're bone-tired from breaking sod or building houses, we'll drop into our beds and dream about this night in a fancy Yankton hotel!" Both sisters laughed.

"Seriously, Charlotte," Lizzy continued. "We have a lot of work in front of us. I'm glad that Mr. Mathews – Mike – will be riding with us to the claims. During the ride, I intend to ask non-stop questions about homesteading."

Charlotte climbed out of the soapy water and dried off. "Then let's do this night up right with a good dinner at that restaurant down the street."

"Now you're in the spirit," Lizzy said.

The following morning, Lizzy and Charlotte met Mike Mathews in front of the Claims Office. Instead of the plaid vest, brown frock coat, and collared white shirt he'd worn the day before, Mike Mathews now looked like a typical farmer. In addition to a broad-brimmed hat, he wore a blue and black striped shirt, gray vest, and dark gray trousers. His brown and white Appaloosa was tied at the hitching post.

"Good morning, Misses," Mike said. "I trust you had a quiet evening in Yankton. It can get rather 'exuberant' at times."

"We did, indeed, Mr. Mathews – Mike," Lizzy said.

"How many hours until we're at the claims?" Charlotte asked.

Mathews checked his pocket watch. "I expect we'll be on the Ward land by noon."

"The 'Ward Land.' I like the sound of that," Lizzy said.

The journey north had literally eaten into the sisters' food stocks, making enough room in the wagons for each woman to sit on the bench while driving the teams. Lizzy's cat was curled up on the bench next to her. Shadow kept pace with Charlotte's wagon. They each clicked their tongues and called "Get up" to the animals.

And the great Dakota adventure continued.

On the ride to the claims, Lizzy peppered Mike Mathews with questions:

"What's the growing season here in Dakota?"

"Have the farmers started planting?"

"Have they finished planting?"

"Do you recommend a soddy or a dugout?"

Then she asked the question that had been nagging her for three hundred miles. "Do our houses have to be in the center of each claim? Or could we build our houses on the shared property line?"

"As long as the domicile is on your property, it qualifies," Mike replied. His eyes twinkled just a bit. "I've heard tell that a couple of brothers down in Nebraska Territory did just that. In fact, they built a common room between their two houses."

"Really?" Charlotte exclaimed. "That's a wonderful idea!"

The sisters continued asking rapid-fire questions, and before they knew it, Mike Mathews said, "There's your land." He pointed to acres of gently rolling land covered in knee-high prairie grass.

"It's beautiful," Lizzy exclaimed. She jumped off her wagon to dig into the prairie soil.

"How can you tell we're in the right spot?" Charlotte asked Mike.

"See those wooden posts?" He pointed to several stakes that seemed to be intentionally placed. "Those posts and those rock piles are what we call 'monumentation.' Surveyors use them to mark claims. Don't move 'em. It's against the law."

"So much to learn out here," Charlotte murmured to herself. She followed Mike's hand as it traced the survey markers along the rolling prairie. Then he pulled a rolled-out map from his saddle bag. "This will help. See how the poles and rock piles follow the landmarks?"

"I do," Charlotte said. "And there's the creek that's on the map."

"I couldn't find a name for it. Guess that will be up to you ladies."

Lizzy approached Charlotte and Mike, holding out a clump of dirt. "This is good soil, Charlotte."

"My little sister, always the farmer," Charlotte said with a smile.

"You're not going to farm, Miss Charlotte?" Mike asked.

"I'll work the land, but I'll never be the farmer that Lizzy is." Charlotte had begun unloading the wagons.

"Please stay for picnic lunch, Mike," Lizzy invited the Claims agent. "Then I expect you'll want to get back to town."

"Lunch would be appreciated, Miss Elizabeth," Mike Mathews said.

They chatted a bit more about homesteading. "I don't see any mounds or hills big enough for dugouts. You'll probably want to start cutting sod for soddies," he suggested. "Like we talked about on the ride here, I can send out a couple of hands to help get you started. There's a lot to do in the first season."

"We are really in your debt, Mike," Charlotte said.

"Just bein' neighborly," Mike answered. "And now, it's time for me to head back to town. Don't be strangers," he called from horseback as he turned his Appaloosa east toward Yankton.

Mike Mathews was nearly out of sight when Lizzy stood up and twirled around, making her full skirt swirl. "We're here, Char. We're truly and finally here!"

"This will be a fine adventure!" Charlotte agreed. She took Lizzy's hands in hers, twirling each other until they were dizzy.

"Come on," Lizzy said. "Let's explore."

Together, they strolled down the center line between the two claims, commenting on likely spots for their new houses, the barn, a well, and all the other comforts of home.

"Building on high ground would be a good idea," Charlotte said.

Lizzy laughed. "Do you see any actual 'high ground'? This land is flatter than anything we had in Missouri."

"Alright…then on a 'rise,'" Charlotte conceded.

"But before we build soddies, we'll need animal pens."

"We can use the wagon canvases for tents," Charlotte suggested. "I can put that together. Heaven knows I slept in plenty of Army tents when I was Charlie Ward."

"That's a good plan," Lizzy said. "I'll gather some tree branches down by the creek for a temporary animal pen."

After-Action Report – Siege of Vicksburg, Mississippi
May-July 1863

The 47-day Siege of Vicksburg was a decisive victory for the Union and for General Ulysses S. Grant. Vicksburg's position on the Mississippi River, midway between Memphis and New Orleans, made it a strategic location for both sides. Grant led a combined force of 77,000 soldiers against 33,000 troops commanded by Confederate General John Pemberton.

In late June, Grant ordered troops to dig tunnels and set explosives under the Confederate defensive works, followed by more than twenty hours of hand-to-hand fighting. The siege continued until July 3, when Grant and Pemberton met between their lines. Grant insisted on an unconditional surrender, but Pemberton refused. Later, Grant reconsidered and offered to parole the Confederate defenders. On July 4, the Siege of Vicksburg was over.

The Confederate surrender gave the Union control of the Mississippi River and split the South in two.

Chapter 14: July 1863
St. Louis, MO

While all the prisoner-of-war camps during the Civil War were criticized for being overcrowded and in poor condition, the Union prisons were generally better than the horrific Confederate prisons, such as Andersonville.

The Gratiot Street Prison in St. Louis was established when the Myrtle Street Prison became overcrowded. The Union Army converted the McDowell Medical College building into Gratiot Street Prison in December 1861. Gratiot Street Prison served as a holding place for prisoners until they could be transferred to larger facilities, so prisoners received better treatment than in some other prison camps.

Still, rations were scarce for the prisoners of war, and disease was rampant throughout the camp. Luke tried to stay with his soldiers, but as an officer, he was moved to another section of the prison.

Because of overcrowding, both the Union and Confederate prisons had begun exchanging prisoners or releasing soldiers during the early years of the War. If POWs agreed they would no longer fight in the conflict, they were released on "parole." After more than two months in the St. Louis prison camp, Luke Jameson was among a group of Confederate soldiers who were paroled with the understanding that they would no longer fight against Union forces.

It was a hot, muggy July day when Luke emerged from the dark, dank confines of the prison. His Confederate gray trousers hung on his spare, nearly starved frame. His hair and beard were long and shaggy and, much to his disgust, were crawling with lice.

Luke left Gratiot Street Prison with one goal: to find Charlotte Ward. Since their meeting in Independence, Charlie (as he still thought of her) was constantly in his thoughts. But before he could do that, he needed to get home. And before he could get home, Luke needed to eat, clean up, and get a job – not necessarily in that order. Because he was released without his sidearm, he had nothing to trade for a hot bath and a meal. Luke scanned the street and saw the livery stable. Mucking out stalls was nothing new to Luke. In fact, after growing up on the Jameson ranch, he was good at it.

At the livery stable, Luke found the owner and offered to clean the stables. Jeremiah Tanner, the livery stable owner, sized up the scarecrow of a man. Tanner didn't think Luke would have the energy or muscle to do the work. Still, Luke was wearing the gray trousers of a Confederate soldier, and Tanner was a Southern sympathizer. He gave Luke a chance to prove his worth.

"There's twenty stalls in there," Tanner motioned to the stables. "I'll pay you two bits a day to muck out the empty ones and fill all the hay racks."

Luke knew he wouldn't be able to find a meal and a boarding house for twenty-five cents, so he started bargaining. "It's a deal if I can sleep in the barn tonight."

"Don't make no never mind to me," the stable owner said.

"Thanks," Luke said. "It's a helluva lot better than where I slept last night."

After cleaning out the stalls and filling the hayracks, Luke found a horse trough to bathe in. A bar of lye soap and a horse brush made short work of the lice in Luke's hair and beard. He'd think about shaving and cutting his hair after he had a full belly.

For now, Luke Jameson felt like a new man. He was clean, and his belly didn't rumble anymore.

Jeremiah Tanner was well-satisfied with Luke's work.

"You know horses, don't ya?" Tanner said the following week. "I see how you move around 'em and how you groom 'em."

"My pa owns a horse ranch out by Columbia in Boone County. Pa said I could ride before I could walk."

Both men knew that was a bit of an exaggeration, but Tanner smiled. "Tell ya what, Jameson. I've got a string of ponies coming in a couple of days. I could use someone to help break 'em and wrangle 'em. Pay is a buck a horse."

Luke considered the offer. "I'd rather take my pay in horseflesh."

"You've got yourself a deal," Jeremiah Tanner said, happy he wouldn't have to part with hard cash.

Working Tanner's new string of horses was tonic for Luke. He didn't miss the sound and the fury of warfare.

And his months in prison had taken its toll on his mind and body. Regular meals, sleep, and physical labor helped Luke regain the muscle he'd lost in prison.

Luke and Jeremiah sat on the corral fence, watching the fresh horses trot around the ring as if they'd been born with saddles. "The farrier comes day after tomorrow to shoe 'em," Tanner said.

"The horses will be ready," Luke said. He knew he'd spend the next few days cleaning and filing the horses' hooves. He was looking forward to watching the farrier work. He'd forgotten how much he truly loved being around horses.

Unlike some farriers who only shoed horses, this man was also a blacksmith, so he also made the horseshoes. Luke observed as the blacksmith sized the horses' hooves, adjusting the metal shoes to fit each horse's individual hooves. The blacksmith/farrier looked up at Luke and handed him the hammer. "Are you ready to give it a try?" he asked Luke.

"I used to watch my Pa shoe horses. He made it look easy. You make it look easier. I'm guessing it's not easy," Luke said.

"You're right about that, but it gets easier with every shoe."

At that point, Jeremiah Tanner walked into the horse yard and saw Luke shoeing a horse.

"No extra charge for teaching your man the basics," the farrier/blacksmith said before Tanner could complain that the blacksmith was neglecting his work.

"Hmmph! Make sure they're shoed right," said Tanner.

"They'll be dancin'," the blacksmith assured Tanner.

Luke worked side-by-side with the farrier/blacksmith, and in the end, Luke could fit, size, and nail on the shoes like he'd been doing it for years. He also learned some of the blacksmith's techniques for working the metal horseshoes on the forge.

It was the end of July when Luke approached Jeremiah Tanner to thank him. "Mr. Tanner, thank you for taking a chance on this old soldier. Working your horses – and mucking your stables – helped me get back on my feet."

"You're a good worker, Jameson. I expect that you're saying you're leavin' me."

"I am, sir. It's time I got on with my life."

"And what's that gonna be, Jameson? Are you going to join up with your old outfit?

"No, I made a pledge when the Blue Coats paroled me. I promised I wouldn't take up arms again. And I'm a man of my word."

"Then you're headed back to your Pa's horse ranch?"

"Yes. But then I'm going to Dakota Territory."

"Startin' over, huh? Are you gonna homestead, then?"

"Not sure. But there's someone I need to find out there."

The longing sound in Luke's voice and the faraway look in his eyes told Jeremiah Tanner that "someone" might be a woman.

"Hmmph," Tanner repeated. "Better pick out that horse you'll be needing for the ride west."

After-Action Report – Battle of Gettysburg
July 1-3, 1863

The Battle of Gettysburg is considered the most important battle of the Civil War. Fresh off a victory at Chancellorsville, General Robert E. Lee marched his Confederate forces into Pennsylvania in late June 1863. On July 1, Lee's troops clashed with the Union's Army of the Potomac, commanded by General George G. Meade, in Gettysburg. The fighting was even heavier the next day, with Confederate forces attacking the Union troops on both the left and the right.

On the third day, Lee ordered 15,000 Confederate troops to attack the Union at Cemetery Ridge. The assault, known as "Pickett's Charge," broke through the Union lines but cost thousands of rebel casualties. Lee withdrew his battered Army on July 4. Stopping Lee's invasion was a significant turning point for the Union Army and for the War.

Union casualties numbered 23,000, while the Confederates lost some 28,000 men — more than a third of the Southern Army. Following the defeat at Gettysburg,

General Lee offered his resignation to President Jefferson Davis, but Davis refused. The Battle of Gettysburg, along with General Ulysses S. Grant's victory at Vicksburg (also on July 4), turned the tide of the Civil War in the Union's favor.

Chapter 15: Summer 1863
Yankton, Dakota Territory

Mike Mathews made good on his promise to find and send honest workers to help the Ward sisters.

Charlotte searched for and gathered eggs from the hens that were now free to roam much of the homestead yard. She was the first to see the strangers ride up.

"Good morning, gentlemen," she said.

"Morning, ma'am," said the rider on a gray and white horse. "Mike Mathews sent us to inquire about work on your land. I'm Gordon Robinson – everyone calls me 'Gordy,' and this here is my cousin, Ed Robinson."

The other rider tipped his cowboy hat in acknowledgment and said, "Howdy."

"We can use the help getting started," Charlotte said. "There's a lot to do, and my sister wants to spend her time plowing and planting." She gestured to the wide-open prairies.

When Gordy dismounted, Charlotte understood why he wasn't in the Army. Gordy's right leg ended at the knee.

"Where did you lose your leg, Gordy?" Charlotte asked.

"Second battle of Bull Run," the former soldier said. "I miss my leg, but it was my ticket home, too." He shrugged. "I'm still handy enough with a hammer and saw."

She turned to the other rider, who was dismounting. Before she could ask why he wasn't fighting, the young man said, "I'd been fighting more than two years when Gordy got shot. I figured my time was up, too. Gordy and me, we came home together."

Charlotte understood that to mean that Ed was a deserter. "And where's home?"

"Kentucky, ma'am," Ed replied. "After Manassas, when Gordy lost his leg, we decided to head back home to Kentucky."

"And we just kept on going west," Gordy added. "We didn't want anything more to do with the war."

"That's why we're here," Lizzy said. She had heard the last part of the conversation. "I take it that Mike Mathews sent you?"

"Yes'm," Gordy said. "Uh, I'm Gordy Robinson. This is Ed Robinson. We're cousins."

The two sisters and the two cousins settled on a wage that included three meals a day.

"The first thing we need is a barn," Charlotte said. "Our soddies can wait until that's done."

"More than one soddy?" Ed asked.

"We've each staked a claim, so the law says we each need to build a house," Lizzy answered. "But we'll build only one barn to begin with. I'm thinking right over here."

"We'll need lumber, nails and such for the barn," Charlotte said. "One of you can take a wagon into Yankton to buy building supplies. We've set up accounts at the general store and the lumber yard."

The Robinsons understood that Lizzy and Charlotte would be fair but firm employers. While the Robinsons concentrated on construction projects, Lizzy and Charlotte began working the land. Lizzy knew that plowing the prairie sod would be a challenge, but she had no idea how tough the virgin land would be.

"I thank the Lord every night for the oxen," Lizzy said one evening as the four sat around a campfire. "I don't think I'll get as much plowed as I'd hoped, but it will have to do."

"I could take a turn with the plowing, if you like," Charlotte offered.

Lizzy shook her head. "Thank you, but I'd rather have you plant the garden. There's a good-sized plot ready to sow the seeds I brought from home."

Thankful that she didn't have to manhandle the team of oxen and the heavy plow, Charlotte readily accepted the gardening task. She raked the over-turned sod into furrows and completed planting garden seeds.

"Now to water the seeds," she said to Shadow. The dog, who followed Charlotte everywhere, trotted alongside as she made her way to the creek with two large buckets.

But the dappling waters tempted Charlotte to forego her gardening chores. She had removed her shoes and socks and hiked her skirts up above her knees to enjoy the cool waters when she heard Shadow let out a low growl.

Charlotte looked around but didn't see anyone. Then, in the shadow of a willow tree, she saw three Indian women and a child wading in the creek.

"Shhh, Shadow," Charlotte instructed her dog. "Let's not scare the neighbors right away."

Shadow stopped growling but stood on alert.

Charlotte recalled meeting Osage and Shawnee Indians as a little girl in Missouri. Her parents had taught her not to fear the native peoples but rather to treat them with respect.

She put up her hand in greeting. "Hello. I am Char...I am Charlie." She pointed to herself and used her shortened name.

One of the women smiled shyly. "Hah-ue." Charlotte hoped that meant "hello" or a similar greeting.

A small girl approached and touched the ruffle on Charlotte's blue-dotted dress. Thinking quickly, Charlotte pulled the blue ribbon from her hair and handed it to the little girl. She gestured that the ribbon was a gift. The little girl smiled.

Shadow watched this exchange and slowly approached the girl. She put out her open palm, and Shadow sniffed the girl's hand.

"Good dog," Charlotte said.

To the little girl, Charlotte said, "This is Shadow." The little girl repeated the name. The girl pointed to her chest and said, "Zitkato....Zee-dkah-doh." Then she pointed to a bluebird in the nearby willow tree. "Zitkato."

"Ah, Blue Bird," Charlotte thought, understood the translation. "Hello, Zitkato." The little girl smiled again.

The women, who had been watching this conversation, waved to Charlotte and called the little girl back to them.

"Wait," Charlotte called out. "What is this water called?" She gestured to the creek.

Not precisely sure of the question, the younger of the three women responded, "Ma mni," and let the water trickle through her fingers.

"Ma mni," Charlotte repeated. "Thank you."

With that, the older of the three women called to the others. They climbed out of the creek and quickly departed. The little girl turned and waved to Charlotte.

"We have neighbors," Charlotte said to Shadow. "And you were a good boy." She petted the German Shepherd between his ears.

The Robinson cousins completed their building projects by mid-summer. A sturdy barn and two small soddies stood tall on the flat Dakota prairie. And to Lizzy and Charlotte's delight, the soddies were connected, with a common room that bridged the property line. Doors on each side of the common room ensured the soddies were two separate houses.

"It seems a luxury that we have two bedrooms and two kitchens," Charlotte observed one summer evening. The sisters were relaxing in the rockers they'd brought from Missouri.

"It does, indeed. But when the inspectors come by – and I'm told that they might – we want to be following the letter of the law," Lizzy replied.

She ticked off their accomplishments to date. "Each claim has its own house, and fields have been planted."

In the distance, Charlotte spotted a rider coming their way. "Looks like we're going to have company." Both women went into their soddies to fetch their shotguns. They understood the dangers that women faced on the prairie.

The rider came into view, and Charlotte could see it was a man who was riding hard. "Hmm, a new neighbor?"

The man called out breathlessly from horseback, "I saw the smoke from your soddy. I'm looking for a doctor, or a nurse, or anyone who can help."

Lizzy looked at Charlotte.

"We can help," Lizzy said. She took the horse's reins and gestured for the man to get down.

"Tell me what happened," Charlotte said.

"It's my wife. She was plowing and it got away from her. She went to catch the team and the plow … well, it broke her arm. It's bad."

Charlotte went inside to grab her medical bag. Emerging from the soddy, she pulled on a shawl and asked, "Is your wife bleeding?"

"She was. I stopped the bleeding, but I can see the bones. I'm no good with this kinda thing," he said in a panic.

"Compound fracture," Charlotte said more to herself than anyone else. "How far away are you?" she asked the man.

"We're about ten miles from here," he said. Then he gathered his senses and said, "I'm Stan Walker. Are you…are you a doctor?"

"I'm Charlotte Ward, and that's my sister, Lizzy. I worked in the field hospitals in the War for a while. If it is a compound fracture, I can help."

Lizzy was leading Charlotte's horse from the barn. "Let's go," Charlotte said.

On the ride over, Stan explained how the accident happened. "We got to Dakota late in the season, so Clara and me, we've been trying to plow and plant as much as we can to make up lost time. I was working on the soddy, and Clara was taking a turn on the plow. I shouldn't have let her do it. She's not strong enough to handle the oxen. But she insisted. Then something spooked them darn animals and she lost control. Next thing I knew, she was lying in field, screaming in pain."

Charlotte and Stan got to the Walker farm before sundown. Inside the soddy, Charlotte found a woman unconscious on the bed. The woman was very young. Charlotte guessed the woman was several years younger than Lizzy, making her eighteen or nineteen.

Her medical training in the Army took over, and Charlotte started giving orders. "Start boiling water," Charlotte instructed Stan. "Let's bring her outside while there's still good light."

In the sunlight, Charlotte could see what she needed to do. She cleaned out the wound with witch hazel and then probed for fragments. Satisfied that it was a "clean" fracture, Charlotte administered a small amount of chloroform to make sure Clara wouldn't become conscious and struggle during the procedure.

Charlotte matched up the bones and immobilized the arm with a temporary splint while she sewed up the open wound. She covered the injury with clean cloths. By then, the sun had nearly set. Charlotte and Stan brought Clara back into the soddy.

"Hopefully she'll sleep through the night," Charlotte told the anxious husband.

"You're not leaving, are you?" he asked.

"No. I've done all I can for now, but I'll stay the night. We'll watch for infection, and you need to keep her comfortable." She measured out a dose of laudanum and explained how much to give Clara to help with her pain.

"So, you're a real doctor?" Stan said.

Charlotte thought about the answer before responding. "I haven't been to medical school, but I trained under two surgeons during the War: Dr. Bernard and Dr. Lee."

"You were a nurse in the war?" he asked.

"Noooo. I was more like a medic or physician-in-training. Dr. Bernard taught me how to do amputations, remove bullets and care for patients after surgery. I wasn't with Dr. Lee for long, but I assisted him with patient care.

Before I left the Army, Dr. Bernard gave me the medical bag you saw."

That seemed to satisfy Stan for the time being.

Clara Walker slept through the night, but Charlotte continued checking her for fever, which might be a sign of infection. In the morning, Charlotte started to make breakfast for the three of them until Stan stopped her.

"That's my job, Doc," he said.

"I'm not an actual doctor," she began.

"You are as far as I'm concerned."

Either the smell of cooking bacon or Charlotte and Stan's conversation woke up Clara.

"Stan…Stan…" she called out. Both Stan and Charlotte rushed to her bedside.

"How are you feeling?" Charlotte asked her patient.

Clara looked up at Charlotte, confused to see the stranger in her house.

"This is Dr. Ward. She cleaned and set your arm last night," Stan explained. "I was riding for Yankton when I saw the smoke from their soddy. It was our luck that we have a neighbor who's a doctor."

Charlotte felt guilty for not correcting Stan, but she also understood that patients needed to trust in their doctors.

Stan helped Clara sit up in bed while Charlotte brought over a cup of tea. Charlotte got a good look at her patient now. Clara Walker had long, black hair platted into braids, high cheekbones, and beautiful, dark brown eyes fringed with thick, dark lashes.

"Doctor Ward, we're in your debt," Clara said.

"That's what neighbors do," Charlotte replied. "My sister, Elizabeth, and I are new to the Territory, just like you are. We came up from Missouri in the spring."

"Where abouts in Missouri?" Stan asked.

"We farmed near St. Joseph. Missouri's been hard hit by the War. We decided to leave that behind. Where are you folks from?"

Stan took his wife's hand and said, "Minnesota. There was trouble there, too. Clara and me, we wanted to leave that behind."

Charlotte decided there was more to Stan and Clara's story, but now was not the time to pry. "Seems that a lot of us have come to Dakota Territory to start fresh," she observed.

She stood, removed the apron she wore when treating patients, and picked up her medical bag. After repeating her orders regarding the laudanum and watching for infection, Charlotte said, "It's been a long night for all of us. I'll leave you now, but if you need anything, please, come and get me."

The Walker homestead was just a few miles northwest of Charlotte and Elizabeth's claims, which, on the frontier, was almost like being next-door neighbors.

The four homesteaders got to know each other well during the summer of '63.

Lizzy was pleased that the Walkers had a bull. "Consider his services payment for your doctoring," Stan offered.

"Calves in the spring," Lizzy said, happy her cows would be bred for another year.

Charlotte was not surprised to learn that Clara Walker was part Indian. She and Stan had married before the Sioux uprising in Minnesota the previous year – the troubles Stan referred to. Clara's mother was Lakota Sioux. Her father's family came from Germany several decades before.

Clara was delighted to hear about Charlotte's encounter with the Lakota women at the creek. "I haven't met any Lakota people yet," Clara said.

"They called the creek 'Ma mni,'" Charlotte told Clara. "What does that mean?"

"Something like 'medicine water' or 'medicine creek,'" Clara said.

"Medicine Creek," Lizzy joined in the conversation. "I like that. Now we have a name for the creek."

After-Action Report – Quantrill's Raiders Attack Lawrence, Kansas

August 1863

On the morning of August 21, 1863, William Quantrill and his guerrillas rode into Lawrence, Kansas, seeking retribution for ongoing conflicts between Free-State Jayhawkers who controlled Lawrence and the proslavery partisans who lived in nearby Missouri. It was estimated that approximately four hundred Raiders entered the town and began ransacking and burning homes, looting stores, and shooting civilians. Quantrill ordered his men to "kill every man big enough to carry a gun." The raiders followed orders, killing 160 to 190 men and boys, approximately twenty percent of the male population, leaving eighty-five widows in the eastern Kansas border town.

Chapter 16: September 1863
St. Louis, MO

Luke selected a strawberry roan gelding from Jeremiah Tanner's stable. He would have preferred a mare, but Tanner was not keen on parting with any breeding stock. In a gesture of goodwill, Tanner threw in an old saddle and blanket that had seen better days.

"The Southern Army is losing a good man," Tanner said as Luke saddled his horse.

"The parole came with a promise that I don't aim to break."

The two men parted company with a handshake.

Luke figured he could be back in Boone County in about two days of hard riding. He patted the horse's withers and said, "Let's make tracks, Rusty."

The ride home was pleasant. The days were starting to cool off as the season turned the corner to autumn. Luke wondered what the weather was like now in Dakota Territory. He thought about Dakota Territory a lot.

Actually, he thought about Charlotte Ward a lot. Her dark brown eyes. The sprinkling of freckles. And her smile. He regretted that he hadn't been bolder in Independence and pressed for a kiss. Was he crazy to think she might have feelings for him, too? She surely hadn't acted like she was sweet on him. So, why was he set on following her to

Dakota Territory? He wasn't sure, but he knew in his heart he had to find her.

He also knew that his ma and pa wouldn't be happy that he was leaving Missouri. Will Jameson had always assumed that Luke would take over the horse ranch someday. Even though Luke had two older brothers, neither had shown any interest in training or breeding horses. "They don't have the 'horse sense' that you and Nellie have," Will would say.

Nellie would be a dandy horse rancher, Luke thought.

He was looking forward to being home. He recalled his last ride back when he brought Charlotte home to be cared for by his mother. And, just like that last trip home, Nellie galloped up to greet Luke as he trotted to the Jameson ranch house.

"Luke! Ma got your letter that said you'd left the Army. She'll be cooking up a storm tonight when she sees you!"

"What's Pa think about it?"

"He said you had done your duty as a proper Missourian."

Luke nodded. In the days before the War, the Jameson family had many heated debates about supporting the Confederacy or the Union. Ultimately, all four brothers joined the Confederate Army or the Missouri State Guard. Ma had been especially vocal about the decision.

"Slavery isn't right. We've never owned a slave, and we never will," she declared.

"It's the Bushwhackers that I'm worried about, Mary," Will had said. "We've seen what those crazy hotheads did to the Schmidts and the Kleins: burned down their barns, killed cattle. Nobody was safe. We're going to have to take sides, and this is secesh country."

Luke was confident that Ma would be happy he was a civilian again.

He was right. Mary Jameson flew out of the house when she heard the horses coming up the path. Of course, Nellie calling out that the prodigal son had returned also alerted their mother to Luke's arrival.

Luke jumped from his horse and hugged his mother. He swept her up and twirled her around as if she were a girl at a dance. "Luke Joseph Jameson, you are a delight! Now put me down!" she laughed.

She stood back and sized up her third son. "You're thinner – but not as thin as I'd expected, you being a prisoner of war and all. The things I've read about those army prisons…"

"Ma, I'm fine. I've been out of prison for a month, working at a livery in St. Louis so I could earn enough to get back to you!" He kissed his mother on her cheek.

Will Jameson heard the commotion from the stables and strode out to shake Luke's hand. "It's good to have you home, son."

"It's good to be home, Pa." In a rare show of emotion, Will gave Luke a quick hug.

Nellie had been right about their mother "cooking up a storm." The dinner table was piled high with fried chicken, mashed potatoes, black-eyed peas, collard greens, cornbread, and, of course, sweet potato pie for dessert.

Luke and Will sat on the porch after dinner, enjoying the evening breezes.

"Every night your Ma prays that the Lord will see fit to return all her sons safe and sound," Will said. "You've done your duty to the Confederacy, Luke, and you've given your word that you won't join up again. That's fine by me. One of your Ma's prayers has been answered."

Luke breathed a sigh of relief that his father accepted Luke's decision to leave the War.

"There's plenty to keep you busy around here," Will continued.

"I've been thinking about that, Pa. The War can't go on much longer, and the other boys will be returning home."

Will remembered his youth when he and Mary decided to leave Kentucky to start their lives in Missouri. "Where are you bound for?" he asked Luke.

Luke had been prepared for an argument with his father. "How did you know?"

Will pulled a long draw from his pipe and said, "Itchy feet. Wanderlust. Whatever you call it. I recollect what it was like to be young. I wanted to strike out on my own, too."

He repeated his question, "So, where are you bound?"

"Dakota Territory."

"You planning to be a sodbuster? Stake a claim?"

Luke shook his head. "I've been thinking about it. When I was in St. Louis, I did a little blacksmithing. Spent some time shoeing horses. They need blacksmiths and farriers in Dakota Territory."

"There's more to it than that, I reckon," the older man said.

At that point, Mary Jameson joined the two men on the porch. Sitting down in her favorite rocker, she said, "Oh, I'm guessing there's more to it, Will."

She saw the surprised look on her son's face and said, "You mentioned to Nellie that Charlotte and her sister were leaving Missouri for Dakota Territory. And you know that Nellie can't keep a secret! How long before you leave us, Luke?"

He blew out a breath. "Can't get anything by you, can I, Ma?" He stood up and started pacing the porch. "As much as I'd like to stay a spell, I've heard that winter comes early on the plains. I'd like to get settled there before the snow flies." He winced and then admitted, "I'm thinking I'll leave in about a week. There's some planning to do."

"Well, plan on taking a couple of horses with you, son," Will said.

"I can't do that, Pa."

"Either you take 'em or the State Guard will 'requisition' them. That's army talk for 'steal.' I'd rather see you have my horses. Besides, you'll need 'em for packing provisions."

In the following days, Will and Luke collected the supplies and some of the equipment that Luke would need for blacksmithing: hammers, tongs, punches, and chisels.

"I can't set you up with a forge," Will said, "but there's a farrier anvil in one of the back stalls. It ain't light, but one of the horses can carry it."

Will and Luke selected two strong horses for the journey: a chestnut stallion and a dappled gray mare. "You'll get some good stock from these two," Will predicted.

Mary and Nellie cooked another feast for Luke's farewell dinner. They sat at the dinner table, held hands, and Mary prayed.

"Dear Lord, thank you for bringing our boy home safe and healthy. Watch over him now as he begins a new journey. May he find happiness at the end of the road. Amen." They all joined in the final "Amen."

Luke was especially struck by his mother's wish that he find happiness at the end of the road. He hoped her prayer would come true.

The following day, Luke packed the stallion and the mare for the journey. Then he saddled Rusty. He hugged his sister and his mother and shook his father's hand.

"I know you're gonna want to make good time on the road, Luke," Will cautioned, "but take it easy on the pack horses. They're carrying heavy loads."

Luke nodded. "I'll be good to them, Pa."

"I'll be back, Ma. Don't you worry. And I'll write to you when I put down some roots." Mary smiled but wiped a tear from the corner of her eye. "Travel safe, Luke."

"I'm coming to visit you, Luke. Better get used to that idea," Nellie called out as Luke turned his horses toward the road. He smiled and waved. "I'm holding you to that, little sister!"

Luke planned to travel along the Missouri River, just like Charlotte and her sister had done once he'd reached St. Joseph. Using the Missouri River as a road map seemed the best way to reach Dakota Territory. And just like the Ward sisters, Luke made camp outside the towns along the way.

Less than two weeks after he'd waved goodbye to Nellie, Luke reached Yankton. Steamboats were docked by the pier, with sailors unloading home goods and parcels. Wagons and horses crowded the dusty roads. Even though it wasn't the size of St. Louis, Luke could see that Yankton was a growing, bustling town.

"Someday, Yankton will be as big as St. Louis," Luke told Rusty. The horse just tossed his head and nickered.

After unsaddling and unpacking the horses at the livery stable, Luke decided to treat himself to a cold beer. There were plenty of saloons to choose from, he noted. The Black Bull looked to be a likely place for a beer and a meal.

Luke stepped up to the bar and ordered a cold draught. "Coming right up, mister," said the barman.

Luke savored that first swallow and said to no one in particular, "That's been a long time coming."

A man next to Luke at the bar took the comment as an opening for conversation. "Howdy. Did you just roll into town?" he asked Luke.

Luke sized up the man. He wore a light brown buckskin coat with fringed sleeves. His buckskin breeches were tied off below his knees just above dark buckskin boots. His black felt hat was decorated with a braided piece of leather holding an eagle feather. Luke had heard tales about mountain men, but he'd never met one before.

The man laughed. "I ain't usually so chatty, but I haven't seen another white man in nearly a year," the man continued. "I been trapping in the Rockies. Name's Carson…Abe Carson."

He nodded his head, and Luke returned the greeting.

Luke figured he didn't have anything to lose by talking with the mountain man. He needed information about Charlotte – although he doubted this fellow would know anything about the sisters.

"Howdy, Abe," Luke responded. "Name's Luke Jameson. I just got to town from Missouri."

"Are you headed anywhere in particular?"

Luke bit his lip, gauging how much information to share with this stranger – this strange man. "Headed west, I reckon." Then he put his cards on the table, "I'm looking to do some blacksmithing."

Abe laughed. "You're the first one who's not here for the free land."

"I'm not a sodbuster. I figure there's plenty of work for blacksmiths and farriers, though."

"Ain't that the truth."

Luke ordered a hot beef and gravy meal while he listened to Abe talk about trapping beaver, living with the Crow in the mountains, and a close encounter with a grizzly bear. He said that when he wasn't trapping in the mountains, he hunted buffalo on the plains.

"Gotta be careful with the buffalo, though," Abe said. "Them beasts will veer off and head right for ya. And they don't stop for nothing."

"I wish I could stick around and hear more, but I've got some business to do in town," Luke said. He knew that Abe would regale him with stories for hours, and while he'd enjoy hearing every one of those stories, it was time to move on.

Abe gave Luke a hearty pat on the back and said, "Get moving, boy."

Not sure how to respond, Luke just smiled and tipped his hat.

Outside, Luke was trying to decide where to ask about the two sisters. He knew Charlotte had *planned* to come to Yankton, but he also knew that plans change. The Claims Office was just down the street, and Luke decided it was a good place to start.

His hunch was right. A brief conversation with Mike Mathews proved to be fruitful.

"You're in the right place, Mr. Jameson," Mike said. "The Ward sisters came through here four…no five months ago. Each of 'em filed a claim out by Shady Bluffs – that's a few hours west of here." Mathews looked Luke up and down. "If I can ask, what's your business with the Misses? They're nice ladies and …"

"Charlie…Charlotte and I met in the…met in Missouri," Luke replied. He was going to say, "met in the war," but he knew that would lead to more questions he didn't want to answer.

"You say they're homesteading west of here? Can you give me directions?" Luke asked.

Mike complied, providing landmarks to help Luke find the Wards.

"Thank you kindly," Luke said. He was leaving the Claims Office when it occurred to him to ask, "I'd like to bring them a…my ma called it a 'housewarming gift.' Any ideas what they might appreciate?"

Mathews thought for a moment. "I haven't seen either of them in town for a couple of months. They might be getting low on coffee and sugar."

"Thanks again," Luke said as he pushed open the office door.

"'Course, if I wanted to impress a lady, I might bring flowers." Mike's eyes sparkled mischievously.

Luke smiled to himself and thought, *Was I that easy to read? Apparently.*

After-Action Report – Battle of Chickamauga

Sept 18-20, 1863

The second bloodiest conflict of the Civil War occurred in September 1863 near Chickamauga, Georgia. The Union Army of the Cumberland, consisting of 60,000 men, was commanded by U.S. Major General William Rosecrans. The Confederate Army of Tennessee, with approximately 65,000 soldiers, was led by General Braxton Bragg. After two days of fierce fighting, the Rebels broke through Union lines. The Confederates forced the Federals into a siege at Chattanooga.

The Battle of Chickamauga marked the end of the Union's campaign in southeastern Tennessee and northwestern Georgia. The Confederate Army secured a decisive victory at Chickamauga but lost twenty percent of its force in the battle.

Chapter 17: October 1863
Dakota Territory

Luke took Mike Mathews's advice and purchased bags of coffee and sugar. As for the flowers, he decided that prairie flowers would be just right for Charlotte.

It was a warm October day when Luke packed up and put Yankton's noise and dust behind him. Truth be told, he was looking forward to a few hours in the saddle to rehearse his "speech."

Charlotte Ward might think he was plum crazy to come looking for her. Maybe he wouldn't start with that. How would he explain his hankering to move to Dakota Territory? As a former Confederate soldier, he couldn't file a claim through the Homestead Act.

"I could be honest and say I came west looking for you, Charlotte," Luke said to his horse. "I could tell her that I couldn't get her out of my head. I could say, 'You've been in my dreams since Springfield. I wanted to kiss you in Independence.' Nah, best not to lead with that, huh, Rusty?"

He spotted a cluster of bright yellow sunflowers near the trail and halted to gather the bouquet. He added some purple flowers – not sure what they were – but they were pretty, he judged. He wet his neckerchief with water from his canteen and wrapped it around the wildflowers so they wouldn't wilt. By his reckoning and the map from Mike Mathews, he should be reaching Charlotte's claim soon.

Luke was accustomed to Missouri's rolling hills with its stately beech and elm trees, so the never-ending, treeless plains were new to him. He reached the top of what might be considered a "hill" on the Dakota prairie. The highland gave him a better perspective on the land spread before him.

Sure enough, there was a homestead about a half mile away. Or was it two homesteads? There were two soddy cabins but only one barn. It was a puzzle, Luke decided.

For the first time in his life, Luke Jameson was unsure of himself. *I've led men into battle,* he thought to himself. *I've faced cannon fire and artillery attacks. I've scouted enemy encampments. Hell, I've been wounded in battle. And I was never this nervous!* Luke chuckled at his case of nerves.

As he trotted up to the soddies with the two pack horses trailing, he scanned the farmyard for signs of life. There were a few pigs in a pen next to the barn. Cows were grazing in a nearby pasture. In the distance, he could see a woman in a cornfield, but he wasn't sure it was Charlotte.

The woman in the field waved to him and indicated she would come to greet him.

Luke studied the woman approaching him. It had been a while since he'd seen Charlotte, but this woman didn't move like Charlotte did. And she didn't have Charlotte's slim figure. Maybe he was at the wrong homestead.

The woman emerged from the edge of the cornfield and removed her hat to fan herself. Golden blonde braids trailed down her back.

"Hello!" she said. "Can I help you?"

"I hope so, ma'am," Luke replied. "I'm looking for the Ward place."

"And you are?" Lizzy asked the strange man in her farmyard.

Luke removed his hat. "Forgot my manners, ma'am. My name's Luke Jameson. I'm a friend of Charlotte's…I think."

Lizzy put her hands on her hips and looked Luke up and down. He was tall and thin, with a scruffy beard and reddish-brown hair on the long side. He wore black trousers with black suspenders, a blue chambray shirt, and a black leather vest. Luke had long ago shed the remnants of his Confederate uniform.

"It's good to finally meet you, Mr. Jameson. Charlotte told me how kind your family was when she was shot."

"Are you…are you Elizabeth?"

Lizzy laughed. "Now, it's my manners that are lacking. Yes, I'm Elizabeth Ward. You can call me Lizzy. Let me get you a drink."

She hurried into the nearest soddy and returned with a tall glass of cool water. "We don't have a well yet," Lizzy explained, "so we get our water from the creek. It's not far from here if you'd like to water your horses," she suggested.

"I'd appreciate that. It's been a warm ride out here."

Lizzy wanted to ask what brought Luke out this way, but she suspected she knew the answer. Instead, she watched as Luke led his horses toward the creek.

The creek that Lizzy directed Luke to provided a reliable water source for the crops, the animals, and the people. A well would be more convenient, but the sisters had decided that was a project for next year. It was also where Charlotte had taken Shadow to wash the stinky dog after he ran through the pig pen.

Wouldn't he be surprised to see Charlotte there? Lizzy thought. *And won't she be surprised to see Luke? I am so easily amused.* Then she giggled at herself.

As Luke walked the three horses to the creek, he surveyed the land around him. The prairie grasses were turning an amber gold. A breeze rippled through the grasses, almost like waves on a lake. He could see a scattering of trees by the creek, mostly willows and cottonwoods. Then he heard someone talking.

"Get in here," a woman said sternly. "I know you don't want a bath, but you should have thought about that before you chased the pigs. Don't make me come and get you. You can't go near the house until you're clean! Get in here!"

The next thing Luke heard was splashing and a dog whining.

Now, at the bank of the creek, Luke saw the woman of his dreams – sort of. Charlotte was wrestling a large dog. Both Charlotte and the dog were in the creek and were soaking wet. She was wielding a soapy scrub brush on the big dog. "Hold still," she scolded the dog.

Luke started laughing.

Charlotte looked up, surprised that she was being watched. "You!" she said. "What…"

"Do you need a hand?" Luke asked.

Then Charlotte realized the ridiculousness of the situation, and she started laughing too. Shadow seized his opportunity to escape, racing out of the water, still covered in soapy water. When he got to shore, Shadow shook the soapy water all over Luke.

Charlotte just sat down in the shallow creek and stared at Luke.

"Luke Jameson. What are you doing here."

"I came to the creek to water my horses. I didn't expect to get a comedy show in the bargain." He pulled off his boots and leather vest and waded into the creek to join Charlotte.

Luke moved a strand of wet hair off Charlotte's face. Then he drew her close and kissed her. Charlotte put her arms around Luke's neck and kissed him back.

They sat in the warm creek water a while longer, with Luke holding Charlotte in his arms. She laid her head on Luke's shoulder and murmured, "This feels right."

"Hmmm," Luke agreed. He pulled her closer and said, "I'm glad I found you."

"The last time I saw you, you were riding back to war," Charlotte said.

"The war is over for me."

She sat up straight and looked at Luke. "Did you get hurt again?"

"No, I was taken prisoner at Cape Girardeau."

Charlotte gasped.

Luke continued, "Then I was paroled through a prisoner exchange if I agreed that I wouldn't fight against the Union again. That was an easy promise to make. Charlie, all I could think about was finding you before it was too late." He kissed Charlotte again.

"Too late?"

"You'd get swept off your feet by some cowboy out here, and I'd lose you."

Charlotte looked into Luke's slate-gray eyes and tenderly touched his cheek. "I'd say we swept each other off our feet."

"You are correct, Miss Ward. Now, let me help you to your feet."

They climbed out of the creek. Luke fetched his horses while Charlotte squeezed the water out of her skirt and gathered the brush and soap.

"You know," she said, "I've thought about our next meeting. But this isn't how I envisioned it. Of course, in a previous meeting, one of your men shot me."

"It might have been a Yankee bullet," Luke countered. "You don't know that. So, you were certain we'd meet again?"

"I hoped so. There were so many things I wanted to tell you."

Hand in hand, they walked back to the soddies.

Lizzy started laughing as soon as she saw the two soaking-wet figures approach.

"I'm sure there's a story here," Lizzy said.

"It's all Shadow's fault," Charlotte replied. "I'm going to get a towel."

"I...I'll take care of my horses," Luke said.

"You can hobble them in the north pasture, or you can put them in the barn," Lizzy offered. "It's up to you."

Luke unloaded the equipment on the two pack horses and left it in the barn. He unsaddled Rusty and put all three horses in the pasture as Lizzy had suggested. Then he returned to the soddies with the coffee, sugar, and flowers.

"It's past lunch time," Charlotte said when she emerged from the soddy farthest from the barn. She had changed out of her wet clothing and now wore a becoming lavender skirt and white blouse. Her golden-brown hair fell in loose waves to her shoulders.

"Can I help?" Luke asked. "Oh, I brought you something." He handed her the housewarming gifts and the flowers.

"Thank you. I love sunflowers. We usually eat inside, but the weather's nice, so let's eat out here," Charlotte said. She gestured for Luke to follow her into the soddy.

Inside, he saw that the small home was tidy. There was a cookstove on the wall opposite the front door. The one-room soddy had a bed covered with a colorful patchwork quilt, a rocking chair and small table, and a long cedar chest. There was an oil lamp on the small table. He noticed that the windows did not have glass panes. Instead, they were covered in oiled paper.

Charlotte followed his gaze. "Oh, that's only temporary. We'll board up the windows before winter. Glass windows are on the list for next year – but it's a long list." She smiled ruefully.

He gestured to the common room that connected the two homes. "I've never seen anything like that before."

"We can explain it over lunch. You can carry that quilt and the jug of water. I'll bring the food."

They picnicked by the creek, or "the scene of my humiliation," as Charlotte referred to the dog-washing episode.

"You're the one who wanted a dog," Lizzy teased. "My cat is self-cleaning."

"Have you ever tried to wash a cat?" Charlotte argued. "You'd be taking your life into your hands.

Besides, Shadow proved his worth when those drifters tried to surprise us. He's a good watchdog."

"And Butter proves her worth every day. You don't have mice in your house, do you?"

The sisters' banter amused Luke. "You two remind me of my sisters – um, in a good way."

"You said you were captured. Can you talk about it?" Charlotte asked carefully.

"There's not much to tell," Luke replied. "I was taken prisoner at the Battle of Cape Girardeau and shipped to Gratiot Street Prison in St. Louis. A couple of months later, I was exchanged for a Union officer, and they kicked me out on the street. As part of my parole agreement, I promised to stay out of the War."

Luke told the sisters about his time with Jeremiah Tanner. "Working at the livery stable reminded me how much I enjoy being around horses. I'm not a proper blacksmith yet, but I'm learning as I go."

"There's plenty of work for farriers and blacksmiths out here," Lizzy said. "In fact, our horses and our oxen all need to be shod. Are you available for hire?"

"I've never shoed an ox," Luke admitted. "I guess it's time to learn."

"You're hired," Charlotte said. "When can you start?"

"I'll set up a forge and get to work," Luke answered.

Charlotte and Luke spent the afternoon exploring. She explained that the creek crossed through her claim and

Lizzy's claim. "The Lakota call it Ma Mni. My neighbor, she's part Lakota, said that means Medicine Water or Medicine Creek."

Charlotte told Luke how she met Clara and Stan Walker. "It was just luck that he found me," she concluded.

They walked back to the soddies. Luke asked, "It's obvious that Lizzy is the farmer here. Do you want to farm, too?"

"She loves the land. Back on the farm in Missouri, I handled the household chores, and she did most of the farm work. I try to do my share here," Charlotte objected.

"Don't get me wrong. But when you were telling me how you helped the neighbor with the broken arm, I could tell that's what you love doing. I could see it when you were in the field hospital. Medicine is your calling."

"You're right. But there's not much call for a doctor out here on the prairie."

"There could be. Mike Mathews said that Shady Bluffs is a likely place for a new blacksmith. As a former Confederate soldier, I can't stake a claim for land. Besides, I don't want to be a sodbuster – anymore than you want to be one."

"But here I am," Charlotte said.

"That's my point. If people knew there was a doctor in the area, you could do something that you love."

Charlotte considered the suggestion. "But the claim…"

"Keep an open mind. I'm going to visit Shady Bluffs after I finish my work here. Come with me. We can have another adventure."

"I like adventures."

"And I like women who like adventures." Luke pulled her into an embrace and kissed her. "I've been wanting to do that since lunch," he said.

"Don't wait so long next time." And they kissed again.

Luke was happy to bunk in the barn. The next day, he began building a forge for his blacksmith work. As luck would have it, the sisters had an old cast iron pot with a hole in the side.

"It's no good to us now," Charlotte said.

"Perfect," Luke said. "Now, I just need a source of fuel."

"Buffalo chips," she suggested. So, she and Luke spent an afternoon gathering buffalo chips to fire the forge.

In anticipation that he might set up shop in Shady Bluffs or another frontier town, Luke had purchased a supply of horseshoes in Yankton. He would use these "blanks" to shape the final horseshoes for the Ward horses and oxen.

With his forge in working order, Luke started with something he knew how to do: shoe horses. After that, he moved on to the oxen. As with horses and mules, oxen need shoes to protect their feet. But unlike horses and mules, oxen have divided hooves and need two shoes per hoof – a total of eight shoes per ox.

Lizzy caught Charlotte watching Luke work one day. Even though it was mid-October, he wore only trousers and a leather apron. He glistened with sweat from the heat of the forge and from working the iron.

"I do believe you are smitten, dear sister," Lizzy teased.

"He is a fine figure of a man," Charlotte admitted. "But don't tell him I said that!"

"Never," Lizzy promised.

At the end of the day, Luke shut down the forge and headed to the creek to wash off the dirt and sweat from the day's work.

Charlotte remembered their first meeting out here. She wanted to follow him to the creek and watch him bathe. Was it wrong? She gave in to her desires and silently followed Luke to the creek. Hiding behind a thicket of chokecherry bushes, Charlotte watched as Luke stripped off his clothes and waded into the water.

After he'd soaped up his torso, Luke disappeared below the water's surface to wash off. He popped out of the water. "Let's see…I believe the phrase is 'get in here.'" Luke echoed the words he'd heard Charlotte call to Shadow. He held out his wet hand. "You wouldn't make much of a spy, Charlie. That white blouse is like a flag of surrender. I dare you!"

Charlotte laughed and walked out of the bushes. "I can't resist a dare."

Charlotte shimmied out of her skirt and blouse, leaving only her chemise. She entered the cool creek water. "Brrr," she said. "It's colder than I imagined."

"Come on. Let's get out," he said huskily. Luke took Charlotte's hand and led her from Medicine Creek. She spread a shawl in the sun while he wrapped a towel around his bare midriff.

Even though Charlotte had seen countless naked men in her time as a medic during the war, she had to admire Luke's body. Her comment to Lizzy that Luke was a "fine figure of a man" was truer than she had imagined. He had broad shoulders, a muscled back, and a narrow waist.

They sat together on the shawl, but Charlotte was still shivering. Luke put his arm around her, and she leaned into his embrace. "I'll warm up you," he said.

"This is nice," Charlotte said. "But just to be clear…"

"We'll take it slow, Charlie. I promise."

So, they sat by the creek and watched the October sun play across Medicine Creek.

After-Action Report: Third Battle of Boonville
October 11, 1863

Confederate Colonel Jo Shelby and his cavalry entered Boonville, Missouri, in Cooper County on October 11, 1863. When the town's defenders realized they could not defend the town from the Confederates, they surrendered to Shelby. Union reinforcements under the command of Brigadier General Egbert Brown arrived the following day. Shelby's Confederates were forced to retreat to the West.

Chapter 18: November 1863
Shady Bluffs, Dakota Territory

While Luke was shoeing the horses and oxen, Charlotte and Lizzy spent their days preparing food for the coming winter. The long shelves in the common room between the two soddies were laden with preserved vegetables and canned fruit.

Pork loins, shoulders, hocks, and ribs hung from rafters in the barn. "That will have to do until we get a root cellar," Lizzy said.

"Add a root cellar to the list for next year," Charlotte said, looking at the hanging meat.

They each finished their work just as the first snowflakes fell on the Dakota prairie.

"It seems early for the first snow," Luke observed at dinner that night. "But then, this is my first Dakota winter. I wanted to check out Shady Bluffs before winter. Maybe find a place to open a blacksmith shop."

"Let's go to town tomorrow," Charlotte said. "We haven't been there for a while, and we need supplies."

"Count me out. Somebody's got to hold down the fort," Lizzy said. "I've got animals to feed."

"Nope, everyone's coming to town. We'll all pitch in on chores," Luke offered.

"And we'll be home before nightfall, Lizzy," Charlotte added. "It's going to be a long winter. Let's see what Shady Bluffs has to offer."

Lizzy knew she wouldn't win this argument, so she graciously accepted their help.

Shady Bluffs was as close to a "newborn" as a town could be. The Main Street, running north to south, was a haphazard collection of wooden shanty buildings, including a general store, a stagecoach station, a saloon, a post office, and a church under construction.

Next to the general store, Charlotte noticed a small office with a sign above the door: Dr. Walter Stone. She pointed to the office and said, "See, there's already a doctor here. I'm out of a job before I even started."

"Let's go meet Dr. Stone," Lizzy suggested.

"I'm headed to the saloon," Luke said.

"Of course you are," Charlotte said.

"That's where people talk. I want to find out what's going on here. It's strictly a business visit," he assured them.

Both sisters smiled in amusement. They parted ways with Luke and headed to the doctor's office.

A bell jingled when Charlotte opened the door to Dr. Stone's office.

"Be with you in a minute," a man called from the back room.

Soon, an older man entered the front office. "Good day. I'm Doc Stone. What can I do for you ladies?" he asked.

Doc Stone had a full head of snow-white hair. A pair of wire-rim glasses sat halfway down his nose. He wore a brown, herringbone fabric vest over a white linen shirt with brown garters halfway up sleeves. Suspenders held up his dark brown trousers. A jacket or coat was hanging on the back of a chair by a rolltop desk.

Lizzy nudged Charlotte.

"Good afternoon, Doctor Stone," Charlotte began.

"Call me 'Doc'," the man instructed her.

She began again, "Doc Stone, I'm Charlotte Ward, and this is my sister, Elizabeth. We have claims between here and Yankton."

"What ails you?" Doc Stone asked.

"Oh, nothing. It's just that…" Charlotte stammered.

"Charlotte has some medical training," Lizzy said. "She's not a doctor, but…"

"Where'd you train?" Doc Stone asked.

"In the war," Charlotte answered. "I served with Dr. Thomas Bernard in the Union Army. Joined up after Springfield."

"I heard they were short-handed in the field hospitals. I imagine you got some solid training. Did you do surgery?" he asked.

"Yes. I learned how to do amputations, remove bullets, treat gangrene, and the like. Of course, most of the time we were fighting dysentery and pneumonia."

"War is an awful undertaking," Doc Stone said. "It brings out the worst in men. But it also brings out the best in some of them. I expect you saw some of both."

"I did," Charlotte answered.

"You're new to town. Where'd you ladies come from?" he asked.

"We farmed by St. Joseph, Missouri," Lizzy said.

Doc Stone eyed the two women. "Just the two of you, then?"

"Yes," Lizzy replied. "We've each staked claims through the Homestead Act. Tell him," she said to Charlotte.

Charlotte cleared her throat and said, "I wanted to introduce myself to you…in case you ever need help in the office."

"Shady Bluffs is a quiet little town. Fact is, that's why I settled here. I pulled up stakes in Minnesota and moved to Dakota after the troubles in '62."

The sisters had heard about the Uprising of 1862 from Stan and Clara Walker. Sioux Indians in Minnesota attacked settlers throughout western Minnesota during the summer and fall of 1862. The uprising was put down with brutal force by the military.

"But I appreciate the offer, Miss Ward. Er, it *is* Miss?"

Charlotte nodded. "The other thing is, well, I need to restock some of my medical supplies, such as laudanum. Can I purchase some from you, or can you order some for me? I can pay in advance."

"No need, Miss Ward. I'm always willing to give a hand to a fellow doctor. I keep a couple of bottles in the back room. Give me a minute."

Doc Stone returned with a bottle of laudanum and handed it to Charlotte. "I don't need to tell you to use it wisely."

He sat down at his desk and removed his glasses. "Being a doctor is a lot like being an undertaker. The less work you have, the better it is for everyone. I wish I could tell you that I'm expanding my practice and could use your help, but like I said, Shady Bluffs is a quiet town. I appreciate that. Maybe in a few years things will change and I'll feel differently."

Then, wanting to end their conversation in a friendly way, he said, "You know, I've heard there are a lot of local medicinal plants by the creek near your claims. Might be a good time to gather some of them."

This got Charlotte's attention. "That must be why the Lakota call it Medicine Creek."

"Hmmm. Don't know about that, but this is a good time to collect rose hips, and you might want to stock up on willow bark."

"Thank you, Doc," Charlotte said. "It was a pleasure meeting you."

"Good afternoon, ladies," he replied.

Their next stop was the general store. Both sisters agreed that the Shady Bluffs Mercantile couldn't hold a candle to Bloom's in St. Joe. But they knew they needed to make allowances for the frontier store.

A well-endowed, middle-aged woman stood behind the counter. "Welcome to my store," she said to Charlotte and Lizzy. "We haven't met. My name is Isabell Vaughn. Are you new in town?"

"We are," Lizzy said. "We're homesteading east of here."

The shopkeeper nodded. "I've been looking forward to meeting you. You're the Ward sisters, if I'm not mistaken. Girl homesteaders are a rarity. Mike Mathews stops in from time to time," she explained.

"Thank goodness!" Charlotte exclaimed in jest. "I was hoping we hadn't gained a reputation yet! I'm Charlotte, and this is Elizabeth Ward."

"Call me Lizzy," her sister said.

Isabell smiled. "It's good to see more women on the frontier. My husband and I came out in '59 on our way to Pikes Peak. Lawrence thought he would strike it rich there. Instead, he passed away before we got to Yankton." She shook her head. "There I am, telling my life story to two complete strangers."

She changed the topic. "Mike said you'd staked claims this spring. I'm surprised you haven't been to town before."

"It's been a whirlwind," Lizzy said. "There was a lot to do this summer."

"We decided a trip to town was in order before winter sets in," Charlotte said as she browsed the dry goods. Then she saw the books, and her eyes lit up.

Lizzy was shopping for more practical items. "Do you have any suggestions on what we might need for the winter up here?" she asked Isabell.

The storekeeper offered some practical suggestions, including crackers, cooking oil, and the like. "But on those long, cold days, I like to keep my hands busy," she said. "Do either of you knit or crochet?"

"When we're forced to," Charlotte said. "I prefer sewing. Mama taught us how to quilt. We brought some fabric scraps from Missouri, but I could use more thread and needles."

Isabell added those items to the purchases. She tallied up the bill, and they settled the account.

"Thank you, Mrs. Vaughn," Lizzy said.

"Please call me Isabell. The next time you're in town, please make time for tea."

"That sounds lovely, Isabell," Charlotte said.

"We've made another new friend," Charlotte told Lizzy as they packed the purchases into their saddlebags. "Now, we should find out what Luke has been up to."

Luke had not covered as much ground as the Ward sisters had. He was standing at the long, polished bar talking to the barkeeper. When Luke saw the sisters enter, he gestured them over.

"Before I escort you ladies back to your claims," Luke said, "I have something to show you."

"We really should be getting back to the farms," Lizzy said.

"This won't take but a moment," Luke said as they walked down Main Street. "In fact, we're here."

They were standing in front of an empty lot on a side street.

"What are we supposed to see?" Charlotte asked.

"This is the location of Shady Bluffs' newest business: the Jameson Blacksmith Shop." He beamed. "What do you think?"

"I think it's very exciting," Lizzy said.

"I've put down a deposit on the lot. I think I can trade work for the building supplies."

"I'm glad for you, Luke," Charlotte offered. "When will you start?"

"If I can borrow one of your wagons, I can pack up this week."

Charlotte was a bit rattled at the suddenness of Luke's decision. "Oh."

The one-word response communicated volumes to Lizzy. "I should…I'll meet you at the horses." She left Charlotte and Luke to talk through his plans.

"You don't sound happy, Charlie," Luke said.

"It's not that. I just didn't think you'd be leaving so soon. What with winter coming on and all, are you sure this is a good idea?"

"I'm not going to spend the winter with you, Charlie."

"But…"

"It's not that I don't want to. I hate to leave you again, but it's too tempting – you're too tempting. I want to do this right, and that means I need to put some distance between us. I want to court you good and proper."

Charlotte nodded. "I understand. But…well, I'll miss having you around."

He hugged Charlotte and murmured in her ear, "You're not getting rid of me, Charlie. Shady Bluffs is just a few miles away. I'll be around so much you won't have time to miss me." He discreetly kissed her ear.

Then, holding Charlotte by her shoulders, he backed away and said, "It's time for us to get back to your home, Charlie. Let's talk about it tonight."

Charlotte nodded. Luke offered his arm, and they walked down the street to join Lizzy.

News of the Day – The Gettysburg Address

November 19, 1863

On November 19, 1863, President Abraham Lincoln commemorated a new cemetery at the site of the Battle of Gettysburg that occurred just four months before. President Lincoln's three-minute speech, which was only 275 words, redefined Lincoln's belief that the Civil War was not just a fight to save the Union but a struggle for freedom and equality for all. The Gettysburg Address, one of the most important speeches in American history, connected the sacrifices of the Civil War with the desire for "a new birth of freedom," as well as the all-important preservation of the Union created in 1776.

Chapter 19: November 1863
Medicine Creek, Dakota Territory

On a crisp morning in November, Charlotte set out to collect the rosehips and willow bark that Doc Stone had suggested. She recalled seeing wild roses growing by the creek, so she headed in that direction with Shadow following as usual.

She began filling a basket with the bright red berries when she saw the Lakota women gathering elm bark. They were pulling it from the trees in long strips. The young girls were coiling the strips and putting them in leather pouches.

"Hello again," Charlotte said.

"Haú kȟolá," said one of the women.

"She is saying hello," said a young woman. "I speak some of your...your words. I am Wachiwi. That is 'Dancing Girl' in your words."

"I am Charlotte."

The two women smiled at each other. Charlotte held up her basket of rose hips. "Rose hips," she said.

Dancing Girl understood. "We collect tree bark for..." She couldn't find the right word, but Charlotte understood it must have a medicinal purpose.

Charlotte watched as the women continued working. "Can you teach me about the bark?" she asked.

Dancing Girl said something to the older woman. The older woman replied, and Dancing Girl translated the response. "She says first we learn to speak. Then she will teach you our medicine."

Charlotte nodded. "Thank you. I have a friend who can help," she told Dancing Girl. Charlotte would ask Clara Walker to teach her the Lakota language so she could communicate with the medicine woman.

The women indicated they were returning to their camp. Charlotte waved goodbye. She was excited and planned to visit Clara the next day.

She recounted the meeting to Lizzy. "That's wonderful, Charlotte. You've finally realized that medicine is your calling."

"Yes. You were right once again."

"It's good that you understand that," Lizzy laughed. "Now, I have cows to milk."

Charlotte and Lizzy had not visited the Walkers since Luke had arrived in Dakota Territory. "You should come, too, Lizzy," Charlotte said to her sister. "Winter will be here before we know it, and then we'll be snowbound in our soddies. Come with me."

Lizzy agreed to accompany Charlotte to visit the neighbors. Despite the promise of another pleasant fall day, Lizzy had moved the cows and the pigs into the communal barn "just in case the weather turned."

"There's plenty of room in here now that Luke and his three horses have moved out," Lizzy said.

Life for the Ward sisters had returned to "normal" after Luke moved to Shady Bluffs, though both sisters had liked having Luke around.

The short ride to the Walker farm was indeed pleasant. Charlotte packed a basket with fresh bread, a jar of preserves, and a small bag of the rosehips she had gathered. Lizzy had followed Charlotte's example and wore a split skirt for the ride. Both women wore heavy woolen jackets and gloves despite the mild temperatures.

As they approached, they could see Stan Walker working on a new addition to the soddy.

"Are you running out of room already?" Charlotte asked as she tied her horse to a fence post.

"Will be soon," Stan said. "Come on inside. Clara will be glad to have some female conversation."

"Clara, darlin', we have guests," Stan called to his wife as he ushered Charlotte and Lizzy into the soddy.

"It's so good to see you again," Clara said. "I've got a pot of coffee on. Please sit down. It's been too long since we've visited!"

Charlotte unpacked the loaves of bread and jam on the small table, and the four sat down to catch up on each other's news.

"You go first, Clara," Charlotte said. She suspected that Clara and Stan had some big news to share.

"I can tell that you know already," Clara said with a Madonna-like smile. "We're having a baby this spring."

"That's wonderful!" Lizzy exclaimed. "I'm so happy for both of you."

Stan beamed with happiness. "That's the reason for the new room."

The Wards told Stan and Clara about Luke's arrival and his move to Shady Bluffs.

"We can use a good blacksmith around here," Stan said. "I noticed our team was in need of shoeing and I'm not up to the job."

"I also have a favor to ask," Charlotte began. "Clara, I've been talking with some women from the nearby Lakota camp. They come to the creek to gather berries and herbs from time to time," she explained. "I want to learn more about their medicine, but there's a language barrier. I don't know their language, and they know only a little English."

"I would be happy to teach you my language," Clara said.

"Thank you, Clara!" Charlotte said.

"I would also like to meet my Lakota sisters," Clara said. "Perhaps I could come with you someday."

Charlotte thought that might put the Lakota women at ease and readily agreed to Clara's offer.

"I'm going to get back to work," Stan said. "I'll leave you ladies to your chit-chat."

As soon as he was out the door, Charlotte said, "Now, how are you feeling, Clara?"

"I'm feeling pretty good. Early on, I was sick in the morning, but that has stopped for the most part. Now I'm just hungry all the time!"

"If anything changes, you send Stan to fetch me," Charlotte said. "Our language lessons will give me a good reason to visit." She sipped her coffee and continued. "Would it be too burdensome for me to have a weekly lesson, Clara?"

"Of course not," Clara replied.

"Wonderful!" Charlotte said.

"Charlotte," Lizzy interrupted. "We should be getting back."

Charlotte and Clara agreed on the date of their first Lakota lesson the following week. The three women said their goodbyes and the Wards headed back home.

On the way, Charlotte said, "We're halfway between our claims and Shady Bluffs. Would you mind if I went to town instead of coming back right away?"

"Now, what could be the attraction of town," Lizzy teased. "Yes, go see how Luke is doing."

The sisters split up, with Lizzy continuing southeast toward the claims while Charlotte rode west to Shady Bluffs.

Charlotte arrived in Shady Bluffs early in the afternoon. She saw that Luke was making good progress on his new shop. Like the other buildings in town, the blacksmith shop was made of lumber. But unlike the other buildings, the blacksmith shop looked more like a barn than a store or office, with a large, double-door entrance.

She reined in at the front of the building and tied her horse to a nearby post.

"Hello?" she called into the dimly lit shop. "Are you open for business?"

Luke recognized the voice immediately. "Charlie!" Putting down the hammer, he strode toward the shop's double doors. He picked up Charlotte and swung her around. Then, before she could respond, he put her down, took her face in his large, calloused hands, and kissed her.

"I've missed you, Charlie Ward!"

Charlotte laughed. "It's been a couple of weeks, but that was a better greeting than I expected."

"I've been thinking about it for a while. There's more where that came from," he said. "What brings you to town?"

"You," she said simply. Then she threw her arms around Luke's neck and kissed him even longer and harder in return.

Finally, they pulled apart. Charlotte looked around the large, mostly empty building. In the center of the shop stood the forge. She could see there would be stalls along one side. A long, sturdy workbench held blacksmithing tools on the other side wall.

"You've made good progress," she commented.

"I haven't had any distractions...until now."

"I'm a distraction? I can…"

Before she could continue, he covered her mouth with his. Still holding her, he said, "You're a welcome distraction."

"I haven't been kissed this thoroughly in…in weeks," she said.

"Then you need to be kissed more often. We'll have to make that happen."

"Yes, we will," she said with a twinkle in her ebony eyes. "Now, tell me about Jameson's Blacksmith Shop. Have you shoed any horses yet?"

"No, but I've mended a couple of shovels and some farm equipment."

"I've got a customer for you. Stan Walker. He and his wife Clara farm about halfway between here and our farm," Charlotte said. "Lizzy and I were visiting them this morning. He mentioned his horses need shoeing."

Luke recalled that Charlotte had made an emergency trip to Walkers' farm to set Clara's arm earlier in the summer.

"While I'm in town, I thought I'd do some Christmas shopping. I saw a book in the Mercantile that I think Lizzy would love," Charlotte said.

"I'll clean up and meet you at the saloon for a bite to eat." Luke kissed her again, a playful kiss on the tip of Charlotte's nose. "More kisses. More often," he said.

Charlotte left Luke to clean up.

Isabell Vaughn was not behind the counter when Charlotte entered the Mercantile. Instead, she was stocking shelves and humming to herself.

"Hello, Isabell," Charlotte called out. "I don't recognize that tune. What is it?"

"It's new. 'When Johnny Comes Marching Home.' It's sad and hopeful at the same time."

She sang the first few lines.

When Johnny comes marching home again, Hurrah, Hurrah,

We'll give him a hearty welcome then, Hurrah, Hurrah.

The men will cheer, the boys will shout,

The ladies, they will all turn out,

And we'll all feel gay,

When Johnny comes marching home.

"I see what you mean," Charlotte said. "It is sad and hopeful."

Isabell stood up and dusted off her navy blue skirt. "It's hard to keep ahead of the dust in here," she complained. "Are you looking for anything special?"

Charlotte pursed her lips. "Yes. The last time I was in here, I saw a book, *David Copperfield*, that I think Lizzy would like. She loves anything by Dickens."

"I still have it!" Isabell said triumphantly. "Between you and me, there's not a lot of call for books by Mr.

Dickens in these parts." She pulled the leather-bound book from a top shelf and handed it to Charlotte.

"Will that be it?" Isabell asked.

"No, I need to find something for a gentleman friend. Any suggestions?"

"Would this gentleman be a fellow Missourian? A blacksmith, maybe?"

Charlotte smiled and said, "You're well-informed."

Isabell tilted her head and said, "It's a small town. Mr. Jameson is a single, good-looking man." The shopkeeper scanned the shelves and pulled down several items for consideration: a wallet, a straight razor and shaving brush, and a small book with blank pages.

"These are all good ideas, Isabell. If I choose the wallet, am I suggesting that he needs to fill it with money? Do the shaving supplies tell him that I think he's untidy?"

She considered the options and said, "I like the idea of a blank book. He can write his own story. That's what we're all doing these days. I'd like one, too." Then she thought about Lizzy's upcoming birthday and said, "Make it three of those blank books."

Isabell wrapped up the purchases. Charlotte thanked her and left to meet Luke at the saloon. As she made her way to the Prairie Rose Saloon, she noticed the clouds were gathering.

While the name Prairie Rose Saloon might sound elegant, the establishment was far from refined. Two large wooden barrels held up the saloon bar. There were no stools at the bar. Instead, patrons stood at the bar but could rest a foot on a railing near the floor. The bar room smelled of beer, sawdust, and men's sweat.

Behind the bar was a large painting of a woman holding a rose between her teeth. Charlotte was relieved to see the woman was "nearly" fully clothed.

Luke was at one of the three tables in the saloon. There was an empty chair waiting for Charlotte to arrive.

"I wasn't sure what you'd like to drink. Billy Rose – he owns the saloon – suggested coffee or tea. I've already ordered turkey sandwiches for us."

"Thank you," Charlotte said as she sat down. "Coffee would be fine." Luke motioned to the bartender to bring a cup of coffee. She fidgeted uncomfortably in her chair.

"What's wrong," Luke asked.

"I'm regretting coming to town," Charlotte admitted. "The weather looks to be turning."

Luke left the table to check the skies. He came back and said, "You're right. You should stay in town tonight."

She shook her head. "Lizzy is going to wonder what happened to me. I don't want to worry her."

"When she sees the bad weather, she'll understand you were safer in town."

"You're probably right. There's not a boarding house here, is there?"

"Not yet. I've been sleeping in the shop. I could make a place for you there. Hopefully you'll be able to control yourself."

"It will be a struggle, but I accept your kind offer."

They finished their meal and returned to the blacksmith shop. The clouds were getting darker, with the promise of snow.

Charlotte led her horse into the shop. "Use that stall in the back," Luke directed her.

While she unsaddled her horse, Luke made a bed for his guest. "I don't have a real bed yet, or even a cot…" he indicated the bedroll on the shop floor.

"I've slept in worse places," Charlotte said.

They settled in for the night, each sleeping in separate bedrolls.

During the night, Charlotte woke up cold and shivering. She pulled her coat over her for added warmth.

From his bedroll, Luke said, "You know, two bodies are warmer than one alone."

Charlotte snorted. But she continued to shiver. She knew that Luke's suggestion made sense.

"Alright. Your bedroll or mine?"

Luke scooped up his bedding and joined Charlotte.

"Get in here," he whispered as he pulled her tight. Charlotte snuggled into Luke's arms, glad for the heat of his body.

Charlotte expected their situation to be awkward in the morning. Instead, she awoke to find Luke making coffee on the shop's cookstove. He brought a mug over to Charlotte, who was still bundled in the bedding.

"Here, this will warm you up," he said, squatting to hand her the mug. "Or I could get back in bed and.."

"Coffee is good and appreciated," Charlotte said as she reached for the steaming cup.

"You're beautiful in the morning, Charlie," Luke said. He was sitting on the bedroll next to her, sipping his coffee. "Have you ever thought about moving to town?"

The question surprised Charlotte. "What? Lizzy and I have our claims to work."

"You can still prove your claim by living on it six months of the year," Luke said. "Yes, I've done my homework, too. You could live in town the other six months. I've heard some homesteaders are doing that – especially in the winter. Think about it," he concluded.

"I'd better think about getting back home," Charlotte countered. "Lizzy will be worried."

"Thanks for the night," Luke said. "I mean it sincerely. It was good to spend some time alone with you."

Luke helped Charlotte saddle her horse. "Uh, I was thinking I might ride out to your place in a couple of weeks. Would that be all right?"

"I know Lizzy would like to see you. And so would I."

She was about to lead her horse out of the shop when Luke stopped her. He gathered her into his arms and pulled her close for a farewell kiss.

"Thank you," she said. "Thank you for the hospitality and thank you for that."

It had not snowed as much as Charlotte had feared, so the ride home was uneventful. When she arrived in the yard, Lizzy came out to greet her.

"How was Shady Bluffs?" Lizzy asked.

"Oh, it was fine. Weren't you worried about me?"

"Sister, you spent more than six months at war. A night in town? I knew you'd be fine. Maybe better than fine."

With that, Lizzy returned to her soddy. *Yes, I do amuse myself,* she thought.

"Well!" Charlotte said out loud to no one.

News of the Day – Proclamation of Amnesty & Reconstruction

December 8, 1863

December 8, 1863, President Abraham Lincoln issued a Proclamation of Amnesty and Reconstruction. This was Lincoln's first step toward healing the nation. In the Proclamation, Lincoln offered a full pardon to Confederate soldiers who took an oath of loyalty and accepted the abolition of slavery. Lincoln understood the need for postwar reconstruction. The Union armies had already captured large sections of the South. The proclamation addressed three issues:

It gave a full pardon for and restoration of property to those who engaged in the rebellion except for the highest Confederate officials and military leaders.

It allowed a new state government to be formed when ten percent of the eligible Southern voters took an oath of allegiance to the United States.

It encouraged Southern states to enact plans to deal with the formerly enslaved people as long as their freedom was not compromised.

Chapter 20: December 1863
Medicine Creek Claim

The winter continued to be mild with little snow, which allowed Charlotte to spend a day a week learning Lakota from Clara Walker. Clara had begun with some basics, such as greetings, familial titles, and names for nature's flora and fauna.

"This spring, after the baby is born, I would like to come to the village with you," Clara said one day. "I miss my inala."

Charlotte thought a moment and said, "Ah, your aunts." She understood that "aunt" and "aunties" were terms of endearment and respect for the matriarchs of the tribe.

"I would like that, too, Clara. I never knew my aunts and uncles or my grandparents. My parents moved to Missouri before I was born, and we never went back East to visit."

"That is too bad. I hope my children will meet their grandparents one day," Clara said.

"I hope so, too. Families are important. That's why Lizzy and I decided to move here together."

Charlotte found that the more Lakota words she learned, the easier it was to understand the cadence of the language. She wrote the new words in her blank book. At the top of each page, she had written a subject or category in her Lakota dictionary.

Even though there were no crops to tend, both sisters found plenty to do in the winter. They took turns fetching water from the creek. Frequently, they needed to break through the ice with an axe to fill their buckets. Rather than haul the water buckets themselves, they led the horses or the oxen to the creek so the animals could exercise. On other days, they saddled their horses and rode out to collect buffalo chips to feed the cookstove. They would return home with enough "prairie muffins" to keep the soddies warm for weeks.

Even when they had completed those winter chores, there were always animals to tend to and housekeeping to fill their days. In the evening, Lizzy often settled into Mama's rocker with Butter in her lap and read a book. While Charlotte enjoyed reading, she preferred spending her evenings sewing and quilting.

Before they knew it, Christmas was upon them. Both sisters looked forward to having Luke visit, but for different reasons.

Lizzy had a pile of shovels, pitchforks, and hoes that needed repairing. "I'd never given much thought to how important blacksmiths are," Lizzy said one evening. "I hope Luke can take some of the tools back to town to mend. I'll need them come spring." She paused, realizing how self-serving that comment was. "Of course, having Luke around for a day or two will be nice."

"Yes, it will be nice to have him around," Charlotte responded. She blushed as she thought about his strong arms around her that night in the blacksmith shop.

Luke arrived early on Christmas Eve. Charlotte knew they had a visitor because Shadow began to bark immediately.

"Hey, boy," Luke said. "It's me." He opened his hand and fed the large dog a bit of beef jerky. By then, both sisters had come outside to see what the commotion was.

"Shadow is easily bribed," Luke chuckled. The dog was already sniffing around for another treat.

"He's a good watchdog," Charlotte said in defense.

"Merry Christmas, Luke!" Lizzy said, changing the subject. "And just on cue, it's starting to snow."

"You ladies get back inside," Luke said. "I'll take care of Rusty, and then I'll be in."

When he entered Charlotte's soddy, Luke was carrying what looked to be a tree branch. "I found this scrub cedar on the way here and thought it would make a good Christmas tree," he explained.

Upon further inspection, Charlotte saw the branch had roots. "You uprooted an entire tree?" she said.

"Well, it's not much of a tree…" he began.

"It will be a beautiful Christmas tree," Lizzy said. "I have just the thing to hold it." She found a pottery crock and "planted" the cedar in it. "There, now we can decorate it."

Luke and the Ward sisters spent the afternoon stringing popcorn and rose hips to decorate the tree. They twisted paper into shapes and hung those on the tree as well.

"Now we just need a tree topper," Lizzy said. "I have an idea!" She began digging in her clothes trunk and returned with the white hair ribbon Charlotte gave her last Christmas. She tied the ribbon into a bow with several loops and placed it at the top of the now-beautiful cedar tree.

"Perfect!" Charlotte declared.

They spent the rest of the evening catching up on news from "back home."

"Not sure how much war news you get out here," Luke said. "Ma sends me clippings from time to time. It seems they've turned the Gettysburg battlefield into a cemetery – which is fitting since so many men died there. President Lincoln gave a speech there. It was a mighty short speech. The newspapers printed the entire thing." Luke paused, thinking about Lincoln's words. "Lincoln said, 'we here highly resolve that these dead shall not have died in vain – that this nation, under God, shall have a new birth of freedom – and that government of the people, by the people, for the people, shall not perish from the earth.'"

The three were silent for a moment, thinking about the friends and family they had lost during the war.

Charlotte wiped a tear from her eye. She said, "Max and so many others."

Lizzy gently patted her sister on the arm. "We won't forget."

"So many others," Luke echoed.

He had intended to tell Charlotte and Lizzy about the skirmish at Boonville and the massacre at Lawrence, Kansas, by Quantrill's Raiders but decided now wasn't the right time for such sad news.

"What other news do you have from your family?" Charlotte asked.

"Ben Fuller – that's Martha's husband – mustered out. He was wounded at Wilson's Creek early in the war. Mary Jane is back home now that she's a widow. And Nellie, well, she's just as wild as ever."

"I like Nellie. She's a … a free spirit," Charlotte said.

"That's the perfect description for that wild cat," Luke agreed.

They talked a while longer, and then Luke said, "It's late. I'd best head for the barn to bed down."

"We won't hear of it," Lizzy said. "The barn was fine when the weather was warmer, but we thought you could sleep in the common room. We've already put quilts in there for you."

"It would be a might warmer," Luke said. "Thank you, kindly."

As Charlotte changed into her nightgown, she wished she were bold enough to invite Luke to keep her warm again.

Luke tossed and turned. Finally, he pulled a quilt from his bed and, wrapping himself in the blanket, went outside.

Charlotte heard him leave the soddy. She pulled on a shawl and joined him.

"I couldn't sleep," Luke explained. "I thought a little fresh air might help."

"I couldn't sleep either. I could make warm some milk for us," she offered.

In the light of the December moon, Charlotte saw Luke grimace. "You don't like warm milk?" she asked.

"Warm milk isn't going to help. You're the reason I can't sleep, Charlie." He turned and looked deep into her eyes. "You're all I think about. I think about holding you, about kissing you, about..."

"I couldn't sleep either," Charlotte said. Luke moved closer and wrapped Charlotte in his quilt. Under the winter stars, they came together in a lovers' embrace. His hands moved from her shoulders down her back until he reached her bottom. All the while, he trailed kisses from her mouth up to her ear and then down her neck.

Glorying in his touch, Charlotte kneaded the muscles in his shoulders and back. When his hands cupped her bottom and lifted her, she wrapped her legs around his waist.

Luke pushed open the door to Charlotte's soddy and carried her to bed. Charlotte shrugged off her nightgown and pulled him down to her.

"Charlie, I've dreamt of this for two years."

From the firelight of the cookstove, he explored Charlotte's lithe body. He circled the brown peaks of her small breasts, then traced a path to her flat stomach. Finally, he found her warm center. He continued teasing and exploring her body until she arched her back in pleasure. Then he entered her, and they both found release.

Charlotte moaned in delight. "That was…that was worth the wait," she said.

"Two years is a long time to wait," Luke whispered.

"No, I mean you are my first. *You* were worth the wait."

"Charlie…Charlotte…I thought…no, I didn't think. I'm sorry."

"Don't be sorry. I've dreamed of this, too. And now, let's get some sleep."

Charlotte slept in Luke's arms, resting on his shoulder. Luke didn't sleep. He stroked Charlotte's hair, felt the rhythm of her beating heart, and marveled at the woman in his arms.

Charlotte woke just before dawn to find Luke gazing at her. She smiled and stretched. "Did you just wake up, too?"

"No. I've been awake. I've been watching you sleep. Did you know that you're beautiful when you sleep?"

Charlotte laughed softly. "No one's ever said that to me."

"It's true. But you're even more beautiful when you're awake. Now I can see your amazing brown eyes."

She kissed him long and deeply. She caressed his bare chest, and he began to respond. "No, it's my turn," she stilled his hands.

Slowly, Charlotte moved her hands over his muscled chest. Briefly, she followed the curve of his biceps. Then, her hands returned to the thick hair on his chest and stomach. At last, it was Luke's turn to moan.

Charlotte shifted on top of Luke and covered his mouth with her own. She guided him into her. He held on to her hips, and they began the dance of love. Sated and a little out of breath, Charlotte collapsed on top of Luke.

Luke, reveling in the morning lovemaking, softly stroked Charlotte's back.

At last, they could hear Lizzy moving around in her soddy. Quietly, they rose from the tangles of their bed and dressed.

Charlotte started a pot of coffee.

"What can I do to help?" he asked.

"After you wash up, you could fetch water from the creek. You'll need to take an axe to break the ice."

The December morning air was bracing. It gave Luke time to consider what to do after last night. After all, he had taken her virtue. Her virginity. He should propose. It would be the honorable thing to do. She might be expecting it. He continued to think about his obligations on his way to the creek.

As Charlotte had said, he needed to break the ice to collect fresh water. A few hundred yards down the way, he saw native women doing the same thing. They waved at him, and he waved back.

Friendly neighborhood, he thought to himself. It appeared that Charlotte and Lizzy had made friends with the local Indians.

Luke returned to the soddy and to the aroma of frying bacon.

"That smells amazing!" he said. He peeked over Charlotte's shoulder and saw pancakes sizzling in the skillet. "I haven't had a breakfast like that since I left Missouri."

"Help yourself to coffee," Charlotte offered. "Lizzy will be here in a couple of minutes." He kissed her on the back of her neck. Charlotte shivered just a bit at his touch.

"Good morning and Merry Christmas," Lizzy greeted them. She carried in her cup of coffee and two packages wrapped in brightly colored fabric.

"And a merry Dakota Christmas to all!" Charlotte replied. "Breakfast is ready."

Lizzy gave a brief blessing, and the three began eating.

"Luke, we don't get much news out here on the frontier," Lizzy said. "You updated us on your family last night, but what have you heard about the war?"

"Ma wrote that there's been some fighting close to home," he said. "Back in October, Joe Shelby – that's

General Joe Shelby – and his boys raided Boonville. There was a skirmish with Federals, and Shelby's unit retreated. That's the third time Boonville has seen combat."

"That's close to your family's ranch, isn't it?" Lizzy asked.

"Yep, in the next county. Too close for my comfort. And the Bushwhackers and Jayhawkers are still going at it," he continued.

"Quantrill's men?" Lizzy said.

Luke nodded. "More bad news, I'm afraid. In August, Quantrill's Raiders went through Lawrence, Kansas, killing the residents and burning the town. Some said it was in retaliation for the deaths of Bill Anderson's and Cole Younger's kin. Those two ride with Quantrill," Luke said. "Others said it was because Lawrence has been a stronghold for Unionists and Jayhawkers. Either way, I heard that nearly two hundred townspeople died in the raid."

"Lizzy met Quantrill and some of his men," Charlotte said.

"How'd that come about?" Luke asked.

Lizzy related the story of Quantrill's men at the farm and the shootout with the Jayhawkers.

Luke shook his head. "I'm glad I got captured and paroled. I want nothing more to do with the war, the Bushwhackers, or the Jayhawkers."

"Dakota is a fresh start for all of us," Lizzy said. "Enough talk of war. It's Christmas morning, and I have gifts for both of you." She handed the wrapped packages to Charlotte and Luke. "Go ahead – open them!"

Luke waited while Charlotte untied the jute string holding her package together. Inside, she found a bundle of fabrics. She eyed her sister and said, "You knew I was running short on quilting fabric. This should get me through the winter. Thank you." She hugged her sister.

Then it was Luke's turn. "It's heavy," he said as he pretended to weigh the package with his hand. He unwrapped the small but heavy gift to find a bullet mold. "It was Papa's," Lizzy said. "I'd packed it with the other implements. Now that you're a blacksmith, maybe you can use this at your shop."

"That's very thoughtful, Lizzy. Thank you. Now it's my turn." He handed packages to each woman.

Lizzy opened hers first. It was a box of lavender-scented soap. Lizzy inhaled the fragrant soap and said, "It's heavenly. Thank you, Luke."

Charlotte received a similar box, but her soaps were rose-scented. "Thank you, Luke. Perfumed soaps are such a luxury out here. And now it's my turn." She returned with the packages she had purchased at the mercantile.

Lizzy opened the Charles Dickens book. She said, "My favorite author! I have wanted to read *David Copperfield*. I have the start of a good library. Thank you, Charlotte."

Just as he had "weighed" the bullet mold from Lizzy, Luke pretended to weigh the small package from Charlotte. "It's not a bullet mold, I'd wager."

He unwrapped the package and saw that Charlotte had given him a small book with blank pages.

"It's a bit unusual, I know," Charlotte began. "But I thought you could use it for sketches, for ideas…"

Before she could continue, Luke said, "This is perfect. You've said that we're starting new lives here. New chapters in our lives. That's what this book is. Thank you, Charlie."

"Oh, go ahead and kiss her," Lizzy said. "I know you want to."

And he did.

After breakfast, Lizzy curled up in the rocker with her new book.

"It's a nice day for a walk," Luke said. "Charlie, could I interest you in a winter stroll?"

Together, they walked down to the creek. "I saw deer tracks when I went to get water," he said.

At the creek, Luke dusted off a fallen log, and they sat. "I've been thinking about last night, Charlie," he began.

"So have I." She smiled warmly.

"I want to do the honorable thing."

Charlotte started laughing. "Oh my, is this a proposal? I'm not a fragile flower, Luke."

She moved into his lap, put her arms around his neck, and kissed him.

"I enjoyed last night just as much as you did," she said when they broke apart. "I do have a question for you, though."

He cocked his head, waiting for her to continue.

"Last night, you said you had waited two years. As I recall, two years ago you thought I was a man. Or did my disguise not fool you?"

"Well, that's the thing, isn't it? I've always been attracted to you. Maybe deep down, I thought you were a woman, but I was dang confused for the longest time." He laughed at the memory.

Charlotte joined in the laughter. "Well, that's quite a confession," she said.

"When did you know you had feelings for me," Luke asked.

"It took a while. You perturbed me as a patient at the hospital in Springfield. But things changed when we were at your family's home. You were different around your family. Then, in Independence, Dr. Lee called you 'my beau.' I told him he was mistaken. I didn't think you were interested in me – I've never had a beau – so I thought we'd just be friends." She shrugged at the memories.

"But about that 'honorable thing, Luke, let's take it slowly."

Luke didn't know if he was relieved or disappointed. Either way, he understood Charlotte's wishes and would abide by them.

Charlotte stuffed and cooked prairie chickens for Christmas dinner. She had expected Lizzy to lend a hand with the holiday meal preparations, but her sister stayed in her own soddy. Charlotte thought that was a bit unusual, but she decided Lizzy must be enjoying her new book.

For dessert, Charlotte served cookies and hot chocolate. After dinner, Lizzy left to read, closing the door behind her.

Luke and Charlotte sat by the decorated tree and talked about their future.

"I'd never thought about blacksmithing until I worked at the livery in St. Louis. I guess everything happens for a reason. What about you, Charlie? I can't see you homesteading forever."

"You're right. Lizzy loves it out here. I want to do more. No, not 'more.' I want to do something different. I was hoping to be the town's doctor. But Shady Bluffs already has Doc Stone. I guess I'll see what the future has in store for me."

This time, when they retired to Charlotte's bed, it was not as awkward. Charlotte allowed Luke to undress her, and she did the same for him. Then, they spent the night enjoying each other and learning how to please one another. Finally, they both drifted off to sleep.

The day after Christmas, Luke hiked to the creek again to fetch water. When he returned, he said, "The weather's going to turn, I think. I'm going to high tail it back to town after breakfast."

Lizzy helped Luke load her broken farm tools for the trip back, and then she quickly made her goodbyes, leaving Charlotte and Luke alone.

"Charlie, it's been, well, it's been the best Christmas ever. And not because of the…"

"I feel the same way. It's been a long time coming." She kissed him goodbye. "Safe travels back. I'll come to town in a few weeks. I want to see the progress you're making on the shop."

After one more long goodbye kiss, Luke mounted his gelding and trotted toward Shady Bluffs. Charlotte watched him ride away, smiling at the memories they had made together.

Thinking to help Lizzy with chores, Charlotte found her sister in the barn milking cows.

"I'll feed the pigs while you milk," Charlotte offered.

"Fine."

Lizzy's curt response surprised Charlotte. "Are you upset with me?" she asked.

"Not so much 'upset.' I'm disappointed and concerned about you and Luke. You'll end up getting hurt, pregnant, or married if you continue down this path," Lizzy said. "I hope you know what you're doing, Char."

"I thought you liked Luke," Charlotte said.

"I do like Luke. But I don't like the direction your relationship is going. It's too soon and too fast."

"Too soon," Charlotte exclaimed. "Luke and I have known each other for over two years. You and I both saw girls back home get married after courting for only a month or two."

"War brides," Lizzy said with a sniff. "But that's not the issue here. We're not talking about marriage. And I'm not being prudish, Char. What you do is your business. But what if he gets you 'in a family way'? We both know the consequences of your nighttime activities."

"For your information, he did propose. But I refused. I don't want to rush things."

"Nature may think differently. We know how babies are made."

"You're just upset that I might leave the claim."

"Since you've brought it up…" Lizzy continued. "It sounds as if you're considering that. You know you could lose the land. If you get pregnant and he offers marriage, you won't be Head of Household anymore. Besides, I don't think Confederate soldiers can stake a claim through the Homestead Act. You'll be putting your claim at risk on top of everything else."

"It's always about the land, isn't it, Lizzy? I can't believe you're more worried about my land than my happiness. You sound like a frustrated old maid."

With that, Charlotte threw the last pail of corn to the pigs and stormed out of the barn.

After-Action Report – Quantrill's Raiders Retreat to Texas

Winter 1863-64

After the raid on Lawrence, Kansas, in August 1863, Quantrill and his band of Bushwhackers retreated to Texas. In October 1863, Quantrill's men attacked Fort Baxter in the southeast corner of Kansas, where they ambushed and killed nearly one hundred Union soldiers.

The Raiders spent the winter of 1863-64 in Sherman, Texas. Quantrill's Raiders' lawless actions continued to embarrass the Confederate command. During their time in Texas, Quantrill's men split into two bands, one led by "Bloody Bill" Anderson and the other by George Todd. The Bushwhackers returned to Missouri in early 1864.

Chapter 21: January 1864
Medicine Creek Claim

The weather turned exceptionally cold in January, but not as cold as the sisters' friendship. Like many siblings, Charlotte and Lizzy had fought when they were younger. But the deaths of first their mother and then their father had formed a bond that transcended traditional sibling rivalries.

Neither sister apologized for the argument. In fact, they didn't speak to each other for nearly a week.

January's harsh weather made up for the mild December. About a week after Christmas, it began snowing. And snowing. And snowing. The wind whipped the snow into drifts that topped the soddy walls.

Sometimes the snow fell so furiously that it was a total white-out. At times, Lizzy couldn't see the barn from her front door. She had heard of homesteaders who had lost their way during a blizzard. Lizzy solved the problem by stringing a rope from the barn door to the door of her soddy.

The snow made everything more difficult, such as fetching water from the creek. Charlotte had resorted to bringing buckets of snow in and letting it melt.

That still left the animals to care for. It was so cold that the hens stopped laying eggs, which meant the sisters no longer had that daily chore to handle. Still, the cows had to be milked, and the pigs, horses, and oxen needed to be fed.

Lizzy trudged to the barn one morning after a particularly heavy snowfall. She had started wearing a pair of Max's old trousers, which she found to be much more practical in the deep snow. She fed the livestock and then turned to milking her three cows. Lizzy was pleased that all three cows would calve in the spring. That meant a steady supply of milk, but more importantly, it meant her herd would increase.

The barn lacked windows, so Lizzy milked by the light of a lantern. When she was done, she picked up the bucket and the lamp, closed the barn door, and headed back to the house. Charlotte would separate the cream and churn the butter.

That afternoon, Lizzy repeated her chores, but when she got to the barn, she saw the barn door was swinging open. Pushing down her panic, Lizzy hurried inside, hoping to see the cows still in their large stall and the pigs bedded down in their pen.

The pigs were there, but the three cows and their calves were missing. Lizzy panicked. The snowfall during the day had covered the cows' tracks. Lizzy wasn't sure which way to search first, but she thought the cattle might wander toward the creek, where they had watered in the summer months.

The winter days were short, and the sun would soon be setting, but Lizzy knew what she had to do. She wrapped her scarf more tightly around her head and face and grabbed a coil of rope and the lantern. Even though she and Charlotte were still not on speaking terms, she poked her head into Charlotte's soddy and said, "The cows are loose. I'm going to search near the creek." And she was gone.

"Wait for me," Charlotte said. But Lizzy had already shut the door and probably hadn't heard Charlotte's offer. Hurriedly, Charlotte put on several layers of clothing. She lit her lantern and left her soddy to follow Lizzy.

The strong winds covered Lizzy's footprints just as they had wiped away the cows' tracks. Charlotte took the most direct path to the creek, hoping Lizzy would do the same. The winds were getting stronger, but the snow had subsided somewhat so that Charlotte could find her way to the creek.

When she arrived at Medicine Creek, she didn't see Lizzy or the cows. Charlotte noticed the creek was still open in some spots. That worried her.

Then she heard mooing. She went in that direction and began calling out to Lizzy.

"Over here," Lizzy shouted back. Charlotte sighed in relief until she saw that Lizzy was in the creek. She had attempted to reach a cow that had walked out on the ice and then fallen into the icy water. That's where Lizzy was – in the icy creek waters.

Charlotte sized up the situation and noticed that Lizzy was still holding the rope.

"Tie the rope around your waist and toss the coil to me," Charlotte instructed.

Lizzy's fingers were numb and nearly frozen. After some fumbling, she was able to tie a tight knot. She tossed the coiled rope toward Charlotte on the shore. It fell short, but Charlotte thought she could venture out a bit on the ice without falling through. She was half-right. One foot went through the ice, but Charlotte was able to grab the rope. She carefully retraced her steps back to shore, all the while calling out reassurances to Lizzy.

"I've got the rope, Lizzy. I'm going to pull you in. If you can, lay flat on the ice while I pull on the rope. Don't struggle. I've got this."

Slowly, Charlotte reeled in the rope, pulling Lizzy in as quickly and cautiously as she could. Charlotte didn't want Lizzy to fall through another weak spot in the ice. Eventually, Charlotte was within an arm's length of her sister. She reached out and pulled Lizzy to shore.

"We need to get you back home and warm you up," Charlotte said.

"But the ..." Lizzy's teeth chattered so violently that she couldn't finish the sentence.

"The cows will have to wait," Charlotte declared. "We can get more cows. I can't get another sister. Here, wrap yourself in my dry shawl. Can you walk?"

"I think so." Lizzy leaned on Charlotte's arm.

They reached the soddies after dark. The moon's light on the white snow provided enough illumination for them to find their way back.

"Home, sweet home," Charlotte said as she helped Lizzy into her soddy. "Let's get those frozen clothes off." She helped Lizzy strip off her blouse and trousers. "The undergarments, too. You are frozen down to your skin," Charlotte chided her sister.

Lizzy finished removing all her clothing while Charlotte fed buffalo chips into the cookstove to warm up the soddy.

"Come over here by the fire," Charlotte said. She began to rub Lizzy's hands and feet, and arms and legs vigorously. "This should help get the circulation flowing. If nothing else, it will help warm you up faster – I think. I haven't treated severe frostbite before."

Charlotte kept rubbing Lizzy's limbs until they were pink.

"How are you feeling?" Charlotte asked.

"Better," Lizzy said. "I'm so tired."

"I think that's a symptom of the frostbite. Let's get some hot coffee into you. Then, if you want, you can rest. But I'll be waking you up regularly to check on you."

Lizzy gave a sleepy smile. "Can I have cream in my coffee?" she asked.

"There's the Lizzy I know and love. Now, sit in Mama's rocker, and I'll bring you a cup."

The sisters talked about childhood memories, about Max's antics, and how much they missed their Missouri neighbors. Finally, Lizzy couldn't keep her eyes open any longer.

"Go ahead and rest, honey," Charlotte said. She pulled a quilt over Lizzy in the rocker and began her vigil.

Just as she had promised, Charlotte woke Lizzy up frequently. While Charlotte was rubbing her sister's hands and feet, she also inspected the fingers and toes. She didn't think Lizzy would have permanent damage, but time would tell.

In the meantime, Charlotte knew that she needed to rescue those cows. But she couldn't do that until Lizzy was on the mend. And she would not let Lizzy venture outside to help!

The next day, Lizzy seemed to be improving. Charlotte bundled up for her trip to the creek.

"Wait, I'm coming along," Lizzy said.

"No, you're not. Doctor's orders. If you want to be helpful, make dinner for us. I'll be back in a bit. And no, I am not going swimming in the creek." That made Lizzy giggle.

Charlotte was able to retrace her steps in the snow down to the creek. Once there, she could see where the cows had been. She wasn't a tracker, so she wasn't sure how many cow and calf tracks she was seeing. She followed the tracks down the shoreline, right up to the edge of the Lakota camp. Two cows and all three calves were in the pen with the tribe's horses.

She wasn't sure what to do next. Had she forfeited the cattle now that they were in the possession of the Lakota? She was deciding on her next steps when a Lakota man approached.

"Hah-ue," he said.

Charlotte now knew that meant "hello," and she returned the greeting. Through hand gestures, Charlotte communicated that she had been looking for the cows.

He motioned to the cows and calves and pointed to Charlotte. "Yours?" he gestured. They exchanged names, and Charlotte learned she had Spotted Horse to thank for rescuing her cows.

Spotted Horse gestured for her to follow him into a tipi. Inside the dwelling, the family was enjoying beef stew. Charlotte now knew where the third cow was. But, if she could retrieve the other five as she hoped, it would be payment well spent.

A woman handed Charlotte a bowl of stew. Charlotte was famished and dug into the savory soup. She gestured that it was delicious.

"But I have to get home. I'd like to take the other cows with me," she said in English. She accompanied the request with sign language that she hoped communicated her intent.

The young woman she had spoken to at the creek last summer, Dancing Girl, entered the tipi in time to hear the request. She said something in Lakota to the family, and they responded, nodding.

"They found the pte gleškal…the cows…at creek. One almost frozen. They brought cows here. They…" She searched for the right word. "They knew you come for cows. They were hungry. They thank you for cow." She pointed to the stew.

Charlotte smiled and nodded in agreement. "Can I take them home now?"

The woman spoke to the family. The older woman in the tipi said, "Pilamaya," which Charlotte recalled from her lessons with Clara meant "Thank you." Charlotte repeated the phrase to the people in the tipi.

Spotted Horse and Charlotte went to the cattle pen. Together, they tied the cows and calves into a line, and Charlotte began the long trek back to the soddies.

Once home, she led the cattle into the barn. Making sure the cattle had sufficient hay and water for the night, Charlotte returned to Lizzy.

"You're back!" Lizzy said. "Did you find them?"

"Yes. The Lakota found them and took them to their camp."

"And?"

"And the mostly brown cow was delicious," Charlotte said.

Lizzy was alarmed. "Oh, no."

"They knew we would come looking for them. The one in the stew was nearly dead when they found her. I don't begrudge them one cow. We still have two cows and three calves. I'm thankful that they were so understanding. A lot of people in Missouri wouldn't have been that generous."

Lizzy knew that to be true. "Where are the cows and calves now?"

"They're in the barn, fed and watered them." Charlotte folded herself into Mama's rocker. "It's been a day. I'm cold and exhausted."

Mischievously, she looked at Lizzy and said, "But I'm not hungry. I'll have to get their recipe for that stew. It was delicious!"

Lizzy knelt by Charlotte and put her head in her sister's lap. "I'm sorry we fought. I didn't have any right to criticize your choices. You should be happy. And I really like Luke."

Charlotte stroked her sister's golden blonde hair. "I'm sorry, too. I was pretty harsh. It's just you and me out here. We must watch out for each other. You gave me quite a scare. No matter what happens, we're sisters forever. I love you, Lizzy."

"I love you, too, Char. I only want the best for you."

And just like that, the sisters returned to their loving relationship, thankful for each other.

After-Action Report – Federal Troops Capture Meridian Mississippi Feb 14, 1864

The Meridian campaign, led by Union General William Tecumseh Sherman, lasted from Feb 3 to March 6, 1864. Sherman's strategic goal was to destroy the Confederate rail center and military post at Meridian, Mississippi, as well as the Rebel resistance in southern Mississippi.

The Confederate troops, under the command of Lieutenant General Leonidas Polk, retreated from Meridian on February 14, at which time Sherman and his troops entered the city. The Union Army destroyed over

100 miles of railroad and burned anything of value to the Southern cause. When Sherman left Meridian to return to Vicksburg, he reportedly stated, "Meridian, with its depots, storehouses, arsenal, hospitals, offices, hotels, and cantonments, no longer exists."

Chapter 22: Spring 1864
Medicine Creek Claim

A robin landed on the fence by the barn.

"The first sign of spring!" Lizzy said out loud. Even though the day was still cold, the farmer in Lizzy was delighted that planting season was right around the corner. She had sorted through her seed stock during the winter and was already planning the garden.

Lizzy reviewed their first year in Dakota Territory. She took mental stock of the claim: the hens were laying again, and a young rooster was making his presence known in the hen house. She estimated there would be two new calves in the barn soon. There would be new piglets, too.

Lizzy was on her way back to the soddies when she saw Stan Walker riding in as if the devil was on his tail.

He was halfway down the path to the soddies when he called out, "Is Charlotte here? The baby's coming! Clara sent me for Charlotte!"

Lizzy took off running to Charlotte's soddy. "Char, get your medical bag. It's Clara – her baby is coming," she called. "I'll saddle your horse."

Charlotte rushed out of the soddy to see Stan jumping from his horse.

"It's the baby, Miss Charlotte," Stan said. "Clara said to fetch you."

Charlotte hurried back inside. By the time she changed into her riding skirt and grabbed the black satchel, Lizzy was leading Charlotte's mare from the barn.

Despite the muddy paths and fields, Stan and Charlotte made good time to the Walker's homestead. Charlotte dismounted and threw the reins to Stan. In the shanty, Charlotte saw Clara squatting against the wall.

"When did your water break?" Charlotte asked.

"At sunrise," Clara answered. "This is my first baby. I wanted a woman – I wanted you – to help."

"Let me see how things are progressing," Charlotte said calmly. "You know, this isn't my first baby."

"But I thought you were a spinster," Clara said. "I mean, I didn't think…"

"Oh, I've never been married. What I mean is this isn't the first time I've helped bring a baby into the world. I helped the midwife in Missouri. I even helped my mama give birth." She remembered how Blanche Ward had died in childbirth and was determined that would not be Clara Walker's fate.

Charlotte washed her hands and said, "I'm going to check the baby's position."

Afterward, she washed her hands again and said, "Everything looks just fine. I'll help you through labor and soon you'll be holding a beautiful baby boy…or girl."

Clara smiled weakly. "I'm so glad we met. I'm even more glad you're here." She grasped Charlotte's hand as another labor pain washed over the laboring woman. Charlotte never winced.

"That was a hard one. It means your body is moving the baby," Charlotte said. "It's a good sign." After a third labor pain, Charlotte checked the baby's progress. "I can see the baby's head, Clara. It won't be long now." Through the next hour or so, Charlotte massaged Clara's back and legs, always whispering soothing words to the mother-to-be.

Stan would poke his head into the soddy from time to time. "How's it going?"

"It's going just as it should, Stan," Charlotte said. "It's my understanding that Clara and the women of her family do not invite the fathers in for the birth. You'll just have to wait outside. I will call you as soon as it's time to meet your new child. Now, along with you!"

Clara continued to labor throughout the afternoon. Finally, late in the day, Charlotte said, "All right, I need one more big push."

With that, Clara Walker delivered a beautiful baby boy. He had Clara's jet-black hair and dark eyes. And, Charlotte asserted, the baby had Stan's nose and smile. "Of course, it's hard to tell so soon," she admitted.

She swaddled the newborn and handed the baby to Clara. "There's just a bit more 'clean up' to do, and then I'll call Stan in."

Stan Walker was in love all over again. "Clara, I'd like to name him after your grandpa and my pa."

The new mother smiled. "John Running Bear Walker is a fine name," Clara said.

"Thank you, Clara and Stan, for asking me to be part of your blessed event," Charlotte said. She touched the baby on his nose, "Welcome to the world, John Running Bear Walker." With that, the baby started wailing.

"What's wrong?" Stan said, sounding worried.

Both women laughed. "You'll get used to that cry, Stan," Charlotte said. "I believe your son is hungry." Stan handed the new baby to Clara, and the crying ceased immediately.

Because it was already dark, the Walkers convinced Charlotte to stay overnight. "I insist," Stan said. "I've heard wolves out there at night, and this time of year they're mighty hungry."

"Fine," Charlotte said. "It gives me some time to hold that new baby."

The Walkers and Charlotte made it through the night with only two interruptions. It seemed that Bear Walker – his father insisted on calling the boy "Bear" – had a very healthy appetite.

When Charlotte arrived back at the soddy, Lizzy was waiting for news.

"It's a boy!" Charlotte called as she unsaddled her horse. "A fine baby boy with black hair like his mama. They've named him John Running Bear Walker. Stan is already calling him 'Bear.'"

"Bear Walker. I like it. It's the best of both worlds." Lizzy assessed her sister. "Did you get any sleep last night, Char?"

"Some. But midwifing always gives me energy. I love delivering babies!"

"Good. You might be delivering a baby calf today. I want to spend the day plowing while the ground is still soft, so please keep an eye on Daisy. She's showing signs, and this is only her second calf."

Lizzy was correct. Daisy was already in labor when Charlotte entered the barn a while later. Even though everything seemed normal, Charlotte decided to be "on call." She carried a chair, a lamp, and some mending out to the barn in case she needed to assist. When Lizzy led the oxen into the barn later that afternoon, she saw that the new calf had arrived.

"It's a bull calf," Charlotte said. "Daisy didn't need any help, and the calf has already had his first milk."

Lizzy inspected the newborn calf and decided he would be a good addition to the herd.

"Now I *am* tired," Charlotte declared. "Giving birth – even watching it – is exhausting!"

Lizzy laughed and said, "And plowing virgin sod is a walk in the park."

"We both deserve a day off tomorrow. What do you say to a trip to town?" Charlotte asked her sister.

"I'd say someone is missing their beau," Lizzy teased. "But yes, I'd like a trip to Shady Bluffs. That's a great idea, Char."

Charlotte and Lizzy were up before sunrise. "Let's take the wagon," Charlotte suggested. "We can stock up on flour, sugar, and cooking spices."

"Don't forget coffee!" Lizzy said. "I've already gathered the eggs and fed the animals. Let's hitch up the wagon."

As the sisters drove the wagon to town, they were treated to the pinks and lavenders of a Dakota sunrise. The fluffy clouds drifted on the horizon as the morning sun rose in the east.

"It's breathtaking," said Charlotte.

"Morning is my favorite time of day," Lizzy agreed.

Their first stop in Shady Bluffs was at Luke's blacksmith shop.

The double-wide barn doors to the shop were open to let in the spring air. "Good morning, ladies," Luke said when he saw the wagon pull up.

"It is a beautiful morning, isn't it?" Charlotte said.

"It is now," Luke said with a glint in his steel gray eyes. "Come on in, ladies. I have coffee on the stove."

Over coffee, Luke filled in the sisters on town news, including the news about Doc Stone.

"I heard he has pneumonia. It's not good," Luke said.

"I saw a lot of pneumonia in the war," said Charlotte. "Who is treating him?"

"Betsy Tomlinson. She owns the diner in town. Betsy's been bringing him hot meals. She's keeping an eye on him, but she's not a doctor," replied Luke. "I was going to ride out to your place to see if you could check on him."

"I'll go over there now," Charlotte said. "Good thing I always bring my medical bag with me." She collected her satchel from the wagon and crossed the street to Doc Stone's office.

Just as the first time she'd visited the doctor's office, the bell jingled upon her entrance. A weak voice from the back room said, "No doctoring today."

"That's why I'm here, Doc," Charlotte said as she found her way to the doctor's residence in the back of the building. "It's me – Charlotte Ward. We met a few months ago. I heard you're feeling poorly."

Doc Stone coughed. Charlotte immediately recognized the phlegmy cough as a symptom of pneumonia. "I came here to help you. Do you mind if I listen to your lungs?"

Short of breath, he simply shook his head to indicate he didn't mind.

Charlotte heard the familiar wheezing and discovered he was also running a high temperature.

"No need to diagnose, Miss Ward. It's pneumonia," Doc Stone said.

"I believe you're right," she concurred. "I saw a lot of soldiers with pneumonia when I worked in the field hospitals."

"Short of draining the fluid from my lungs, there's not much you can do," the doctor said.

"Yes. I've seen the procedure done, but I've never done it."

"I've done it, but it's too late for that," Doc Stone said.

"All right. I can keep you comfortable and stay with you."

"Thank you, my girl."

Charlotte familiarized herself with Doc Stone's medical supplies. She made a pot of peppermint tea for him and administered a small dose of laudanum. After he fell into a more restful sleep, she returned to Luke's blacksmith shop.

"Lizzy is at the mercantile," Luke told Charlotte. Then he stepped closer and pulled her to him. Charlotte had anticipated the kiss and eagerly put her arms around his neck. They kissed full on the mouth, a deep kiss filled with love and longing.

"I've missed you, Charlie," Luke murmured as he began kissing her ear. Charlotte ran her fingers through Luke's thick hair.

"Hmmm, I've missed you, too," she said.

Reluctantly, they pulled apart. "I'll be in town for a while, taking care of Doc Stone," Charlotte said.

"Is that good news?" Luke asked.

"I'm afraid not," replied Charlotte.

"What's not good news?" Lizzy asked as she joined Luke and Charlotte. She had been waiting outside the shop for the "right time" to enter.

"Doc Stone is not doing well," Charlotte said. "I've promised him that I'll stay to take care of him."

Lizzy nodded. "That's the right thing to do, Char. I'll need to take the horse and wagon back home. Will you be all right without a horse?"

"She can use one of mine," Luke offered. "I have Rusty and the two horses I brought from the ranch."

"This is certainly your week for doctoring, Charlotte," Lizzy observed. "Two babies and now a doctor with pneumonia."

"Two babies?" Luke questioned.

"Oh, I'll tell you about it later," Charlotte promised. She turned to her sister, "You'd best be on your way back home before it gets dark. Remember, there's a shotgun under the seat in case you run into wolves or coyotes…or worse."

Lizzy chuckled. "I can take care of myself, Char. Didn't I survive the Bushwhackers and Jayhawkers?" She hugged her sister. "We're both pretty self-sufficient, I'd say."

Looking at Luke, Lizzy sternly said, "But you, sir, you take care of my sister."

"Yes, ma'am," he answered with a smile.

Over the next few days, Charlotte spent very little time with Luke. When she wasn't caring for Doc Stone, she was taking care of Doc Stone's patients.

A bartender from the Prairie Rose came in with a nasty cut he'd received in a bar fight. Charlotte stitched up the gash and gave him an ointment to take home. "Keep it clean, and if it gets red and hot, come back right away," she told her patient.

A homesteader west of town rode in with a badly burned arm and shoulder. When Charlotte asked what caused the burn, the patient could not – or would not – say. She suspected he had been burned in a still explosion while making moonshine. Charlotte treated the worst burns with a poultice and wrapped the injury with a clean bandage.

In the evenings, Luke would come by the doctor's office to keep Charlotte company or invite her to dinner.

"How's he doing today?" Luke asked on the third day Charlotte had been in Shady Bluffs. They were in the front office while Doc Stone slept fitfully in his back room.

She shook her head. When he touched a wisp of curl that had escaped her hair net, Charlotte leaned her face into his hand.

"Charlie," was all he said. He pulled her into his lap and covered her mouth with his. They stayed that way for several minutes, holding each other and enjoying the nearness of each other.

Doc Stone's coughing broke up their embrace. Charlotte extricated herself from Luke's arms and left to check on her patient. Luke stayed in the front of the office.

Charlotte reappeared, looking devastated and defeated.

"He's gone," she said.

"He was a good man. The people of Shady Bluffs relied on Doc Stone."

"He gave me instructions to follow if he died," Charlotte said. "We need to call on the minister. Pastor Hess will take care of the arrangements."

Luke left to fetch the minister. By the time Luke and the minister arrived, Charlotte had tidied up the room where Doc Stone had lived and died.

Pastor Hess assured Charlotte that Doc Stone was in good hands and thanked her for caring for the physician in his final days.

"I wish I could have done more," Charlotte said. "He and I both knew that pneumonia can be deadly. I saw a lot of soldiers die from it during the war."

"You were a doctor in the war?" Pastor Hess asked.

"That's where Charlie – uh, Miss Ward and I met," Luke offered. "In a field hospital after the Battle of Springfield."

"I didn't realize you had medical training," the pastor replied. "The town is going to need a new doctor."

"She treated Doc Stone's patients while he was ailing," Luke said. "And before she came to town this week, she delivered the Walker baby."

"Would you be interested in filling Doc Stone's place?" the pastor asked.

Charlotte was taken aback. "But I'm not…" she began.

Before she could refuse, Luke said, "She's homesteading east of here…but she could make it work."

"Luke…"

"Talk it over with Lizzy," Luke suggested.

The pastor said, "We'll pray on your decision, Miss..er..Doctor Ward." Then, he and another parishioner helped move Doc Stone's body to the church for funeral preparations.

After they'd left, Charlotte rounded on Luke. "Luke Jameson! You know that I don't have a medical degree. What are you thinking?"

"That's just a piece of paper, Charlie. If it makes you feel better, we can let people know that. And if you're still not comfortable with it after a time," he looked long and hard at her, then finished his sentence, "you can call it quits. But that's not the Charlie Ward I know.

"You'd be good for this town," he continued. "And the town would be good for you. You've said it yourself that you're not a sodbuster. Lizzy can work her claim, and I'll help you work yours part-time. You can live in town half of the year and on the claim the other half."

"Well…" she said.

"What do you say, Doctor Ward?" He framed her face with his large hands and kissed her.

After-Action Report – Brandy Station Encampment
Winter 1863-64

After the Union Army's unsuccessful advance against the Army of Northern Virginia during the Mine Run Campaign, General George Meade withdrew his forces to a winter encampment at Brandy Station. More than 100,000 cold and tired soldiers occupied Culpeper and Fauquier counties in Virginia from December 1, 1863, to early May 1864. When the roads dried up and temperatures warmed up, the Union army left its winter quarters to begin the bloody Overland Campaign.

Chapter 23: Spring 1864
Shady Bluffs

Just as Luke had suggested, the sisters discussed the idea of Charlotte assuming Doc Stone's medical practice.

"I love being a farmer," Lizzy said. "But you – you've always been a healer, Char. This is your chance to follow that dream."

So, Charlotte split her time between the claims at Medicine Creek and the town. Lizzy did not begrudge her sister the opportunity.

Lizzy loved the feel of Dakota dirt. It was black and loamy. It was different from the red soil in Missouri. Not better – just different. Last year, she had come to love the earthy smell of her "Dakota dirt." It was good for growing, and every spring she anticipated a bountiful harvest in the fall.

She had already plowed last year's corn fields and put an additional twenty acres under the plow. Following Doc Stone's death, Charlotte returned from Shady Bluffs to help with spring chores. There was always a lot of work on the farm, but especially in the spring.

Today, Lizzy would plant her garden. She had big plans for her household garden. As much as she loved seeing acre upon acre of ripening corn, there was something more personal, more intimate with a kitchen garden. This garden plot, which straddled both claims, was larger than her garden in Missouri had been.

It was a warm April day, perfect for planting. Lizzy had raked and hoed the garden plot, and it was now ready for planting. Of course, she would plant a variety of root plants, including potatoes, turnips, beets, radishes, carrots, and onions. There would also be peas, beans, squash, and corn.

Lizzy spent the better part of the day creating furrows and planting the seeds she had saved from last fall. When she had completed her planting for the day, Lizzy hitched up the wagon and led the horse to the creek to fill water barrels. As she approached, she could hear the laughter and convivial conversations of her neighbors, the Lakota women from the nearby camp.

Since the incident with the lost cows, Lizzy and Charlotte had made it a practice to be more neighborly with the Lakota. They occasionally visited the Lakota camp and brought bread or muffins. In turn, several of the Lakota women had stopped by Lizzy and Charlotte's home. They brought beautifully beaded bands and bags as gifts for the sisters.

The language lessons from Clara helped Charlotte and Lizzy communicate with their neighbors.

"Hah-ue," Lizzy said in greeting to the women. They responded by waving. The little girl called Blue Bird approached Lizzy. She was holding an iridescent shell. Lizzy smiled and said,

"Wašté – pretty."

Blue Bird nodded and repeated, "Pretty." It was Lizzy's turn to nod in agreement.

Lizzy helped the women forage for wild asparagus, which they shared with her. Then, the women and Blue Bird left for their camp, and Lizzy finished filling her water barrels.

On her way back to the farm, Lizzy mused about the people she and Charlotte had met since arriving last year, like the Walkers, Isabell Vaughn, and their Lakota neighbors.

And now that Charlotte was Shady Bluffs' town doctor, she was meeting a lot more people. Suddenly, Lizzy felt isolated out on the frontier, a feeling she had never experienced in Missouri. She resolved to make an effort to meet more people.

But, she told herself, *it would have to wait until she had finished spring planting.*

Charlotte was cooking dinner when Lizzy returned from the creek. Lizzy was cheered to see her sister. It helped her shake off the feeling of isolation.

"I didn't expect to see you again so soon. You were just here the day before yesterday," Lizzy said when she entered Charlotte's soddy. "Here, I have fresh asparagus for dinner."

"Thank you. I thought you would be too busy planting to go foraging," Charlotte said.

"I went to the creek for water. Blue Bird, Dancing Girl, Evening Star, and some of the other Lakota women were there," Lizzy said. "You know, I didn't realize how alone I feel out here. I've decided I need to meet more people."

Charlotte cocked her head and looked at her younger sister. "Is this the Lizzy who always said she enjoyed her 'alone time'?"

"I'll never be the gad-about that you are, Char. You thrive when you're with new people. I prefer to spend my evenings with a good book and Butter in my lap." She patted the cat at her feet.

"Come to town with me next time. The room at the back of the doctor's office is large enough for both of us."

"That would be nice. Thank you for the invitation," Lizzy said.

"You're always welcome, you know." Charlotte changed subjects, "What chores will we have tomorrow? Put me to work."

Together, the sisters planned improvements for their claims. "We need a well," Lizzy said. "It's fine to fetch water from the creek when the weather is warm, but I want our water closer."

"Agreed," Charlotte said. "And I want a root cellar. I saw the size of your – of our garden. We're going to need a root cellar to hold the bounty you're growing." After some discussion, they agreed to hire someone to dig the well and the root cellar.

"Do we have enough in savings to pay for it?" Lizzy asked.

"Mmm, I think we can barter for some of it," Charlotte suggested. "But we'll need to go to Yankton to look for hired help."

They decided to go to the "big city" the following week. Charlotte went into Shady Bluffs to check on patients and to let Luke know their plans. When she approached Doc Stone's office, she noticed there was a new sign hanging above the door.

"C. B. Ward – Doctor & Surgeon" was painted in white letters on a large wooden sign.

She stood in the street, mouth agape, looking up at the sign when Luke approached. "My Ma would say, 'Close your mouth before a bug flies in.'" He pointed at the sign and said, "It was time, Charlie. What do you think?"

"C. B. certainly avoids telling people that the doctor is a woman," she replied.

"Shouldn't make a lick of difference," he said.

"To some people it will," she countered.

"Then they don't deserve to see Dr. Ward," he answered. He picked her up and carried her inside the doctor's office.

"What are you doing? Put me down!" she said with a laugh.

"Carrying you across the threshold," Luke said as he set her on her feet.

"That's a tradition for newlyweds," she pointed out.

"I'm changing the tradition." Luke pulled Charlotte into an embrace and kissed her. As they kissed, Charlotte realized she had missed having Luke's arms around her.

"It's good to have you back in town," he said between kisses.

"I'm glad to be back in town." She returned the kisses, then flipped the sign in the doorway to "The Doctor Is In."

"Tell me what's new," Charlotte said.

"I got a letter from Nellie," he said. "There's more fallout from Quantrill's raid on Lawrence last summer. Seems they wintered in Texas, but there was a lot of fighting and jockeying for leadership. They broke into a bunch of smaller gangs."

"Is that good or bad?" Charlotte asked.

"Not sure yet. They're not as big, but there are more of them to make trouble. Guess we'll have to wait and see."

"What about news in Shady Bluffs?" she said.

"There's talk about measles in some of the outposts," he answered. "Most likely came with a wagon train that passed through a while back."

Charlotte considered this. "I had measles as a child, so did Lizzy and Max. Mama kept us out of school even after the spots were gone. It's very contagious. Where did you say it was reported?"

Luke filled her in on the details while Charlotte took inventory of her medical supplies. "Lizzy and I are going to Yankton to find someone to dig a well and a root cellar. While we're there, I want to stock up on medicine."

"I promised I'd help out at the farm. I could dig the well," Luke offered.

She considered. "That would be much appreciated, Luke. But I don't want to take you away from your business."

"The horses can wait another week for new shoes," he said. "I'm caught up on farm equipment repairs, so I could ride back with you."

"And I can wait to restock my pharmacy," she said.

Luke loaded his extra horses with the equipment necessary to do the job: shovels, picks, and buckets, along with posts to frame the well.

They arrived at the soddies at twilight. Charlotte called out to her sister, "Lizzy, I found someone to dig our well."

Lizzy wasn't surprised that Luke had volunteered. She welcomed the riders and said, "You're just in time for dinner."

It had been a while since Luke had visited the claims. He entertained Lizzy and Charlotte with anecdotes about the townspeople and the homesteaders who came to town. "It's a growing city," Luke told them. "Why, three more homesteaders staked claims just last month," he said.

"Did you meet any of them?" Lizzy asked.

"Sure did. They all needed a blacksmith to mend tools or shoe their horses and oxen."

He described the new homesteaders in detail. "One family had twelve kids – twelve of 'em. And I thought I came from a big family! There was another family with two young'uns and another on the way. And then there was a single gent from Illinois or Wisconsin. He's homesteading south of here, if I'm not mistaken."

"It is so good to get news from the outside world," Lizzy said.

"Lizzy is feeling a bit isolated out here now that I'm in town more. We're still planning to get away to Yankton – the big city," Charlotte said.

After dinner, Lizzy insisted on clearing the dishes. "You two go for a walk," she ordered.

The evening sky was bright with a full moon and a blanket of stars. "The heavens unfold on the prairie in a way that seems to never end," Charlotte observed. "It makes me feel like I'm part of something so much larger."

"For me, it's a feeling that I'm not closed in. There aren't any hills and nary a tree to block the view." Luke caught her hand and squeezed it. "It's a good feeling."

Back at the soddies, they sat on a bench and listened to the night sounds: crickets chirping, the wind whispering in the prairie grasses, and an owl's occasional "whoosh" as it hunted.

Charlotte yawned and leaned into Luke. "It's been a long day," she said. She took his hand and led him into her home.

As she unbuttoned her blouse, Luke asked, "Can I do that?" Slowly, Luke undressed Charlotte, kissing her shoulders, her breasts, and her stomach. He placed her on the bed and then quickly undressed and joined her.

Charlotte moved her hands over Luke's strong, muscled back. He rained kisses along her neck and down her breasts, all the while holding on to her hips as they came together as lovers. Charlotte fell asleep with her head on Luke's shoulder, a position that she had come to think of as her favorite place.

The next day dawned bright and sunny. When Charlotte awoke, Luke was already outside gathering his equipment and looking for a likely place to begin digging. Lizzy was with Luke, pointing to a spot for the new well.

"We could place it on the boundary line," Lizzy was saying. "But if one of us sold our claim, that could cause problems. I'd like it closer to the barn, which puts it on my claim." She looked up to see Charlotte joining them. "Charlotte, what do you think about that location? It's not on your claim…"

"That makes perfect sense for watering the animals, Lizzy. We can put the root cellar by my soddy if that makes you feel better." The sisters agreed to that compromise.

Because they were close to the creek, the water level was higher than in other parts of the prairie. By the end of the day, Luke had struck water.

"That's a good day's work, I'd say," Luke said as he climbed out of the large hole. "Tomorrow, I'll frame it up and add the river stones you've collected."

That evening, everyone was so exhausted from the physical labor needed to dig a well that Luke nearly fell asleep at the dinner table.

"Let me make up the bed in the common room," Charlotte offered. Luke did not object.

The following day, Luke finished work on the well, and they celebrated. Charlotte stuffed and baked a hen for the feast. Lizzy set the table with Mama's good china.

"Here's to us!" Lizzy said as she lifted her glass in a toast. "And here's to a year on the Dakota frontier!"

"Oh, my," Charlotte said. "It's gone so fast. Has it really been a year?"

"Here's to the Ward sisters, making a new life for themselves," Luke said.

Once again, Lizzy shooed her sister and Luke out the door, saying, "It's a beautiful evening. Don't waste it! Now go."

It took little persuading for Luke and Charlotte to follow Lizzy's orders.

Arm in arm, they walked toward the setting sun. "It's like a painting, isn't it," Charlotte said of the sky.

"It's gonna be hard for me to leave tomorrow," Luke said.

"Because you'll miss these sunsets?" Charlotte teased him.

Luke stopped, stepped in front of Charlotte, and framed her face with his large, calloused hands. He looked into her dark, dark brown eyes and said, "No, because I'll miss these eyes, I'll miss these lips… I'll miss you, Charlie. I know you have plans to live on the claim and in town, but we should talk about that. We need to make this work," he made a circling motion with his hand,

"Give me time, Luke."

They stood together on the prairie, holding each other and kissing. When they broke apart, they returned to Charlotte's soddy. But they didn't sleep.

In the morning, Luke packed up his horses. Charlotte and Lizzy thanked him again for digging the well and waved goodbye. Luke got halfway down the path, turned his horse around, and galloped back to the yard. Leaning down from his saddle, he gave Charlotte one more goodbye kiss.

"We need to talk," he said. Charlotte nodded mutely.

As he rode away, Lizzy looked in askance at her sister, but Charlotte just shook her head.

Having a working well was a luxury for the sisters. Next on their "to-do" list was a root cellar. Lizzy had also added a smokehouse to the growing list.

Charlotte decided to establish regular office hours in her role as Shady Bluffs' doctor. She would see patients with non-emergency medical issues two days a week. That left her time for her chores on the claim, as well as handling emergency calls. On her way to town in early May, she crossed Medicine Creek as usual. Down the way, she saw several women from the Lakota camp filling water pouches. She rode over to greet them.

To her alarm, she saw they had the tell-tale rash that might be measles. She had heard stories about the devastating effects of measles, chicken pox, and influenza on native people, and she knew this was serious.

Quickly, she dismounted and helped the women fill their water bags. Then Charlotte asked if she could carry the bags for the women. They gratefully accepted the offer.

In the Lakota camp, Charlotte immediately sought out Evening Star, the Lakota medicine woman. Charlotte wasn't worried about being infected herself since she had survived the disease as a child and was now immune to measles.

Using the Lakota words she had learned from Clara, Charlotte understood that many members of the tribe had "rotting face sickness" – the Lakota name for measles. Apparently, a member of the camp had an encounter with someone from the wagon train who was infected.

She knew there were no medicines to cure or treat measles. Instead, she and Evening Star quarantined patients with symptoms and encouraged rest and plenty of fluids.

As Charlotte went from tipi to tipi to determine the severity of each patient's illness, she decided she couldn't handle this alone. She needed Lizzy's help.

Finding Spotted Horse, who did not appear to have measles, she asked if he would bring a note to her sister.

Within an hour, Lizzy arrived at the camp, bringing chicken soup ingredients. Together, the sisters nursed their Lakota neighbors. Charlotte made soup for her patients, while Lizzy helped spoon-feed some of the weakest ones.

On the second day in camp, Blue Bird's mother, Dancing Girl, asked Charlotte to look in on her daughter.

The little girl was very weak and was running a high temperature. Charlotte stayed with Blue Bird throughout the night, applying cool cloths to help reduce the fever. On the third day, Blue Bird's temperature came down, and she could sit up on her own.

While Blue Bird's recovery was something to celebrate, four members of the Lakota band did not survive the disease. Charlotte and Lizzy heard wailing from several tipis while they were in camp. They joined in mourning with their neighbors.

Charlotte stayed in the Lakota camp for five days. When she determined that there were no new cases of measles in the camp and that the remainder of her patients were recovering, she bid a farewell to Evening Star, Dancing Girl, Blue Bird, Spotted Horse, and the other Lakota she had come to know during the outbreak.

After-Action Report – Battle of the Wilderness
May 5-7, 1864

The Battle of the Wilderness was Ulysses S. Grant's first major engagement after being named General-in-Chief of the Union forces. It occurred over three days, from May 5 to 7, 1864, in Spotsylvania County, Virginia. More than 100,000 Union soldiers faced off against General Robert E. Lee's troops, which numbered just over 60,000 men.

The battle's outcome was inconclusive. The Union army suffered more than 17,500 casualties, while some 13,000 Confederates died in the battle. Despite the losses,

Grant refused to order a retreat, having promised President Abraham Lincoln he would not halt his army's advance.

Chapter 24: Summer 1864
Shady Bluffs

The War continued in the eastern theater throughout the summer of 1864.

In Missouri, the Bushwhackers, led by William Quantrill, "Bloody Bill" Anderson, and George Todd, terrorized Union sympathizers while getting a taste for horse stealing and train robbery.

In Dakota Territory, Lizzy's love of the land was transforming the rich prairie soil into productive farmland. Thanks to timely rains, the corn fields flourished. At the same time, the vegetable gardens promised an abundant harvest in the fall.

In Shady Bluffs, Charlotte's medical practice grew as people came to rely on her common-sense advice and steady surgical hands. Luke Jameson was also becoming a fixture in Shady Bluffs. Luke's belief that people would always need horses and oxen shoed was correct. His business thrived as more and more homesteaders moved into the Dakota frontier.

Along with the homesteaders, shopkeepers, bankers, and saloon owners came the outlaws. Former Bushwhackers and army deserters from both sides of the conflict were drawn to the frontier's sparsely policed towns. On a particularly hot, dry day in August, a group of these men rode into Shady Bluffs. Their first stop was the doctor's office.

Charlotte heard the familiar ding of the doorbell and entered the front office to find four men filing in. Shadow, who often came to town with Charlotte, raised his head and gave the men a menacing look.

"Easy, Shadow," she told the dog. "Can I help you?" she asked the men. She assumed the leader – whoever he was – would speak for the group.

"We're lookin' for the doc. Joe here took a bullet in the gut," said a tall man dressed in a worn duster and brown slouch hat. He pointed to a man supported by two other men. The injured man had a large blood stain just above his belted trousers. He and the two men holding him wore the gray kepi caps associated with Confederate soldiers. All the men had beards and long, disheveled hair.

Charlotte assessed the group. "Bring him into the exam room," she instructed.

"Is the doc back there?" asked the first man.

"I will be in a moment," she answered. "I'm C.B. Ward."

"Never heard of a lady doctor," mumbled one of the men holding the bleeding man.

Charlotte was used to this attitude from strangers. "I'm the only medical practitioner in town, gentlemen. If you'd rather have someone else treat your friend, I'd suggest Yankton. It's a half-day ride to the east." She eyed the injured man and said, "He might make it there."

Joe moaned, which forced his three companions to make a snap decision. "Do what the lady doctor says, boys," the spokesman said. They half-dragged, half-walked the wounded man into the exam room as Charlotte had requested.

Charlotte peeled away Joe's bloody vest and unbuttoned his shirt to examine the bullet wound. She could tell that the injury had occurred a day or two ago. "How long ago was he shot?" she asked.

"We was ridin' through…" one of the men began to answer.

"It was a couple of days ago," the leader interrupted.

"Hmmm," Charlotte said. "Looks like the bullet is still in there. You all can wait outside."

"Can't do that, lady," said the lead man.

"And why is that?" Charlotte inquired.

"Need to keep an eye on Joe…and to…to answer any questions you might have," came the reply.

This wasn't the first time a patient had been less than forthcoming, and Charlotte didn't really care.

"Well, it will get very crowded in here with all five of us. I'd suggest that you two," she indicated the men who had carried Joe into the office, "find your way to the saloon. Your friend here can stay with Joe."

The two drifters, as Charlotte had begun to think of them, agreed and left for the Prairie Rose Saloon.

Charlotte laid out her surgical tools: a scalpel, probe, retractor, and bullet forceps. "If you insist on staying, please stand over there," she told the last remaining man. "You can call me Doctor Charlie. What should I call you?"

"Name's Clay," he responded.

"First, Clay, I'm going to give Joe a dose of laudanum to relax him. It will make the procedure safe for … him and for me. Then I'll clean the wound, and I'll look for the bullet."

Clay grunted in agreement.

Once the laudanum had done its work, Charlotte went to work on her patient. The wound was dirty, and that concerned Charlotte. "Why didn't you get help sooner? I saw cleaner bullet wounds on the battlefields," she said.

"You were in the war?" Clay asked.

"Yes," she answered distractedly. Charlotte concentrated on probing for the lost bullet. At last, her instrument clicked on something foreign. "There you are!" she exclaimed.

She exchanged the probe for the bullet extractor and began to maneuver the bullet into position to remove it.

Joe began moaning again. "I can't give him more laudanum," she said to Clay. "You'll have to hold him still." Clay moved in and secured Joe's shoulders and upper torso.

It wasn't long until Clay heard the "clang" of the bullet hitting the metal tray. "Is that it?" he asked Charlotte.

"I'm going to open the incision a little wider and check for internal damage," she replied. "If the bullet nicked the bowels or an organ, we'll have more problems."

Using the scalpel, Charlotte quickly and competently opened the incision. Then, with the retractor, she inspected the tissue and organs.

"I'm not finding anything suspicious," she said. "I'll sew up the incision, but I'd like Joe to stay overnight just to make sure there's not any hemorrhaging."

"Any what?" Clay asked.

"Heavy bleeding. I want to make sure the wound is starting to heal. You can take him if you want, but it's against doctor's orders."

"You're a bossy one," Clay retorted.

Charlotte squinted her eyes. "I'm guessing you wouldn't say that to a male doctor." She threw up her hands and said, "It's up to you, but don't bring him back here if there are complications."

"If we leave him here, are you gonna babysit him all night?" Clay asked.

"I'll be on call if that's what you're asking," she said. "Help me move him to the bed against the wall."

"Fine. How much do I owe you?" said Clay.

Charlotte named her fee, and Clay paid in greenbacks. "Thank you," she said. "You and your friends can pick up Joe in the morning."

Clay left Charlotte's office just as Luke entered. Luke saw the patient in the exam room.

"What's that about?" he asked.

"Bullet wound," Charlotte answered. "They wouldn't say how, or where or when, so I'm guessing it was something illegal."

"I heard talk of drifters and deserters making their way up here. They're looking for work and for trouble."

"These men – there are four of them – are here for trouble," Charlotte surmised.

"None of my business," Luke said. "I'm here to take my favorite gal for dinner." He looked again at the patient in the other room, "Can you leave him for a while?"

"We'll have to make it a quick dinner, but yes, he'll be fine for a bit."

They had dinner at the new diner in town, and then Luke walked Charlotte back to her office. "Want me to stay the night in case your patient wakes up and gets belligerent?" he asked.

"Thank you, but I think I can handle it. Besides, I have Shadow to back me up," Charlotte said. "He's pretty protective."

It was an uneventful night. In the morning, the three comrades returned to collect Joe. Charlotte gave Joe a clean dressing for the wound and told him to drink plenty of fluids – water preferably – and watch the incision for infection.

Joe's buddies helped him mount his horse, and the four rode out of town.

After Charlotte cleaned up the office, she walked over to the blacksmith shop. Inside, she noticed several horses waiting to be shod. There was farm equipment, along with kitchen pots and pans, that required repairs.

Luke was finishing filing the back hoof of a large, black stallion.

"Who does he belong to?" Charlotte asked, referring to the stallion.

"The territorial sheriff," Luke said. "I think he might be on the trail of your patient and his associates."

"Wouldn't surprise me," Charlotte answered. "They left this morning."

"Which way were they headed?"

"I'm the last person they'd tell," she said. "What did they do?"

"Robbed a bank in Nebraska," Luke said.

"They're long gone now," she said. "I just came by to let you know I'm going back to the farm this morning."

"Not without this," Luke said. He pulled her into an embrace and kissed her soundly.

"And that's the other reason I came by," Charlotte said with a smile.

On the way back to the claims, Charlotte stopped at the Lakota camp. She enjoyed talking with the women and adored watching Blue Bird play with Shadow. The little girl had taught the large dog to fetch, and the two could play for hours.

Charlotte arrived at the farm midafternoon. Lizzy had finished milking the cows and had let them out into the pasture to graze.

"I wondered if you'd be coming back today," Lizzy said.

"I'd planned to return yesterday, but a patient with a bullet wound came in. Luke thinks they – he was with three other men – might have been bank robbers."

Lizzy shivered. "Did you know that when you treated him?"

"I suspected they were up to no good, but it's not my place to judge. I removed the bullet and sent them on their way. What have you been up to?"

Lizzy smiled. "Oh, just watching the corn grow."

"That reminds me," Charlotte said. "I found someone to help dig a root cellar for us. Jerry Tomlinson, he's Betsy's husband, said he'd do the work. He'll bring his own tools."

"When can he start?" Lizzy asked.

"I told him I'd ask you first, but if you approve, I'll ask him to come by next week when I'm in town again."

"Good," said Lizzy. "We'll have vegetables to pickle and store soon." Lizzy thought a moment and said, "Do you think he could build us a smokehouse? Remember Papa's smoked hams? Can't you just taste it?"

"Can't hurt to ask. I bet Betsy might like to put your Missouri hams on her restaurant's menu."

After dinner, Charlotte said, "I feel like going for a walk. How about you, or are you too tired."

"I never tire of the prairies, especially this time of year," Lizzy said.

Charlotte whistled to Shadow, and the three headed west toward the setting sun.

After-Action Report – Sherman's March to Atlanta

Summer 1864

General William T. Sherman's march to Atlanta, Georgia, began in early May 1864 when he faced off against General Joseph Johnston near Chattanooga, Tennessee. Through a series of skirmishes and assaults, the Union troops pushed the Rebel armies to retreat to the fortified city of Atlanta in July. Sherman's strategy was to capture Atlanta by cutting its railroad lines and starving the Confederate soldiers as well as the citizens of Atlanta. The last line was cut on August 31st, forcing Confederate Lieutenant John General Hood to abandon Atlanta on September 1, 1864. The city surrendered to Union forces the next day.

The Northern Armies lost 34,500 soldiers; approximately 35,000 Confederate soldiers died in the four-month campaign. The March to Atlanta was a major victory for the Union and helped assure President Lincoln's re-election in November 1864.

Chapter 25: September 1864
Medicine Creek Claim

Lizzy filled two baskets with fresh garden vegetables. She handed one to Charlotte, and she took the other basket.

"I think that should do it," she said. "I know how much Blue Bird and Dancing Girl love the potatoes and carrots from our garden."

"We could take the horses, but it's such a nice September day. Do you mind walking?" Charlotte asked.

As they walked toward the camp, they talked about their progress on the claims in the past year. The sisters and their Lakota neighbors had become especially close after the measles outbreak. Working side by side through those harrowing days and nights had formed a bond that all the women valued.

"I can't believe it's been a year and a half since we came to Dakota," Charlotte said. "It was good to come here. Once again, you were right, Lizzy."

"The ghosts are gone, Char," said Lizzy.

"Yes, we left them behind." She patted her sister's arm.

Up ahead, they could see the smoke from Lakota cooking fires. When they reached the camp, they saw members of the Medicine Creek band hurrying about.

Women were sharpening knives, men were packing ponies, and travois were waiting near the corral.

Seeing Evening Star by her tipi, Charlotte approached the older woman. "What is happening?" Charlotte asked.

"Tatanka," Evening Star answered. "Tatanka were seen by the great river. We go to hunt."

"You're going now?" Charlotte asked. The woman nodded as she continued her preparations.

"We brought vegetables," Lizzy said as she joined her sister and Evening Star. "Can we leave them in your tipi? Will you be returning here?"

"Yes. We will bring the meat back to dry." She pointed to drying racks behind her tipi.

"Soon, they will be heavy with meat," Evening Star said with a smile.

The sisters left their baskets of vegetables in Evening Star's tipi and wished their friends a good hunt.

"That would be so exciting to see a buffalo hunt!" Lizzy said as they returned home.

"Exciting and dangerous," Charlotte cautioned.

When they reached the farm, they saw Luke's horse tied to the fence post.

"Hello, stranger," Lizzy said. "It's been a while since you've been out here."

"Yes, what brings you?" Charlotte said. "You were so busy at the shop that I didn't think you could break away."

"Some things take precedence. I come bearing flowers…and the mail," Luke answered. "It's the least I could do for my favorite homesteaders."

He handed them bouquets of fall prairie flowers along with several letters.

"I also brought a couple of prairie chickens for dinner," he said. "They're dressed and in a pot inside."

"You are the perfect guest!" Charlotte said. "Let's get some lemonade and enjoy the September sun before we eat."

He carried the table and chairs outside, and the three of them enjoyed lemonade and chatted.

"We just came from the Lakota camp," Lizzy said. "They're getting ready for a buffalo hunt! Wouldn't that be exciting?"

"My sister is a thrill-seeker," Charlotte said teasingly.

"Who's the thrill-seeker? You're the one who went off to war, Char," replied Lizzy.

"Ladies, ladies, break it up," Luke said in jest. "So…buffalo? No one in town said anything about a buffalo herd nearby." He turned to Lizzy, "It would be exciting – but have you ever seen a full-grown buffalo up close? They're enormous. They make your cows look like toys."

Charlotte opened one of the letters that was addressed to both sisters. "This is from your sister Martha," she remarked.

"Yes, I received a letter from Ben and Martha, too," Luke said. "These came in the same bundle from my family. I thought the letter would be of interest."

Charlotte scanned the letter and then handed it to Lizzy. Lizzy read the letter, as well.

"So, what do you think?" Luke asked.

"If I understand it, your sister and her husband want to buy our family farm," Charlotte said.

"That's right," Luke said. "You never did sell it, just pulled up stakes and came here, isn't that right?"

"Yes," Lizzy said. "The war was making it hard to farm. And after the Bushwhackers and Jayhawkers shot up the house, well, it didn't seem like home anymore."

"And the ghosts," Charlotte murmured to herself.

Lizzy patted Charlotte's hand, then continued. "We still hold the deed to the farm, but since we were Unionists, we weren't sure we'd be able to keep the land if the Confederacy won. So, we didn't wait around for an offer," Lizzy shrugged.

"As I understand it, Ben – he fought on the Union side – receives a pension for his war injuries. They've been saving up and have some money for a down payment," Luke said. "Are you interested in selling?"

"Of course!" said Lizzy.

"Yes!" said Charlotte.

"It sounds unanimous," Luke said. "I was hoping you'd be willing to help them out. They've always wanted a farm of their own, and this would be a big help."

"Have they seen what they'd be buying?" Lizzy asked.

"Actually, they have," Luke said. "They rode up to St. Joe earlier this summer when I wrote that your farm might be available."

"You put this together for us?" Charlotte said. She leaned over and kissed him on the cheek. "Thank you."

"It's the least I could do for my favorite homesteaders," he said again.

They celebrated that evening with the prairie chickens Luke brought and fresh vegetables from the garden.

"That meal puts the diner to shame," Luke said as he pushed back from the table.

"I'll do the dishes with water from our very handy well. Why don't you two to take a stroll before the sun sets," Lizzy suggested.

Luke caught Charlotte's hand in his. This time, they walked toward the creek.

"I remember the first time I saw you out here," Luke said with a laugh. "You were trying to bathe that dog of yours in the creek."

She laughed at the thought. "I was a sight, wasn't I?"

"Yes, you were," he said softly in her ear. "It was a sight I'd longed to see for months."

She turned into his waiting arms, and they kissed.

Carefully, Luke laid Charlotte down on the mound of leaves, and then he joined her.

"Charlie," he whispered, "I love you."

"I love you, too, Luke," she responded.

They made love under the branches of the willow tree. Afterward, Luke said, "Marry me, Charlie."

Charlotte's eyes flew open. "Marriage? I always thought I'd be a spinster."

"Why on God's green earth would you ever think that?"

"Well, Papa used to tease me that I was too headstrong. And the boys at school said I wasn't pretty enough to be a girl."

"You *are* headstrong – but I'd say that you know your own mind. And those schoolboys, they must have been blind. You are the most beautiful woman I've ever known." He kissed her soundly to emphasize the point.

"You didn't answer my question. Will you marry me, Charlotte Ward?" Luke asked.

"Yes, Luke Jameson, I will marry you. There is nothing I'd love more than to marry you." She kissed him to seal the pledge.

"I'll still be the town doctor," Charlotte said.

"I wouldn't expect anything different, Charlie," said Luke. "It's getting dark. Best get back."

He pulled her up from the bed of leaves.

On returning to the claim, Charlotte said, "We'll have to tell Lizzy. I wonder what she'll say."

Luke just smiled.

Lizzy had already gone to bed by the time they returned to the soddies. "I guess the news will have to wait until breakfast," Charlotte said.

Luke no longer slept in the common room. Instead, he shrugged off his clothes and joined Charlotte in her narrow bed.

"The first thing I'm doing is making you a proper bed," Luke promised.

"Hmmm," Charlotte responded. "I like sleeping in your arms."

"Well, that doesn't have to change just because I'll have leg room."

Charlotte laughed softly and put her head on Luke's shoulder.

In the morning, Charlotte made coffee and brought a cup to Lizzy in her soddy.

"Good morning," she greeted her sister.

"Good morning to you," Lizzy said as she added a splash of fresh cream to the cup.

"I have – we have news for you," Charlotte began.

"It's about time!" Lizzy said. "I thought he'd never pop the question."

"What?" Charlotte said.

"Char, you two belong together," Lizzy replied. "Besides, Luke may have dropped a hint or two."

"But won't this change things here?" Charlotte asked. "The claim…my farm..."

"The claim was filed in your name, and since he's a Confederate soldier, he can't stake a claim through the Homestead Act anyway.

"And now, if Luke's sister and brother-in-law buy our farm in Missouri, we'll have money to pay off your claim if we have to. I'll keep working the farms full time. You can be the town doctor, just like you've always wanted," Lizzy said.

Charlotte hugged her sister and then wiped a tear from her eye. "I was worried that you…that you would be…"

Lizzy picked up the thought, "That I'd be hurt? Oh, Char, I'm so happy for you." And then she started crying, too.

That was when Luke walked in and saw the sisters hugging and crying. The look on his face made the two women stop crying and start laughing.

"Should I be worried?" he asked.

That question brought more laughter. Finally, Charlotte caught her breath long enough to say, "Lizzy has given her approval."

"Whew!" Luke said with a whistle. "I wasn't sure when I saw the two of you crying. I should have known better, what with three sisters of my own."

They spent the rest of the day making plans. The three discussed dates and decided that a fall wedding would be nice.

"Let's talk with Pastor Hess when I'm back in town," Charlotte suggested.

After-Action Report - Centralia Massacre
September 27, 1864

In a last-ditch effort to turn the tide, Confederate forces launched an invasion into northern Missouri in September 1864. Confederate General Sterling Price, the Missouri State Guard, and "Bloody Bill" Anderson joined forces to capture two key Missouri cities: St. Louis and Jefferson City. As part of the strategy, Anderson and his band of Bushwhackers engaged in a skirmish in Boone County. Anderson and his gang stopped a train outside of Centralia, Missouri. They then captured and executed twenty-four unarmed U.S. Army soldiers on September 27, 1864. They set fire to the train and left the civilian passengers to deal with the mutilated bodies.

The Centralia Massacre, as it became known, was an example of extreme violence that periodically characterized the Missouri-Kansas border war. Both Frank and Jesse James were among the guerrillas who took part in the massacre.

Chapter 26: Autumn 1864
Shady Bluffs

Luke walked into Charlotte's office in time to hear Doctor Charlie say, "Now, promise me you won't try any more 'trick riding' for a while." She spoke to a young boy, about ten or twelve, while the boy's mother looked on.

"Honestly, Doctor Charlie," the boy's mother said, "I don't know what gets into the heads of young boys!"

"It's a good thing they heal fast," Charlotte said. "Keep the splint on for at least three weeks – longer if you can. If the broken bone gives you any more problems, come back and I'll take another look at it."

"Thank you, doctor," the woman said.

"Doctor Charlie – I like the sound of that," Luke said. "But not as much as 'Mrs. Jameson.' Soon you'll be 'Doctor Charlie Jameson.' I'll have to update your office sign." He kissed her on the tip of her nose. "I'm here to escort you to the church. Pastor Hess is waiting for us."

Charlotte untied the full apron she wore when she worked. After she grabbed her shawl off the wall hook, Charlotte turned the sign on the door to "The Doctor Is Out."

Luke, Charlotte, and Pastor Gregor Hess selected a date for the wedding.

"Two weeks from Saturday would put the ceremony on October 22nd," Pastor Hess confirmed. "Now, who will be giving you away, Miss Ward?"

Without pausing to consider, Charlotte said, "That would be my sister, Elizabeth Ward."

The Lutheran pastor cleared his throat and said, "That's most unusual."

"You'll find that the Ward sisters are most unusual women, pastor," Luke said. He turned to his bride-to-be and said, "Lizzy is the perfect choice."

With the church plans completed, Luke returned to the blacksmith shop. Charlotte decided she needed to shop for the wedding. When she entered the Shady Bluffs Mercantile, Isabell Vaughn greeted her with, "I hear that congratulations are in order! Have you set a date, Charlotte?"

"We just did – October 22nd," Charlotte replied. "That's enough time to make a new dress, isn't it? I found a pattern in my Godey's Lady's Book that I'd like to try." Charlotte opened the July 1860 issue to a simple yet elegant dress with full sleeves and lace trim that ran from the V-shaped waistline to the hem. The trim made a square corner at the hemline and followed around the back of the dress hemline to the front again and up to the waist. The dress featured a long bow with matching lace trim on the back.

"It's beautiful!" Isabell exclaimed. She scanned the fabric on her shelves and said, "If you're partial to peach shades, this organdy fabric would be lovely on you."

Isabell pulled a length of fabric from the bolt and held it up for Charlotte to consider.

"It is pretty. What about the lace trim?" Charlotte asked.

"I can order that from the city," Isabell offered. "By the time you and Lizzy have the dress ready for a fitting, the lace will be here."

Charlotte was never one to fret over fashion decisions. "That's wonderful, Isabell. I'll take the peach organdy with me, along with thread and lining and such. I'd like Lizzy to have a new dress, too, but I don't know if we have time to sew two gowns."

Isabell tapped her chin with her index finger. "Blue is her color, isn't it?" She ran her hand across the bolts of fabric until she found a bolt of soft, blue wool. "I saw a pattern for a bolero jacket that would be perfect for this fabric."

"Bolero? I'm not certain I know what that is," Charlotte said.

Isabell pulled out her own issue of a new Godey's and found the page she was looking for. "See, it's a short jacket, open in the front. It's worn over another dress. Very stylish, and it wouldn't take long to sew."

Charlotte's eyes lit up at the suggestion. "Isabell, you're a marvel! Yes! Wrap up the blue wool."

Charlotte left the mercantile with an armful of packages and a heart bursting with excitement. Her first thought was to share her purchases with Luke; then she remembered that the groom shouldn't see the wedding dress before the ceremony.

She planned to return to the farm and needed to leave town soon. The days were shorter in October, and she didn't have Shadow to ride with her. She stopped at the post office and was pleased to find letters from Ben and Martha Fuller and from Luke's mother, Mary Jameson.

Before walking to Luke's shop, Charlotte read the letter from Martha, Luke's sister. She and her husband planned to move to the Ward farm in the spring, and they would send the money with Nellie.

With Nellie? Charlotte thought. *Why would Nellie bring the money?*

She decided the answer must be in the letter from Mary Jameson, but that letter was addressed to Luke.

Heading to the blacksmith shop, Charlotte crossed the street just in time to see several men entering the Prairie Rose Saloon. Charlotte recognized one of the men as Joe, the drifter with the gunshot wound she had treated in August.

Her first thought was, *looks like he recovered.* Then she recalled that a marshal had been looking for some outlaws when Joe, Clay, and the other two passed through Shady Bluffs. *I wonder what brings them back to town?* she thought.

"I'm headed home," she told Luke as she entered the blacksmith shop.

"Soon, this will be home," Luke said. He gathered her into his arms for a kiss. "We should add more living space behind the doctor's office."

"That's a good idea," she said distractedly.

"I thought you'd be more excited. Something's on your mind," he said as a statement rather than a question.

"Remember those drifters who came through town last summer? One of them had the gunshot wound. I think I just saw that man go into the Prairie Rose," she said.

"They're back?" Luke replied. "We really need a lawman out here."

"What would a lawman do? He can't arrest them for passing through."

"No, but he could keep an eye on them. I think I'll go have a beer."

"Before you go and get yourself into trouble, I have news from Missouri."

She waved the letters and said, "Your sister and her husband are moving to the farm by St. Joe. But Martha said something odd…that Nellie would be bringing us the money."

Luke frowned in confusion.

She handed Mary Jameson's letter to Luke and said, "Maybe this letter from your mother can explain why Nellie is coming."

While Charlotte waited, Luke read the letter from his mother. Then he read the newspaper clipping she had enclosed. As he put the letter and clipping back in the envelope, he said, "Seems like Nellie is making good on her promise. When I left the ranch to come up here, her last words to me were, 'I'm coming to visit you.' I laughed it off at the time. But the real reason, Ma says, is that the Bushwhacker attacks have gotten a lot worse and closer to the ranch. Ma wants Nellie somewhere safe – like Shady Bluffs."

"Did someone in your family get hurt?" Charlotte asked.

"No," Luke said. "But Bill Anderson's gang stopped a train in Centralia and murdered twenty-four unarmed Union soldiers. They're calling it the 'Centralia Massacre.' Ma thinks that's too close for comfort, and she's shipping her baby up here for a spell."

"The Bushwhackers are robbing trains now?" Charlotte exclaimed. "They always were on the other side of the law, but this is terrifying. I understand why your mother is worried about Nellie – she's her youngest child. You'd best write and let her know that Nellie is welcome. In fact, have you told your family that we're getting married?"

"I planned to, but, well, I've been busy."

"You'd best write to them today. And find out when Nellie will be arriving," Charlotte suggested.

"We're not even married yet, and you're already bossing me around," he teased.

"I'm the oldest sister – I've had plenty of practice," Charlotte teased back. "And while I'm at it, if you're still planning to go to the saloon, please don't get into trouble, Luke."

"Wouldn't dream of it," he said.

"I love you," she replied. With that endearment, she kissed him and said goodbye.

He watched her walk down the dusty street to her office and thought, *What a woman! What a woman! I am one lucky man.*

The Prairie Rose Saloon was doing a brisk business for an afternoon. Luke spotted the four drifters playing poker at a corner table.

Luke watched the poker game from the bar as he nursed a beer. Finally, he approached the table. "Can anybody join?"

"We'll take your money if you're willin'," said one of the men.

Luke sat down and put coins on the table. "Deal me in, boys," he said.

Two of the drifters still wore their Confederate kepi caps, which gave Luke an opening. Summoning his best Missouri drawl, Luke said, "I had one of those. Lost my kepi at Gratiot Street Prison."

"You was in prison?" asked Clay. Luke had determined that Clay was the leader of this gang.

"Yep. I served under General Marmaduke at Cape Girardeau. Got captured and sent to Gratiot." He shook his head, remembering the horrors of the army prison.

"After a few months, they paroled me. Overcrowding. I went home to Boone County for a spell, and now I'm here." He shrugged as if the details didn't matter.

"Damn war. Damn Yankees," said Joe.

"Keep it down, Joe," warned Clay. "Don't know who's listening here." Clay turned to Luke and said in a low voice, "Boone County is sesech country."

Luke nodded. "I served under Braxton Bragg, then Marmaduke. Two of my brothers joined up with the Missouri State Guard. My oldest brother fought for General Forrest in Tennessee. Where'd you boys serve?"

"Here and there," Clay said evasively. "We was in the Guard, too."

"It got too hot down there, if you know what I mean," said the man named Tucker. Luke wasn't sure if that was his first or last name. He had a scruffy, red-tinged beard and hair that hung to his shoulders. The fourth man in the group didn't say much. He wore a kepi like Tucker's, but his hair was shorter and dark.

"The frontier is a good place to lay low," Luke agreed.

"Enough jawing," Clay said. "Deal the cards."

Luke played a few more hands, careful not to win or lose too much. "The next round is on me, boys," Luke said as he folded his final hand. "It was good talkin' with y'all. I'd best get back to work."

The drifters didn't say outright that they'd been riding with Bushwhackers, but comments here and there told the story. One of the men mentioned they'd wintered in Texas. Luke was certain that they'd been with either Quantrill or Anderson. They may not have been at Centralia, but Luke thought these "drifters" had probably participated in the Lawrence massacre. It wasn't a big leap to assume they continued operating on the other side of the law.

Luke just wondered what business they had in Shady Bluffs.

Returning to the blacksmith shop, Luke was more convinced than ever that the violence of the war was headed for Shady Bluffs. The frontier town needed a sheriff to keep the peace. He decided to go to Yankton and talk with the marshal. In the meantime, he answered his mother's letter and asked when Nellie would be arriving.

He set out for Yankton the next day. Because he planned to stock up on supplies, he trailed a second horse. When he arrived in Yankton, Luke's first stop was the post office, and then he headed over to see Mike Mathews. As the town's claims agent, Mathews was often "in the know" about what was happening in the Territory.

Mike was finishing up some paperwork when Luke entered. "Good afternoon, Mr. Mathews."

Mathews pushed his spectacles up on the bridge of his nose. "Jameson, right? Did you find the Ward sisters?"

"I did indeed, Mr. Mathews. In fact, Charlotte Ward and I are getting hitched in a couple of weeks. Say, that won't void her right to the claim, will it? Her being a married woman and all."

"The claim was filed in her name when she was Head of Household. If she completes the requirements, the deed will be in her name," Mathews confirmed. "But I also heard tell that Charlotte is the new town doctor. As the duly appointed claims agent, I'll be checking that she's still living on the claim as per the Homestead Act requirements."

"Oh, she's still living on the claim. She comes into town a couple days a week to see patients now that Doc Stone passed."

"That was a shame. Doc Stone was a good man," Mike Mathews said. "Is there something I can do for you?"

"I'm in town to pick up supplies for my blacksmith shop – wrought iron and steel and such. But I'm also here to talk to the sheriff."

"You got trouble in Shady Bluffs," Mathews asked.

"No, but I want to keep it that way," Luke replied.

"Then you're looking for Sheriff Wilson, Ben Wilson," Mathews said.

Luke thanked Mathews for the information and mentioned that he'd be at the Black Bull Saloon later if Mathews wanted to join him.

"I might take you up on the offer. If I don't get there, congratulations on the impending nuptials."

Luke found Ben Wilson in his office down the street. Entering the sheriff's office, Luke introduced himself. He explained that he was originally from Missouri and had served in the Confederate Army, but that life was behind him now.

"I expect I'll see plenty of Rebs…er, Confederate soldiers come to the Territory once the war is over," Wilson said. "We just don't want 'em bringing the war with 'em."

"I agree, Sheriff," Luke said. "That's why I'm here. I think we might have some Bushwhackers staking out our town. I'm wondering what the plans are for appointing a sheriff or deputy to Shady Bluffs."

"We're stretched thin out here, Jameson. Are you looking to be deputized?" Wilson asked.

"No, I'm plenty busy with my blacksmithing. I just wanted you to be aware of the situation. This is the second time I've seen those fellas in Shady Bluffs. It doesn't seem like a coincidence to me."

"Tell you what. Until we can get a deputy in Shady Bluffs, I'll pay a visit from time to time," the sheriff offered.

"Fair enough. Thank you, Sheriff Wilson." They shook hands, and Luke left in search of the ironmonger.

He completed his purchases of wrought iron and steel, the materials he needed for horseshoes and farm equipment. Having completed his business with the sheriff and the ironmonger, Luke stopped in the Black Bull Saloon for a beer before heading back. He thought he might stop at Charlie and Lizzy's claim first.

Luke had hoped to see Mike Mathews at the saloon, but when the claims agent didn't show up, Luke paid for his beer and left.

As he rode down Yankton's main street, Luke spotted a familiar-looking horse. The buckskin quarter horse was tied to the railing outside a boarding house. On closer inspection, the horse had the Jameson brand on its butt. Luke pulled up sharply and dismounted. He tied Rusty and the pack horse next to the buckskin horse and entered the boarding house.

He tipped his hat to the woman at the desk. "Excuse me, ma'am. I'm looking for…"

Before he could finish the sentence, Nellie burst into the room and threw her arms around her big brother. "Luke!" she exclaimed. "I just got to town!"

"Whoa, Nellie," Luke said with a laugh. "It's good to see you, little sister. But how is it that Ma and Pa allowed you to make the trip to Dakota Territory on your own?"

"Oh, I wasn't alone. The Clemmons family was coming up this way, and I rode with them to the Nebraska border. They headed due west, and I followed the river to Yankton. I was going to send word to Shady Bluffs while I waited for you."

"It's lucky I had business in Yankton, then," Luke replied. "Are you too tired to ride a couple more hours, or do you want to stay the night?"

"I've already paid for the night," Nellie said.

The woman at the desk heard the entire conversation. "If you haven't unpacked yet, we can refund your money," she offered.

"That settles it," Nellie said. "Let's ride!"

Luke was eager to get on the road, too. On the way to the Ward sisters' claims, Nellie filled in Luke on family news.

"Martha and Ben are expecting their first baby in the spring," she bubbled. "I'm finally going to be an auntie! And remember Johnny Andrews from Callaway County? He's courting Mary Jane now that she's out of mourning. Matt is still in Tennessee. Ma hasn't heard from Mark, but John wrote that he's joined a Confederate unit."

"Take a breath, Nellie," Luke laughed.

"Your turn," the girl suggested.

"Not much to tell," Luke said. "Except Charlie and me...we're getting married in a couple of weeks."

"Not much to tell!" Nellie exclaimed. "And I'll be here for the wedding! Wait till Ma hears about this. You *did* write to her, didn't you?"

"Yes. The letter was posted in Yankton – along with questions about when you'd arrive. We'll have to send her another letter letting her know that you arrived safe and sound."

It was getting dark when Luke and Nellie arrived at Lizzy's and Charlotte's farms.

When Charlotte saw Luke's horses coming down the path, she put an extra plate on the table. Then she realized there was a second rider, so she added a fourth plate.

"Lizzy, we have company," she called to her sister in the other soddy.

Lizzy went outside to see Luke and Nellie dismounting. "Lizzy, this is my baby sister Nellie. Nellie, this is Elizabeth – Lizzy – Ward. She's Charlie's sister."

Nellie shook Lizzy's hand like she'd seen her father and brothers do. "Howdy – I mean, nice to meet you, Miss Ward."

Lizzy laughed, saying, "It's nice to finally meet you, too, Nellie. I hear you'll be visiting for a while."

"That's what Ma said," Nellie said.

By then, Charlotte had joined the group. Before Luke could greet his bride-to-be, Nellie launched herself at Charlie, giving her a sisterly hug. "Charlie, I'm so excited that you and Luke are getting married! We'll be sisters! And I'll be here for the wedding!"

"We're happy you're here, too," Charlotte said.

Lizzy assessed the situation and said, "Nellie, let's get you settled. I can bring in your bags if you'd like to unsaddle your horse and stable her in the barn."

Luke and Charlotte waited until the girl had disappeared into the barn.

"I've said it before, but your Nellie is a whirlwind," Charlotte said. "I didn't expect she would be in Yankton already."

"Neither did I. It was lucky I went to town when I did," he replied.

Sheepishly, he said, "I was kind of hoping that Nellie could stay here with you and Lizzy. I don't have a proper place for her to stay at the shop."

"Of course, she can stay with us," Charlotte said.

"We wouldn't have it any other way," Lizzy confirmed as she re-joined Charlotte and Luke outside.

"I imagine you're both hungry after the ride," Charlotte said. "You're in for a treat. We're having Lizzy's first ham from the smokehouse tonight." They waited for Nellie, then gathered at the table in Charlotte's soddy.

Over dinner, the sisters explained the idea for the connected soddies. "It was a blessing last winter," Lizzy said.

They talked about the wedding, and it was decided that Charlotte would alter one of her dresses for Nellie since they were both tall and slim.

"I have just the dress for you, Nellie. It will look wonderful with your red hair," Charlotte said.

Luke checked the horses one last time and then went to his bed in the common room. He and Charlotte had agreed to this sleeping arrangement both because of Nellie's presence and in preparation for their wedding vows.

Charlotte was the first one up in the morning. She had already gathered eggs for breakfast when Luke joined her in the kitchen. Putting his arm around her waist, he nuzzled her neck.

"Good morning, Charlie," he whispered.

She turned into his waiting arms and kissed him. "And a good morning to you, too. With all the excitement of Nellie's arrival, we didn't talk about your meeting with the sheriff. How did it go?"

"About as I expected. They're spread thin. He offered to deputize me – but I turned him down. He did agree to stop in Shady Bluffs more often to keep an eye on things."

"That's as best as we can do," she agreed.

Luke packed up and headed to town after breakfast. Nellie was excited to stay with Lizzy and Charlotte. She finally remembered to retrieve the leather wallet that contained half of the payment for Wards' farm and handed the cash to Lizzy and Charlotte.

With only a couple of weeks until the wedding, Charlotte, Lizzy, and even Nellie worked on the dresses for the big day.

On a cool October afternoon, Luke Joseph Jameson and Charlotte Blanche Ward were united in holy matrimony at the Shady Bluffs Lutheran Church with Pastor Gregor Hess presiding. Charlotte wore a very becoming peach dress with brown and white lace trim. Lizzy walked her down the short aisle in a dark blue dress topped by a pale blue bolero jacket. Nellie Jameson, the maid of honor, looked unusually feminine in a long-sleeved pink dress.

As attractive as Lizzy and Nellie were, Luke could not keep his eyes off Charlotte. He probably wouldn't remember what Charlie's wedding dress looked like, but he would never forget the sparkle that lit up her dark brown eyes when she took his hand before the pastor.

Most of Shady Bluffs' townspeople turned out for the wedding and the celebration at the blacksmith shop. They toasted the newlyweds and enjoyed ham sandwiches and potato salad. Isabell Vaughn, who loved to bake, provided a wedding cake with peach frosting for the event.

After-Action Report – Battle of Westport
October 23, 1864

Sometimes referred to as the "Gettysburg of the West," the Battle of Westport was fought on October 23, 1864, near Kansas City. It was one of the largest battles fought west of the Mississippi River, with more than 30,000 men engaged: 22,000 Federal troops and approximately 8,500 Confederate soldiers.

The Battle of Westport was the turning point in General Sterling Price's Missouri Expedition. It forced the Confederate Army to retreat, ending the Confederate offensive west of the Mississippi River and allowing the Union Army to maintain control of Missouri.

Chapter 27: Winter 1865
Dakota Frontier

If Charlotte had expected married life to change her routine drastically, she was mistaken. She continued to divide her time between the farm and Shady Bluffs, riding back and forth when the winter weather cooperated. But now, she and Luke lived together in the expanded room behind the doctor's office. He had converted the blacksmith shop's sleeping quarters into a storage room but kept the cookstove.

With Nellie staying at the farm, Charlotte felt less guilty about neglecting her farm chores. Nellie was more than happy to lend a hand. For her part, Lizzy was much more careful about closing gates and barn doors. She didn't want another incident like last winter when the cows escaped.

Their cattle herd of two cows and three calves had grown to seven animals by last spring. Five more calves were expected in the coming year.

Charlotte, Lizzy, and Nellie visited their neighbors on mild winter days. Nellie was delighted with Bear Walker. The little boy was nearly a year old and alternated between crawling and walking.

Over cups of sweetgrass tea, the women chatted about life on the frontier. That was when Clara Walker confided that Bear would have a new sister or brother by summer.

"That is so exciting!" Lizzy said. "I imagine Stan is very happy."

"He is," Clara began, "but I would like to give birth with my mother and aunties. He does not want me to travel back to Minnesota."

"It could be dangerous and uncomfortable to travel in those last months of pregnancy," Charlotte admitted. "What about bringing some of the women from your family here for the birth?"

Clara's eyes lit up. "Yes! They could spend more time with Bear, too. That is a very good idea. We could make a trip this spring when I can still travel and invite them to come." Then she paused, "But we don't have anyone to feed the animals while we're gone."

"If I'm still in Dakota, I could do that," Nellie offered. "It's not that far from Lizzy and Charlotte's claims."

The four women talked with Stan about the idea, and he agreed to bring Clara and Bear to Minnesota for a few days in the spring after planting was completed. Nellie would watch over the Walkers' farm animals.

On the way back to their farm, Charlotte said to Nellie, "That was very kind of you, Nellie. Thank you."

"My ma always wished she could go back home to see her kin," Nellie said. "It's just neighborly to help out."

The sisters also introduced Nellie to their Lakota neighbors. On another temperate winter day in December, they packed their horses with smoked pork, bags of potatoes, and fresh bread and rode to the Lakota camp.

While there were some Indian tribes still in northwestern Missouri, Nellie had not had any contact with them. Meeting the Lakota people was another adventure that opened her world even further.

Charlotte's command of the Lakota language was improving, so she could talk at length with Evening Star, Dancing Girl, and Spotted Horse. They told her that the buffalo hunt last fall had been successful. Their cooking pots were full throughout the cold winter. But more than food, the Ward sisters and Nellie learned how important buffalo were to the Lakota way of life. Along with meat, buffalo supplied the means for the Lakota people to live on the Dakota frontier, from clothing and tipis to tools and blankets.

December also brought Christmas to the Ward farm. Like the previous year, Luke brought a small cedar tree to decorate. Nellie was thrilled and took charge of decorating. In addition to popcorn and berries, she found several abandoned birds' nests and added those to the holiday tree.

By now, Charlotte and Lizzy considered themselves "old homesteaders" and were comfortable in their frontier home. While they still exchanged small gifts, a book for Lizzy and sewing shears for Charlotte, they agreed to use the money they'd received from Ben and Martha Fuller to expand the farms. Lizzy suggested purchasing a more reliable plow and additional breeding stock.

They did splurge on a Christmas gift for Nellie. Luke and the sisters gave Nellie a newer saddle for her horse. She beamed when they brought her to the barn to show her the gift.

"Your old saddle was a hand-me-down from Matt, if I recollect," Luke told Nellie. "This one's not brand new, but it's in pretty good shape. It was time you had something that fit you and your horse better."

Instead of replying, Nellie threw her arms around her big brother and hugged him.

It was March when Lizzy found Charlotte letting out the seams of her dresses.

"I wondered about this, Char," Lizzy said. "Have you told Luke yet?"

"I hadn't told anyone yet," Charlotte replied. "Remember all the miscarriages that Mama had? I wanted to keep this to myself as long as I could," Charlotte said.

Lizzy put her arms around her older sister and said, "I know you're worried that your pregnancies will be like Mama's. Her pregnancies were hard on her. She was always sick. But you're different. You're younger and stronger."

"I hope you're right. I haven't had any morning sickness, and I do feel good," Charlotte said. "Still, I've put off telling Luke in case he wants me to stop seeing patients. I don't want things to change just because I'm having a baby."

"I think you're underestimating him," Lizzy replied. "And you're going to have to tell him sooner or later. You're starting to show."

Charlotte blew out a breath and said, "You're right, as usual. I'll tell him when I go to town."

The road to Shady Bluffs was muddy with runoff from the spring snows. Charlotte was glad she had decided to ride her horse rather than hitch up the wagon. She recalled how the wagons had sunk to their axles in that farmyard near Nebraska City.

Spring was in the air. Charlotte was encouraged to see small, green buds on the trees by the creek. Shadow trailed alongside. From time to time, the dog ran off to chase a jackrabbit. His antics made Charlotte laugh as the dog zigzagged through new spring grass.

The streets in Shady Bluffs were even muddier than the country roads, Charlotte observed. As always, her first stop in town was at Luke's blacksmith shop. She greeted Luke with a quick kiss.

"Get in here," Luke said, repeating the oft-used phrase as he opened his arms to her. Even though he was a little sooty from the fire, she eagerly walked into his embrace.

"I've missed you, Charlie," Luke said.

"I've only been gone a few days, but I've missed you, too," Charlotte said. She started giggling as Luke kissed the ticklish spots on her neck. "There's that saying, 'absence makes the heart grow fonder,'" she said.

"There's more than my heart growing fonder," Luke said as he pulled her into a tight embrace.

"Luke Jameson! You're incorrigible!" she said, enjoying the flirting.

"And you love it," he replied.

"Hmmm. I do," she said.

Before the couple could continue their romancing, they heard someone clear their throat. The newlyweds broke off their embrace and stepped apart.

In the shop's doorway, a man was holding the reins of a large bay stallion. "My horse lost a shoe," the man explained.

"Bring him in," Luke said to the customer.

"I'll see you at dinner tonight," Charlotte said as she left the shop. She recognized the man as Clay, one of the drifters who brought the gunshot patient to her office last summer. Charlotte would mention that to Luke that evening.

On her way to her office, Charlotte stopped at the new post office. There were letters from Luke's mother and his sisters in Missouri. Charlotte looked forward to hearing Luke's family news over dinner. Then, she would give him some family news of her own.

She entered the doctor's office and turned the sign to The Doctor Is In. Charlotte didn't expect to have many patients but was surprised when a mother and two children followed her into the office. The mother was carrying the younger child.

"Doctor Charlie?" the young mother said. "Mrs. Vaughn over at the general store directed me here. My Sally, she has a terrible cough. Can you help her?"

"Of course. Come on in," Charlotte said. Before she examined the little girl, who appeared to be about two years old, Charlotte wanted more information. She asked their names, how old the children were, and where they had been recently.

"You're new in town," Charlotte began. "Are you passing through or do you plan to stay in Shady Bluffs? I ask because it's helpful to know where you've come from. Sometimes that helps narrow the diagnosis."

"We were in a wagon train headed to Oregon, but Sally took a turn for the worse. People on the train started saying she had whooping cough, so we dropped out," the mother, Mrs. Ferguson, said.

Charlotte washed her hands and put her ear to the little girl's chest. She could hear the tell-tale barking cough that signaled croup. Knowing that croup and whooping cough symptoms are similar, Charlotte asked more questions.

"She doesn't seem to be running a fever. Has she been sneezing a lot? That would point to whooping cough."

The mother shook her head 'no.'

Charlotte continued the examination. If Sally's tongue and hands had a bluish tint, that could mean whooping cough, too.

"Based on what I'm seeing, it looks like a bad case of croup. But dropping out of the wagon train was a good precaution. I can give you some cough medicine. The best thing you can do is set up a croup kettle. Where are you staying?"

"We're camping outside of town," said Mrs. Ferguson.

Charlotte nodded. "Make sure she's getting plenty of rest and put her under a steam tent to help open her lungs."

"Yes, doctor. Thank you," the mother said with relief.

Charlotte measured a week's worth of cough medicine for the little girl and handed it to the mother. "Just a teaspoon at a time," Charlotte cautioned.

Mrs. Ferguson thanked Charlotte again and left the office with her children.

Charlotte collapsed into her desk chair.

What if that had been whooping cough? she thought. *Maybe it's not such a good idea for me to be doctoring while I'm pregnant.*

Charlotte had to give some thought to how to deal with this issue. She was the town doctor and that carried considerable weight and responsibility. Charlotte washed her hands again and, taking extra precautions, changed into a clean dress. She tossed her apron into the washing bin.

She stopped in the mercantile, more to chat with Isabell Vaughn than to shop. Isabell always seemed to know what was happening in town.

"Good morning, Charlotte! You're looking well today. Marriage agrees with you," Isabell said.

"Thank you, Isabell," Charlotte replied. "I'm in town for a couple of days and need to pick up some groceries."

"You've come to the right place," the merchant said. "Did you hear that Shady Bluffs may be getting a bank? Isn't that wonderful news? And speaking of banks, did you hear about the string of bank robberies in Nebraska? According to the Yankton newspaper, the law thinks it's a gang of Bushwhackers that have come north from the war."

"We don't get much news on the farm," Charlotte answered. "But it wouldn't surprise me. Luke said the Federal soldiers are closing in on guerilla fighters."

Charlotte browsed the fabrics and found a pretty yellow cotton gingham. She fingered the fabric and smiled. "This would make a nice summer dress, " she told Isabell.

The shopkeeper looked up from the counter where she was tallying Charlotte's groceries. "Yes, that just came in. It's hard to get cotton fabric these days. I'm afraid it's priced accordingly."

Frowning, Charlotte said, "Well, that's for another day, then. That is good news about the bank. Shady Bluffs seems to be growing. The bank, the new post office…I even heard there's another saloon open on the edge of town. I had a family come into my office earlier. They were from a wagon trail headed to Oregon."

Isabell nodded. "Shady Bluffs is growing. Say, I heard that Lizzy has smoked hams and side pork for sale. I'd be willing to trade for that yellow gingham."

Charlotte brightened. "I'll let Lizzy know. That's her side business. How much do I owe you today?"

They settled up, and Charlotte walked back to the apartment at the back of the doctor's office. On her way, a group of ten or a dozen men on horseback galloped down the Main Street, reining in at the new saloon. She wasn't sure, but she thought she recognized Clay and Joe, the drifters from last summer. *They seem to turn up regularly,* she thought.

Back home, she unpacked the groceries and realized she was exhausted. She knew that expectant mothers needed more rest, so following the doctor's orders, Charlotte laid down for a short nap.

When Charlotte heard Luke enter the office's living quarters, it was dark outside.

"Charlie, are you still working?" Luke called out from the small kitchen.

Quickly, Charlotte rose from her nap, smoothed her hair, and replied, "I'm in the bedroom. I'll be out in a moment."

Luke assessed his bride and said, "Busy day?"

"A couple of walk-ins," she answered. "How was your day?"

"It's spring. Everyone needs their farm tools mended. There's a pile of plows and harnesses waiting for me at the shop."

From behind her, Luke wrapped his arms around Charlotte and kissed the nape of her neck. "I love coming home to you, Charlie," he whispered.

She twisted around in his arms so they were face to face, mouth to mouth. Kissing him in return, Charlotte said,

"And I love having you come home to me. What is that wonderful aroma I'm smelling?"

"I stopped at the diner on the way home," Luke said, "Betsy makes a humdinger of a chicken pot pie."

"The answer to a prayer," Charlotte said. "I'm famished, and I haven't started dinner. By the way, there are letters from your family on the table."

Betsy's chicken pot pie was even better than it smelled. A flaky crust was filled with tender chicken pieces and assorted vegetables in a savory chicken gravy. While they ate, they compared their workdays.

"I was in the mercantile today. Isabell said that Shady Bluffs will soon have a bank."

"Yep. We need a bank, but banks draw outlaws," Luke said. "Did she mention the bank robberies in Nebraska?"

"She did. Isabell said the Yankton newspaper thought it might be Bushwhackers up from the South."

"I'd have to agree. The Bushwhackers said they banded together to fight Yankee soldiers. But it seemed to me that they spent a lot more time stealing horses and terrorizing civilians. Lately, they've turned to robbing banks and trains. And they're moving into fresh territory," Luke stated.

"The man who brought in the stallion while you were in the shop," Luke continued. "I think he's part of a gang. Of course, I can't prove it. It just doesn't seem to add up, though. He and the men he rides with don't seem to have steady jobs, and they can spend hours in the saloon.

Before you ask, I've talked with Deputy Driscoll from Yankton about it."

"What did the deputy say?" Charlotte asked.

"Same thing that Sheriff Wilson said. Until these 'drifters' are caught doing something against the law, he can't take any action. Seems to me that they're cooling their heels in Dakota after doing some 'business' in Nebraska."

Charlotte rose to clear the dinner table. "You made dinner. Why don't you read those letters from your family while I wash the dishes. Then let's go for a walk."

It was a mild spring evening as the couple walked arm-in-arm down the boardwalk. They strolled away from the hustle and bustle of the town's saloons and soon reached the boundary between the town and the prairie.

Luke pointed out three stars in the southern sky. "See those three stars in a row? That's Orion's belt. Orion the hunter," he said. "As a boy, I learned that the stars stood for strength, attention to detail and good luck."

"I'd never heard that before," Charlotte said. "But it seems appropriate, since I have a secret to tell you."

She stopped and took Luke's hands in hers. "We're going to have a baby."

"My darling Charlie!" Luke exclaimed. "That is wonderful news! The best news ever!" He wrapped her in a tight embrace and gave her a long, deep kiss.

Then he pulled away and held her by her shoulders. "When?"

"Later this summer. July or August."

"That gives me time," Luke said. "We'll need a proper house. Do you want to live in town or at the farm?"

"Goodness, I hadn't thought that far ahead," Charlotte said. "I guess that's where Orion's 'attention to details' comes into play."

"Of course, you'll stop doctoring now," he said.

"No, that's *not* in the stars for me," Charlotte said adamantly. "I want to keep my medical practice."

"My blacksmith shop is doing fine. We don't need you to work."

"Luke, you don't understand. *I need to work.* I always wanted to be a doctor. And even though I don't have the certificate from a medical school, people around here count on me when they are sick or injured. I am needed in Shady Bluffs."

"My wife and the mother of my children should not be working," he said, his voice rising.

Charlotte shook her head. "Apparently, you haven't been paying attention…to me, to your mother, to the women around you. We are always working. Whether I'm at home or in the doctor's office, I'll always be working. And I like working. I like being Doctor Charlie."

"But the baby…" he started.

"When the baby comes, he or she will be Doctor Charlie's baby." She rose up on her toes and kissed his cheek.

"Does that make me 'Doctor Charlie's husband'?"

"You can ponder that one."

"We're not done discussing this, Charlie," Luke said determinedly.

After-Action Report – Appomattox Campaign
March 1865

On February 18, 1865, General Lee wrote to the Confederate Secretary of War, "You must not be surprised if calamity befalls us."

At the time, Lee and his forces were encamped in and around Petersburg and Richmond, Virginia. General Grant's troops had cut off three of Richmond's four railroad lines. When the fourth line was blocked, Lee's Army would have no option other than retreat.

In time, Lee's supply lines were broken, and his soldiers were hungry and in need of supplies. When the Northern Army reached Farmville, Virginia, on April 7, General Grant sent a letter to Lee asking for the surrender of his army. The reply came back: "Not yet."

Chapter 28: April 1865
Shady Bluffs

Lavender pasque flowers, the first flowers of spring, blanketed the prairie and signaled that spring had come to Dakota Territory. Lizzy didn't need the flowers to tell her spring had arrived.

Eagles were sitting on giant nests in the tall trees by the creek. Spotted fawns were scampering behind their mothers along the creek bed. It was spring! A time for new babies.

She was so happy for Charlotte and Luke and for Clara and Stan. During a visit to the Lakota camp, Lizzy and Nellie had learned that Dancing Girl and Spotted Horse would be welcoming a new baby this year, too.

Lizzy was especially grateful that Nellie had decided to stay in Dakota Territory a while longer. She had come to rely on the young woman to help with farm chores, for companionship, and to keep things lively on the claim. Luke had once described Nellie as "a force of nature." That was an understatement. Every day was a new adventure for Nellie Jameson.

"Lizzy!" Nellie called out as she rode up to the barn. "I was just at the Lakota camp. They said the buffalo have returned. Spotted Horse said I could ride with them in the next hunt."

"That's quite an honor, Lizzy. I'm a little jealous, but I'm not the rider that you are. When will they hunt?"

"Spotted Horse said they'll give the calves time to mature, so it will be a while. But they have scouts keeping an eye on the herd."

"That's good animal husbandry," Lizzy said. "Speaking of which, can you please move the cattle to the east pasture?"

Lizzy was busy plowing a new field. She was determined to increase the size of her croplands and put more of the tough prairie sod under cultivation each year. She watched as Nellie herded the cows and calves to fresh grass. That's when she saw the riders coming in from the south.

About a dozen men, most of them wearing long dusters, were headed toward the farm. Lizzy left the plow and ox team in the field and walked to the homestead. She arrived about the same time as the visitors. The riders reminded Lizzy of the men who rode with Quantrill. Most of them had shoulder-length hair and scruffy beards. A few men wore slough hats, and others wore the gray kepis that Confederate soldiers favored. She scanned the group for familiar faces but didn't recognize any of the riders.

"Good morning," she said. "Can I help you?"

"Just trying to get the lay of the land," said one of the men. "Is your man around?"

Lizzy was always wary of strangers who might be trying to determine if she was a woman alone on the frontier.

"Out hunting," she replied. In the corner of her eye, she saw Nellie disappear into Charlotte's soddy and then re-emerge carrying a shotgun.

"Mind if we water our horses?" the man continued.

"The creek's just over the rise," Lizzy said, nodding toward Medicine Creek.

"Not very hospitable of you," the man said.

Nellie cocked the shotgun. That got the attention of the men.

"We don't want no trouble, ladies. Just wanted to wet our whistles. Let's go," he said to the other men.

Lizzy and Nellie watched the men ride toward the creek. "Want me to trail them, Lizzy?" Nellie asked.

"No. Let's not poke the hornet's nest," Lizzy replied. "But let's keep our shotguns with us from now on. Those men reminded me of the ones who rode with Quantrill. If they're Bushwhackers – or former Bushwhackers – they're looking for trouble."

"I thought I'd left those outlaws back in Missouri," Nellie said. "That's why Ma sent me up here."

"The war's winding down," Lizzy said. "They're looking for new places to loot and plunder. And they're trying to stay one step ahead of the law down South."

She shook her head, worried about the encounter. Lizzy decided that she and Nellie would make a trip to town this week to let Luke know about the riders.

By the creek, the gang dismounted and let the horses drink their fill. "That was one uppity female. Like that lady doctor in town," Clay Hancock said to his companions.

He wasn't aware of the relationship between Doctor Charlie and Lizzy, but both women had stood up to him, and he wasn't used to being challenged by the weaker sex.

The gang – they had been Bushwhackers – had wintered in Nebraska along the Niobrara River. It was there, along what would become known as the Outlaw Trail, that Clay Hancock's gang grew in strength. The four-man crew he'd brought to Dakota Territory the previous year now numbered a dozen hard-bitten outlaws.

"Where to?" asked Tucker, one of the original four.

"Let's keep on to Shady Bluffs," Clay decided. "At least we can get something stronger than creek water."

They passed the massive buffalo herd to the south on the way into town. That gave Clay Hancock an idea. He didn't say anything to his men yet. He needed to learn more about those big, shaggy beasts before forming a plan.

The gang was happy to find that Shady Bluffs now had two saloons. The new establishment, closer to the outskirts of town, was rowdier and bawdier. Four Aces Saloon was just what his gang was looking for.

Luke didn't see the riders come into town. And, since they tied their horses to the railing on the far side of the saloon, Luke didn't see the horses either.

He finished shoeing the last team of oxen. Luke had become adept at working on the cloven-hooved farm animals. After shutting down his forge, he headed for home. But his work wasn't done for the day. He'd promised Charlotte that they would have a proper house before the baby came. He planned to work on the new house they were building just outside of town. If his calculations were correct, the town would grow to meet their new home in no time.

Now in her fifth month of pregnancy, Charlotte was barely showing. She wasn't worried, though. Her height gave the baby more room to "spread out," she explained to Luke. Charlotte knew their baby was healthy – he or she – continued to make their presence known. And now Luke could feel the baby kicking. He was in awe.

"Good evening, darlin'," Luke called out as he entered the back door of the doctor's office.

Charlotte greeted her husband with a light kiss.

"You look especially beautiful today," he said. He pulled her into him and kissed her back. "How was your day?"

"Just fine. The Hanson boy – the oldest one – broke his arm climbing a tree. I set the bone. There was another brawl at the Four Aces. That's a rough saloon," she said.

"There's a reason it's on the outskirts of town."

He filled two plates with pork chops, applesauce, fresh asparagus, and fried potatoes, and they sat down to dinner.

After taking a first bite, Luke continued, "The upside of having Four Aces here is that Deputy Driscoll is spending more time in Shady Bluffs. He thinks the sheriff's office in Yankton will re-assign him as a permanent deputy here."

"That's wonderful news," Charlotte said.

"Well, there's more," Luke winced. "Until then, he wants me to be a part-time deputy." Luke knew his wife did not want to hear this news.

"It won't be for long, Charlie. And if you don't want me to do it, I won't. But Shady Bluffs is growing, and I want this to be a safe town for our family."

"You said 'part-time.' Does that mean George will deputizing other men, too?"

He nodded. "Hank Johnson, the new banker. He knows how to handle a gun. Served in Union cavalry. Besides, he's a bear of a man. His size will be enough to settle some disputes."

Charlotte agreed to the temporary arrangement.

Clay Hancock found just who he was looking for at the Four Aces. The old guy was standing at the bar, dressed in fringed buckskins from hat to boots. He even wore tall moccasins just like the Indians, Clay noticed.

"Hey, old timer, can I buy you a beer?" Clay said as he struck up a conversation.

"Ain't sayin' no to a free beer, sonny," the man replied.

"I haven't seen you around these parts before," said Clay.

"I don't cotton much to town life," the old timer said. "Spend most of my time in the mountains. Towns make me itchy."

"You a trapper?" Clay asked.

That's all the encouragement the man needed. "Hells bells, laddie, I've been trapping since I was a young'un. Name's Abe, Abe Carson. No relation to Kit. Though him and me both shot our share of buffalo."

Clay knew then and there he'd found the right man. "Buffalo, huh? I bet you've got stories." He motioned to the bartender, "Barkeep – another round for me and my friend."

Abe spent the better part of the night spinning tales about his time with the Crow and the Sioux. "The Sioux," Abe said, "they know how to hunt those beasties. They get the buffalo moving – stampeding – and then they pick out the best of the herd. It's somethin' to see."

Clay absorbed as much information as he could from the mountain man. When Abe started talking about going to rendezvous with old trappers, Clay lost interest. He got the information he was looking for. Now, he just needed the right time and opportunity.

Back on the claims, Lizzy moved the cattle into a fenced pasture by the barn. She didn't worry about milking the cows since the calves would take care of that. The pigs were fed, and Nellie had gathered eggs, so they hitched up the wagon. Nellie and Lizzy stopped by the smokehouse and loaded a dozen hams and bacon into the wagon for the trip to town. Lizzy was excited that the farm would provide another source of income.

On the way to Shady Bluffs, Nellie and Lizzy looked for more signs of spring.

"The pasque flowers are my favorite," Nellie said when she spied a patch of the lavender blooms. "Look, there are some wild daisies."

"I love lilacs," said Lizzy. "I saw lilac bushes growing by the creek last year. We should plant some by the house. They're so fragrant."

"Ma used to make sachets with lilac and lavender," Nellie recalled. "I wonder if Isabell would sell our sachets?"

"We can ask when we're in town. I'm sure Char has scraps of fabric we could use." The women discussed that and other business ideas until Shady Bluffs came into view.

"Let's poke around the new house that Luke and Char are building," Nellie suggested.

"You beat me to the idea," Lizzy laughed.

The house, made of actual lumber, would be a modest size, Lizzy thought. But there was plenty of space to add more rooms.

"I'm jealous that Char won't be battling bugs and worms falling from the ceiling," Lizzy said. "Maybe a wood-built house should be on my wish list – after a new plow, of course."

"You're always the ever-practical farmer, Lizzy," Nellie quipped.

"Needs and wants, Nellie. Needs and wants," Lizzy replied. "Besides, we've only been here two years. We've made good improvements to the claims in that time."

They stopped at the mercantile before going to Charlotte's office.

"Good morning, Isabell," Lizzy called out. "I have a load of hams and smoked pork in the wagon. If you're interested in some, we'll pull the wagon around to the back of your store."

"Your Missouri smoked hams? They fairly fly off the shelf," Isabell exclaimed. "I guess pigs do fly." They all laughed at her joke.

"We can leave half the load here," Lizzy said. "I promised a delivery to Betsy at the diner."

Together, the three women unloaded the hams and side pork. When they were done, Lizzy and Isabell agreed to settle up later.

"Let's stop at Charlotte's office first," Nellie said. "It's nearly lunchtime. We could eat at Betsy's."

"Good idea."

Nellie drove the wagon the short way to Charlotte's doctor's office. She asked Lizzy, "Mrs. Vaughn is a good businesswoman, but I've not heard about a Mr. Vaughn. Is she widowed?"

"I believe so. I don't know Isabell's story, and it's none of my business.

Nellie nodded but chewed her lip in contemplation. She loved a mystery.

Charlotte was in the back, dusting and re-stocking her pharmacy, when she heard the doorbell. She was happy to see her sister and sister-in-law in the front room of the office.

"Good morning, Doctor Charlie!" Nellie said. "Don't you just love how that sounds?"

"I do, but your brother doesn't," Charlotte replied. "We're still going round and round about whether I'll keep the medical practice after the baby arrives." She patted the small mound on her midriff.

"You are barely showing, Char!" Lizzy said. She almost mentioned their mother's pregnancies in comparison, but she knew that those were bad memories for Charlotte. Instead, Lizzy said, "But you certainly have the glow of a mother-to-be!"

That made Charlotte smile. "Thank you. I'm feeling much better in this stage of the pregnancy. Not nearly as tired – but just as hungry!"

"Then our timing is perfect," Lizzy said. "We're here to take you to lunch at Betsy's Place."

"You don't need to ask me twice. Should we stop and get Luke?" Charlotte asked.

"No, this is a 'ladies' lunch.' No men allowed," Nellie said.

"Even better," Charlotte said.

"I'll drive the wagon over," Nellie offered. "We have a delivery of hams and side pork for Betsy."

"Thank you, Nellie," Lizzy said.

Their ladies' lunch allowed all three women to catch up on family news and news about their neighbors.

"I'm going to stay at Walker's farm while they visit Clara's family in Minnesota," Nellie said. "I'll take care of the animals while they're gone."

"I hope her mother and aunties can come back in time for the baby," Lizzy added. "Our Nellie gets around. She was at the Lakota camp yesterday. They've invited her to go on the next buffalo hunt!"

"How exciting!" Charlotte said. "One of my patients mentioned that the herd isn't too far from here."

They talked about the new house, baby clothes, and spring planting.

"I'm sorry I haven't been more help," Charlotte said. "Maybe now that I'm not so tired, I can come out and help."

"Don't worry about it, Char," Lizzy cautioned. "There's plenty of time for that after the baby comes. You'll have two aunties at the farm to fuss over the little one."

By the time lunch was finished, Betsy's son had unloaded the wagon. Betsy came out of the kitchen to thank Lizzy for the delivery.

"Lunch is on the house, ladies. Your hams and smoked pork will bring in plenty of customers once the word gets out that Missouri ham is on the menu," she said.

They thanked Betsy and decided their next stop should be the blacksmith shop. Luke was busy making nails and bolts when the ladies entered.

He looked up from his work to see his sister and Lizzy. "Hey, sis! Are you pulling your weight at the farm?" he asked Nellie.

"More than pulling her weight," Lizzy answered. "I shouldn't say this, but she's more helpful around the farm than Char ever was!"

"I never said I was a farmer," Charlotte protested.

"I never accused you of being a farmer," Lizzy teased back.

Luke looked at his sister and said, "Ah, don't you love the sound of sisters quarreling."

Then, they all heard the rumbling sound of thunder.

"I didn't think we were getting storms today," Luke said as he headed for the shop's double doors to check the skies.

"That's odd," Lizzy said. "I didn't notice any clouds earlier."

Luke saw dust clouds south of town and understood what was causing the thunder. He rushed back to the three women.

"It's a stampede! Get in the wagon! Get out of town, all three of you," he yelled.

"You're coming, too. Right, Luke?" Charlotte asked.

"I'll try to help turn the stampede," he said. "Take the wagon and head out of town east, away from the stampede."

Now, people were standing outside their stores and houses, their attention turned to the approaching dust cloud.

Charlotte, Lizzy, and Nellie hurried to their wagon. Nellie helped the two sisters up to the bench but didn't join them. "Nellie, what are you waiting for?" Lizzy shouted.

"I'm going to help Luke," she replied. Before they could argue, Nellie ran back into the blacksmith shop to saddle Luke's stallion. She'd ridden that horse at home on the family's ranch. She knew the horse had the stamina and power to outrun a stampede. Luke joined her as he saddled his horse, Rusty.

"I've never been in a cattle stampede, Luke. What do you want me to do?"

"That's not cattle, Nell. It's buffalo. I'm not going to tell you that you can't help. You won't listen anyway. So, follow my lead. We'll try to turn the big bulls at the front of the herd. If we can't, run for your life! Don't be a hero. Get out of the way!"

The sound of the thundering beasts was getting closer. The ground was shaking. Luke raced down the town's main street, yelling to people. To run. To hide. To find a safe place.

But where to go? The herd was speeding directly for Shady Bluffs.

The sound increased, becoming a deafening roar.

People scrambled for horses, not bothering with saddles or hitching the horses to wagons. Sometimes, two people sat on one horse. Other townspeople ran for the shelter of root cellars or climbed onto the roofs of buildings.

The thundering herd grew closer. Luke and several other men motioned that they would try to turn the lead animals. But the bulls at the head of the stampede did not obey. Even though some of the buffalo veered off from the herd and headed in other directions, the mass of moving animals was not to be deterred, and they kept moving northward toward the town's Main Street.

By the time the herd reached the edge of town, Luke could see there was no use stopping or steering the animals. He looked frantically for his sister. She had been keeping pace with the other outriders, but Luke had lost sight of her.

Where was Nellie? Then he spotted his big, chestnut-colored stallion racing alongside the herd.

He yelled to his sister, hoping she would hear him above the din. "Nellie! Nellie! Get the hell away from there!" Instinctively, he made a flanking maneuver, just as he had during the war. When he was within shouting distance, Luke called out, "Come with me!"

Nellie reined in her horse and followed Luke. Together, they were able to peel off some of the outside animals and push the buffalo away from town. But it wasn't enough. The main body of the herd continued to gallop toward the frontier town, trampling everything in its path.

The structures on the south side of town were the first to be destroyed. The buffalo ran over, not around, fences, outhouses, homes, and barns. Everything in the herd's path was crushed. As the animals reached the center of town with its more densely packed buildings, they seemed to use Main Street as a funnel. Still, the stampede damaged most of the town's business establishments: the stores and saloons, office buildings and shops, the church, and the bank. Luke's shop, on a side street, seemed safe for now.

Charlotte and Lizzy watched the destruction unfold from the crest of a hill outside town. What they didn't know was that the stampede was just the first act.

After-Action Report – Lee Surrenders, April 9, 1865

General Robert E. Lee's Army of North Virginia confronted General Ulysses S. Grant's Army of the Potomac on the rolling hills around Appomattox Court House on April 9, 1865. For a week, Grant's troops had been blocking Lee's attempts to march south for supplies and ammunition. With the arrival of thousands of Union infantry, including the U.S. Colored Troops, Lee realized the fight was over and sent a letter to Grant agreeing to a surrender. Grant replied, telling Lee to select a meeting site.

The terms of the surrender stated that Confederate soldiers would be paroled after surrendering their weapons and military property. If they agreed to not take up arms again against the United States, the U.S. government would not prosecute them.

Grant telegraphed President Lincoln that Lee had surrendered. Within hours, most of Washington, D.C., celebrated the news.

Chapter 29: April 1865
Shady Bluffs

Charlotte and Lizzy watched in horror as the stampeding buffalo turned buildings into kindling. From their vantage point east of town, they saw the beasts smash through fences, tip over wagons, and, yes, trample people who got in their way.

Mesmerized by the sheer power of the buffalo, they followed as Luke, Nellie, and other riders attempted to steer the moving mass. For the most part, the riders were unsuccessful in their efforts. Instead, Luke and the other riders looked for people on foot.

Luke scooped up a boy and swung the youngster behind him in the saddle. Darting away to a safe distance, Luke helped the boy dismount. Then Luke raced back into the swirling dust cloud, looking for other survivors. Nellie followed her brother's lead and pulled a young woman onto the chestnut stallion. She delivered the woman safely to Char and Lizzy's wagon.

The stampede through Shady Bluffs lasted only minutes. But in that time, the animals left few buildings standing. The buffalo continued running north out of town. By the time the herd reached the horizon, most of the animals had lost interest in running and were beginning to graze on the prairie grass.

The sound and fury of the stampede ceased. Now, the only sounds that could be heard were the cries and wails of people in the aftermath.

"We need to get back there," Charlotte said. Lizzy clicked her tongue and snapped the horses' reins to drive into town or what was left of it.

As they rode west into Shady Bluffs, there was another stampede of sorts. Lizzy saw the outlaws – the Bushwhackers – who had stopped at the farm the day before. At first, the sisters thought the men were racing into town to help. Then they realized this was a gang of looters, of predators, ready to pick clean the town.

The Bushwhackers looked for the bank, the mercantile, the saloons – any place they might find money or other valuables. They carried cash and valuables out of buildings that were only half-standing. Several men attempted to open the bank's safe and eventually resorted to shooting the lock off the metal box.

Seeing this, Lizzy pulled up the team's reins, stopping the wagon. "What are you doing, Lizzy?" Charlotte demanded.

"They did this!" Lizzy pointed to the Bushwhackers who were looting the town. "This was the reason for the stampede. And they'll shoot anyone in their way."

"We still need to get back to town," Charlotte exclaimed. "People are injured. I need to be there. Give me the reins." She reached for the leather straps.

Lizzy knew there was no use in persuading her sister to stay away. Charlotte was the kind of person who ran *into* a burning building, not away from it. Her enlistment in the army to rescue their brother was proof of that.

"I'm driving," Lizzy insisted. "Where to first?"

"Let's see what's left of my doctor's office. I didn't bring my medical bag to lunch. Hopefully, it's still usable. I'll need it."

When they got to the doctor's office, the woman Nellie had rescued raced off to find her family. Lizzy helped Charlotte search through the rubble for the black bag.

"Found it!" Charlotte called out triumphantly. She opened the latch and inventoried her equipment. "There are a couple of broken bottles, but the instruments are undamaged," she told her sister.

"We should split up," Charlotte said. "We can cover more ground that way. When you find someone who's injured, call out."

Lizzy nodded and struck out. Both sisters began looking for broken bodies.

Charlotte didn't have to look far before discovering Isabell Vaughn trapped under a fallen timber.

"Need help here!" Charlotte called out.

Luke reined in his horse and jumped down to help his wife. "I won't waste my breath suggesting that you stay clear of this disaster," he said. He lifted the lumber on top of Isabell and carried the shopkeeper to a clearing.

"My leg," Isabell mumbled. "It's my leg."

Charlotte followed him. "Thank you for not scolding me. You have more sense than I gave you credit for."

"You don't," he retorted. Then he looked at the shambles that used to be Shady Bluffs. Cries of grief and pain could be heard from every direction. "I take it back. This town needs you, Charlie. What can I do to help?"

"Are the Bushwhackers still looting?" she asked.

"Nope. They took what they could find and skipped town. You're right about them being Bushwhackers."

"That's one less thing to worry about," Charlotte said as she pulled up Isabell's skirt to examine the woman's legs. "A compound fracture," Charlotte said more to herself than to Luke.

Then, addressing Luke, Charlotte said, "I'm going to need bandages and laudanum from my office. Can you go back, sort through the debris, and bring back what you find?"

"On it," he said.

Charlotte addressed her patient. "Your leg is badly broken, Isabell. I'll need to clean the wound, reposition the bone and splint it. Before I do any of that, I'll stabilize the leg and give you something for the pain. Do you hurt anywhere besides your leg?"

"My right shoulder," the woman answered.

"Can you move your arm," Charlotte asked as she examined the woman's shoulder and collarbone. Isabell was able to comply.

"The bones don't appear to be broken. Maybe a severe sprain."

Isabell nodded weakly.

Luke returned with the requested supplies, and Charlotte immediately administered a laudanum dose. "I'll let the painkiller do its work, then I'll work on the broken bone," she told Isabell. "I'll be back."

Charlotte had heard Lizzy calling for Doctor Charlie. When she arrived, Charlotte found Lizzy cradling a baby. "I think his mama is dead," Lizzy said, pointing to a body in the rubble. A tear made a wet track down Lizzy's dirt-stained cheek.

Checking the mother's pulse, Charlotte confirmed what Lizzy had feared. "She's gone. Is the baby hurt?"

"He doesn't appear to be," Lizzy said. "I found him underneath his mother. She was shielding the baby with her body."

A shiver ran through Charlotte. "A mother's instinct." She shook the thoughts from her head and said, "Make a bed for the baby in our wagon. We'll sort out next of kin later."

Lizzy carried the baby to their wagon and made a nest for the infant.

In the meantime, Nellie raced up. "Luke said to look for people who might be trapped or hurt. The Four Aces saloon got hit hard." She and Charlotte hurried over to the remains of the saloon.

"It was one of the first buildings in the path," Nellie said. "Some of the folks didn't have a chance to escape."

Charlotte took in the information as she surveyed what was left of the saloon. The walls had collapsed. The tall, false front of the building was shattered and lying in pieces.

She said, "Go get Luke. Ask him to bring as many men as possible. Bring shovels or pry bars...whatever they can find to dig out the victims."

Nellie ran off to find her brother and relay Charlotte's orders.

Charlotte stood very still. She was listening. Listening for cries of help. Listening for moaning. Listening for signs of life.

Then she heard a woman's calling. "Hello? Can anyone hear me? I need help."

"I hear you," Charlotte answered. "Keep talking." She needed to determine where the woman was. "I'm Doctor Charlie. What is your name?" Charlotte asked.

"I'm Tillie," the voice answered.

"Are you hurt, Tillie?" Charlotte continued talking. She thought she had located the source of the voice. The woman seemed to be on the far side of the demolished saloon.

"I don't know. Yes," the woman said with a cry. "I can't feel my legs."

"You're pinned down," Charlotte said. She had found the woman and grabbed for Tillie's hand. "I've got you, Tillie. I have men coming to rescue you. We'll get you out."

Luke came running. He was carrying a shovel and a pry bar. "I got your message. Nellie is rounding up more men."

Charlotte whispered to Luke, "There's a woman named Tillie trapped here. Let's start removing the debris carefully, piece by piece."

"Tillie, don't you worry. Luke Jameson, the blacksmith, is here. We're going to start digging you out. I'm going to let go of your hand and help Luke. Don't panic."

Together, Luke and Charlotte began lifting pieces of broken lumber, fence railing, and even pieces of glass from the shattered mirror behind the bar. Bit by bit, they were making progress. But Charlotte was worried they would not get to Tillie in time.

A huge man, well over six and a half feet tall and weighing three hundred pounds, approached on a run. Charlotte had to admit the big man moved faster than she thought possible. This must be the new banker Luke described as "a bear of a man."

"Luke, your sister said you needed help. I've got more men coming."

"You're just in time, Hank. Help me move the saloon's bar," Luke said.

Luke Jameson was not a small man by any means, but Hank Johnson towered over the blacksmith. Together, the two men lifted the heavy, solid-wood saloon bar off the buried woman.

Charlotte moved in to examine Tillie. She smiled at the woman. "It's good to put a face to a name, Tillie. I'm Doctor Charlie. Where does it hurt?"

"I can't feel my legs," Tillie sobbed again. "I can't feel my legs."

"They might be pinched. Give them time to get circulation back. Do you hurt anywhere else?" Charlotte asked. "Does your head hurt?" She had noticed blood on the back of Tillie's head.

"Yes, yes, my head hurts. A lot," Tillie said.

"You're in good hands, Miss Tillie," said Hank. "Doctor Charlie knows her medicine. She was a doctor in the war, you know."

That startled Charlotte. She didn't realize that people in town knew her story. Of course, they did. Luke, or maybe Doc Stone, had told people that Charlotte had been a medic in the war. Her wartime experience helped people trust that she knew what she was doing.

She bandaged Tillie's head wound. Then she rechecked Tillie's legs for feeling. Still nothing. That was worrisome. But rather than panic her patient, Charlotte assured Tillie that it might take time to get feeling back.

"You need to rest, Tillie. You have a head wound, so I'm not going to give you any laudanum. But if the pain gets worse, let me know. I'm going to check for other people who are hurt. I'll be back. Rest."

With that last word of medical advice, Charlotte picked up her black satchel and responded to a call for help down the street. Hank and the other men continued sifting through the wreckage of the saloon. They found three bodies but no other survivors.

Charlotte, Lizzy, Nellie, and Luke worked until nightfall. The death toll was not as horrific as Charlotte had feared it might be. Still, seven people, including the mother of the baby that Lizzy found, had died in the stampede.

The fatalities were carried to the churchyard. When Charlotte had made her "rounds" – just as she had during the War – she realized that more than two dozen people had been injured during the stampede. Some of them had superficial wounds. Others, like Tillie, might be paralyzed.

Isabell Vaughn's fractured leg was among the more severe injuries that Charlotte could treat. She had asked the men to carry Isabell back to Luke's shop, one of the few buildings the stampeding herd had spared. From the light of the forge and a couple of lanterns, Charlotte cleaned and set Isabell's thigh bone. She braced the leg with sturdy splints – there were plenty of pieces of wood to choose from – and wrapped the broken leg with clean bandages.

Isabell was sitting up, sipping chamomile tea, when Lizzy and Nellie entered Luke's shop. Lizzy was still carrying the baby.

"We've checked around, and it seems that both parents died in the stampede," Lizzy said. "This little one is an orphan."

"He's not crying," Charlotte observed. "Is he alright?"

"His tummy is full. I found a bottle, and Nellie helped rig a nipple on it," Lizzy said.

"He's been fed and burped. And diapered," Nellie added.

Charlotte smiled. "Well, that's what we all want, isn't it? Let me see the little guy."

Lizzy passed the baby over to Charlotte. Just then, Luke entered the shop. He stopped short when he saw his wife holding the baby. Whatever he was going to say went clean out of his head.

Charlotte looked up and saw Luke. "You have that dazed look like when I first saw you in the field hospital. That time, you'd been knocked in the head."

"That's kind of how I feel right now – seeing you holding a baby. It hit me like a brick!" he replied.

"You have a couple more months to get used to it, brother," Nellie said.

"You came in to tell us something?" Lizzy prompted Luke.

"Yeah…yeah." He shook his head, then focused on Lizzy's question. "After the dust settled, I sent the Hanson boy to Yankton to fetch the sheriff. He and his deputies should be here tonight…tomorrow morning at the latest."

"Those Bushwhackers are long gone," Nellie said.

"But they left a trail," said Hank Johnson as he joined the group in the blacksmith shop. "I haven't seen this much destruction since...well, since the war," the banker said. "Even if the sheriff doesn't catch 'em, there will be wanted posters out there. I have a duty to get back the money they stole from the bank. It wasn't my money. It's the hard-earned money of the folks in Shady Bluffs."

"Mr. Johnson," Lizzy began, "a lot of people come to the bank for help. Do you know of a young couple who may have just come to town...a couple with a baby?"

"Can't say that I do, ma'am," said Johnson. "Is that the baby in question?" He gestured to the baby that Charlotte was rocking in her arms.

"Yes," Lizzy answered. "I found him underneath his mother. She had been crushed by a falling building. His papa was found later. The buffalo had run over him."

Johnson winced. "Horrible way to die," he said. "What about the baby? Does he have any kin?"

"That's what we're trying to discover," Lizzy said. "We don't even know their names. They must have just arrived in town. I'm Lizzy Ward, by the way. Charlotte's sister.

"Nice to make your acquaintance, ma'am," Hank answered. "My name's Hank Johnson. I just moved to town a few weeks ago." He liked what he saw in the shorter, more compact Ward sister. While Lizzy may have been covered in dirt and dust from the rescue activities, there was something about the buxom, blonde-haired beauty that stirred Hank Johnson. He decided to keep an eye on this Ward woman.

Hearing the exchange between Hank and Lizzy, Luke said, "We'll keep looking for their wagon and belongings. That might give us a clue – if it wasn't destroyed in the stampede. For now, I think we should all get some shuteye. Since this is one of the last buildings that's still sound, you're all welcome to bed down here."

He looked at his younger sister. "Nellie, there are some blankets in that trunk. Can you give me a hand?"

Nellie sometimes bristled at being bossed around by her older siblings but didn't mind obeying in this instance. She found the blankets and a couple of quilts that Charlotte had made and handed them out to the people in the shop. They all settled in to get some much-needed sleep.

In the morning, Luke had coffee brewing before anyone woke up. At least, he thought no one was awake. Then he saw Lizzy feeding the baby.

"I didn't hear a peep out of him all night," Luke whispered to Lizzy. "Was he fussy?"

"Not a bit. I had a bottle ready for him this morning. He's a good baby." She glowed, and Luke knew what that meant. If they did find the baby's family, Lizzy's heart might break. For now, he'd keep that to himself.

Other folks started stirring and stretching. Luke greeted each of them with a hot cup of coffee.

"Much appreciated, Jameson," Hank said as he gulped the black brew. "I'd best check what's left of my bank. My house is gone, that's for sure. Luckily, my horse was stabled outside of town. Times like this, we need to be grateful for small blessings."

Hank gazed at Lizzy and the baby. Then he slapped Luke on the back and said, "Thanks for the hospitality. I'll be riding with the sheriff when the posse gets here."

"So will I," Luke responded.

As if on cue, the sheriff and a half dozen deputized lawmen reined up outside the blacksmith shop.

"Howdy, Luke," said Sheriff Ben Wilson. He dismounted and motioned for his companions to do the same.

Wilson called Yankton his home office, but as the Territorial Sheriff, he was responsible for keeping peace in the vast regions of Dakota Territory. He *was* the law.

"We got the gist of what happened from the boy, Tim Hanson," Wilson said. "But this," he gestured to the mass destruction in the town, "is beyond anything I've ever seen."

Wilson and the posse members helped themselves to coffee while Luke and Hank briefed the sheriff on the Bushwhackers.

"There were about a dozen of 'em," Hank said. "A couple of folks here said the gang headed back south, where they came from."

"Down Niobrara way, I expect," Wilson said. "We brought a tracker with us. But it would be mighty helpful if we had someone with us to help identify members of the gang."

"I can do that," Luke offered. "I saw them here a couple of times. They must have been scouting the town. I shoed one of their horses. And played poker with four of 'em."

"Poker, eh?" said Wilson. "Say, do you stamp your horseshoes?"

"I do," Luke said. He pulled a used shoe from a pile and showed Sheriff Wilson the small "J" imprint at the toe of the metal horseshoe.

Wilson took the horseshoe. "Mind if I give this to my tracker?"

Luke shook his head. "It's all yours."

The rest of the posse followed Sheriff Wilson outside. As they prepared to mount up, Luke took leave of the women in his life.

"Nellie, I'm leaving you to hold down the fort – the shop – while I'm gone. Lizzy, I expect you're headed back to the farm." Both women nodded in agreement and made themselves scarce.

"Charlie," Luke's voice was heavy with emotion. "My Charlie." He wrapped her in an embrace. She lifted her face to his, and they kissed as if they were parting for an eternity.

"Take care of yourself, Luke Jameson. You have someone waiting to meet you soon."

He caressed Charlotte's swelling middle. "I love you, Charlie. You take care of yourself and our little one."

After a last kiss, Charlotte stroked his face and said, "Always."

Sheriff Wilson, Deputy Driscoll, Hank, Luke, and the other men in the posse knew the general direction the Bushwhackers had headed. But the stamped horseshoe turned out to be the advantage they needed to pick up the outlaws' trail.

The posse tracked the Bushwhackers to the Outlaw Trail along the Niobrara River while the townspeople of Shady Bluffs set about cleaning up their town.

Lizzy promised to return as soon as she had tended to the livestock on the farm. She began to hand the baby to Charlotte, but the older sister protested.

"He's yours, Lizzy." Then Charlotte smiled and asked, "Have you thought of a name for him?"

It was Lizzy's turn to smile. "I'd like to call him Max."

Charlotte wiped a tear from her eye. "It's perfect." She looked at the baby in Lizzy's arms and said, "Goodbye for now, Max Ward. I'll see you soon."

Then Charlotte did something that she rarely did: she kissed her sister on the cheek. "I don't tell you how much I love you and rely on you, Lizzy. Thank you for all you do."

Lizzy beamed. "I love you, too, Char. This is quite a day! A new baby. And a heartfelt thank you from my big sister! It's going to be a good day."

She placed Max in the nest she'd made in the wagon the day before. Climbing onto the box bench, Lizzy said, "Git up" to the team.

There was a lot of cleanup to do in Shady Bluffs. Charlotte spent her day treating patients. A makeshift clinic had been set up in the church. She felt a bit of déjà vu as she entered the church. The setup was like the converted church in Independence when Frank James had whisked her back to the front lines of the war.

The war. How it had changed things. But soon it would be over. Everyone could get back to their lives. But nothing would be the same as it was before. Of that, she was certain.

It must be the pregnancy that's making me emotional, Charlotte thought. Still, that was one of the biggest changes in her life. A husband. A baby. Her own family.

She smiled to herself as she tied an apron over her day dress. And I'm a doctor to the people here.

Doctor Charlie made her rounds, stopping to chat with each patient, noting their responses, and helping them heal, both physically and emotionally.

News of the Day – Lincoln Is Assassinated, April 14, 1865

Amid the celebrations that marked the end of the War, President Abraham Lincoln was assassinated by John Wilkes Booth, an actor and Southern sympathizer. The War ended for Abraham Lincoln on April 15, 1865.

Epilogue: Summer 1865
On the Dakota Frontier

It was a scorching hot day in July when William Jacob Jameson burst into the world. To his father's delight, the baby had his mother's dark brown eyes.

Luke cradled the newborn in his arms while Lizzy and Evening Star completed their midwife duties. Charlotte was grateful that Evening Star was there. Lizzy had suggested they ask the medicine woman when it was "Charlotte's time." Evening Star had decades of experience as a midwife.

Lizzy had taken to motherhood with the same passion that characterized all aspects of her life. She adored her adopted son. After a fruitless search, no one was able to find any family or even distant relatives for the orphaned baby. Now, Lizzy couldn't imagine a life without her son.

Charlotte and Lizzy guessed that Max was about two months old when Lizzy rescued the baby, so they celebrated Max's birthday on Valentine's Day. That seemed fitting since Lizzy called Max "her sweetheart."

As for the Bushwhackers, Sheriff Wilson was correct when he said that the stamp Luke used on his horseshoes was the break they needed to find the outlaws. The posse tracked Clay Hancock and his gang as the Bushwhackers fled south. After a shootout by the river, the Bushwhackers surrendered.

Hank Johnson recovered the money stolen from his bank, as well as the cash and valuables the outlaws had robbed from stores and houses in Shady Bluffs the day of the stampede.

More importantly, Luke, Hank, and the other men returned home safely to their families. With them, the men brought news of the end of the war.

The South had surrendered.

The End

Lizzy's story continues in *Iron Horse Claim: On the Dakota Frontier*.

About the Author

CK Van Dam is a daughter of the Dakota prairies. With degrees in History and Journalism, she has embarked on a second career to create stories about the strong women who have built our nation and our world.

Her debut novel, *Proving Her Claim*, received two Spur Awards from Western Writers of America: Best Western Romance and Best First novel. The inspiration for the book came from historical records that found 42 percent of women homesteaders successfully proved up their claims, while only 37 percent of the men received title to their lands.

Lone Tree Claim, the second book in the "Claim" series, tells the story of a Civil War widow who comes to Dakota Territory after the devastation of war. As a woman alone on the frontier, she fought nature as well as powerful cattle ranchers.

The inspiration for *Medicine Creek Claim* came from the story of two sisters, Mary Ida and Edith Ammons, who homesteaded in Dakota Territory in the early 1900s.

She is currently working on the story of another pioneer woman in Dakota Territory.

Learn more at ckvandam.com

Made in the USA
Monee, IL
28 December 2024